I0825178

THE CAPTIVE AND THE FIRST BLOOD GAME

THE CAPTIVE AND THE FIRST BLOOD GAME

NEW YORK TIMES BESTSELLING AUTHOR
K.A. LINDE

RED TOWER
BOOKS™

This book is a work of fiction. Names, characters, places, and incidents are the product of the author's imagination or are used fictitiously. Any resemblance to actual events, locales, or persons, living or dead, is coincidental.

Copyright © 2018 by K.A. Linde. Previously published as *Blood Match*. All rights reserved, including the right to reproduce, distribute, or transmit in any form or by any means. For information regarding subsidiary rights, please contact the Publisher.

Entangled Publishing believes stories have the power to inspire, connect, and create lasting change. That's why we protect the rights of our authors and the integrity of their work. Copyright exists not to limit creativity, but to make it possible—to ensure writers can keep telling bold, original stories in their own voices. Thank you for choosing a legitimate copy of this book. By not copying, scanning, or distributing it without permission, you help authors continue to write and reach readers. This book may not be used to train artificial intelligence systems, including large language models or other machine learning tools, whether existing or still to come. These stories were written for human connection, not machine consumption.

Entangled Publishing, LLC
644 Shrewsbury Commons Ave., STE 181
Shrewsbury, PA 17361
rights@entangledpublishing.com

Edited by Sylvan Creekmore
Cover design by LJ Anderson and Bree Archer
Edge design by Bree Archer
Interior design by Britt Marczak

Paperback ISBN 978-1-64937-972-6
Ebook ISBN 978-1-64937-533-9

Manufactured in the United States of America
First Edition October 2025

10 9 8 7 6 5 4 3 2 1

MORE FROM K.A. LINDE

BLOOD TYPE

The Monster and the Last Blood Match

THE OAK AND HOLLY CYCLE

The Wren in the Holly Library
The Robin on the Oak Throne

ROYAL HOUSES

House of Dragons
House of Shadows
House of Curses
House of Gods
House of Embers

ASCENSION

The Affiliate
The Bound
The Consort
The Society
The Domina

To the girls who fell for the vampire
and never looked back.

The Captive and the First Blood Game is a dark supernatural romance filled with vampires, the humans they rely on for survival, and the machinations of a company that wants to rule it all. As such, the story includes elements that might not be suitable for all readers. Violence, gore, blood, needles, suicidal ideation, references to torture (off page), kidnapping and confinement, drugging of a drink, death of a loved one, emotional and physical abuse, depictions of mental illness including a break from reality, and dark romance themes including control, jealousy, possessiveness, owner/pet dynamics, and graphic sex are depicted in the novel. Readers who may be sensitive to these elements, please take note, guard your hearts, and step into the monster's prison…

Chapter One

"Every breath and every heartbeat and every minute of every day was spent waiting for you," Reyna whispered against his skin.

His perfect skin. The hard-muscled chest, the cold feel to him, the awareness of his body pressed against hers. She had waited so long for this. So very long.

"Becks," she said. She ran her hands against his jaw and forced him to look down at her. A bottomless sea of onyx enveloped her. "Say something."

"I love you," he said like a prayer.

Her breath caught. She'd waited to hear that for so long. At her low points, she even tricked herself into believing Beckham had never said those words. That maybe he had never admitted to being part of the rebel group Elle. Maybe Beckham had never put all of his trust in her hands only for her to rip it away in one horrifying flight of dizzy terror.

But he *had* said those words. And she *had* run out of his penthouse after he had bitten her, only to be kidnapped by Visage.

This was her reality.

Now he was here and saying those words she'd so longed for.

"I love you, too." She wrapped her arms around his neck and held him close. She wanted to feel him, solid and immovable. To know that she couldn't shake him—that nothing could tear him away from her again.

A tear slipped down her cheek, and he brushed it aside with his thumb. "Shh, Little One."

"I can't believe you're really here."

"You never have reason to doubt me."

His thumb brushed across her lips as she read hot desire in his eyes. It had been so long since she'd had his hands on her and seen that look cross his face. Her body heated, and a flush suffused her face.

She said the words she'd been dying to say: "I never should have run that night."

"I know, but you're here now."

After that there was no talking. Beckham pushed her backward and onto the bed. It creaked beneath her weight. She reached out for him, but he ignored her and took her threadbare dress in his hands, ripping it straight down the middle. She was naked underneath save for a pair of cotton panties, but he looked at her as if she were encased in silk lingerie. She had been, once. It felt like a million years ago.

At the sight of her, a primal growl escaped his lips. He shucked his black shirt to the ground and stepped out of the black slacks. The length of him was visibly hard and bulging against his boxer briefs. All she wanted was to touch him, to feel him inside of her again—but Beckham was in control. She'd once quaked under his gaze. Now she was shaking for entirely different reasons as his body covered hers.

His lips closed over her nipple, sucking it into his mouth. Her back arched off the bed as her hands dug into the sheets. His hips pressed her down into the mattress, and she felt the full length of him press against her core while his hand kneaded the other breast. She swiveled her hips, wanting the release, wanting everything he would give her. Then his fangs grazed her nipple and she nearly fell apart.

"Becks," she moaned.

He just shot her a ruthless smirk as he moved to her other nipple. Her panties were soaked, and she needed them gone. As if he read her mind, he slipped his hand under the material and found her wet and wanton. A feral noise of pleasure breached his lips. Then he took the thin fabric in his hands and yanked it down her legs.

"Please." She wasn't above begging. "I've waited so long."

"I won't bite you," he said, his face sliding down between her legs. A fang nipped at the sensitive artery in her inner thigh. "But I bloody well want to."

Did she even care if he bit her? It would be a relief after what she'd endured. A relief to feel that connection so acutely. She wouldn't press him this time. She remembered how they'd gotten carried away. He'd taken too much, drunk too deeply, and she'd almost died. They needed to take it slow.

The blood. Not the sex. She needed that right now.

His finger slicked through her wetness and used it to draw circles around her clit. Her fingers dug grooves into the mattress as she vibrated from the sensation. She was so close that she didn't know if she'd be able to hold out before he was inside of her.

Then his eyes found hers again. That dirty smirk returned as he sped up. "Come for me."

And she could hold out no longer. Her body contracted and a gasp escaped her as she released at his ministrations. Her body hummed as she came down from the orgasm and watched through hazy, sex-drunk eyes as he removed his boxers.

He took his cock in his hand. He pumped it up and down as he watched her return to earth. "This is my favorite view of you," he said as he settled back between her legs.

"Fucked?" she asked with a laugh.

He grinned. "Mine."

Then with one powerful thrust, he seated himself to the hilt within her. She cried out. Despite her prior orgasm, she was still tight, and he stretched her to the max. No warning or preamble, just his cock inside of her, filling her to completion.

Her walls clenched around him as he slowly pulled out and then quickly drove inward. Once, twice, three times. Each pull brought her right back to that razor-thin edge she had been hovering on earlier. Even though she had just come, her body was primed and desperate for him.

"Ready for me again already?" he asked.

"So close," she admitted as he bottomed out in her again and a wave of pleasure shot through her core. "So very close."

"Not yet," he commanded.

She forced herself to hold back even as he drove into her again and again. She could wait. Oh God, she could wait.

Then his rhythm changed from methodical to relentless. He set his own course to owning and claiming her body. Reclaiming everything that they'd lost in his one moment of weakness. In her one moment of panic.

She could see in his eyes what that loss had cost him. The toll it had taken on him, how he would never forgive himself for giving in to his urges, for finally relinquishing control. His eyes said he'd never do it again. In them was a promise.

"Becks, come with me," she cried, finally reaching for that strong jaw to bring his lips down to hers for one more kiss.

Their lips collided as he owned her body where he refused to own her blood. Taking everything she would give him but not everything he wanted. Not everything *she* wanted.

Their eyes met, both so close. She was on the precipice and knew they would finish together.

• • •

Reyna woke up screaming.

She jolted upright in her plush king-size bed with its too many pillows and too much softness. Her hair was plastered to her face. Sweat coated her body, soaking through the thin white shirt she'd worn to bed.

Her eyes adjusted to the dim lighting, and she looked around the small room. Everything was in place. Nothing had changed. Not a damn thing.

Beckham wasn't here.

It had been a dream. A sick dream. A desperate, horrible dream.

Her hand moved to her cotton panties and found the slick wetness *was* real. The ache still building in her lower half from lack of release. The aftereffects of the dream.

It had felt so real. So very real. She had felt him moving inside of her. She had seen the love in his eyes. She had known his remorse.

That was her imagination at work. Conjuring his face just to torture her with his absence. She ached to see him one more time, to remember the feel of his body and the love in his eyes, only to twist the knife deeper when she remembered that he hadn't found her and she hadn't escaped.

It had been fifty-five days since she'd last seen his face. Reyna made a mark in the notebook next to the bed.

Fifty-six.

CHAPTER TWO

As if it wasn't bad enough that she had woken up from that dream, it had to be a Thursday, too. A fucking Thursday.

On Thursdays she had to give blood.

Reyna shucked the covers off of her legs and stalked to the adjoining bathroom. She still didn't consider it *her* room. She hoped that she would never think of it like that. It might have a jetted tub, waterfall shower, an enormous bed, and a library to make any bookworm jealous, but that didn't make it anything other than what it was—a prison cell.

She may have everything she could ever need, but she had nothing she actually wanted. No access to the outside world. No news of Beckham. No news of her brothers, not that she'd dare ask. The last thing she wanted was to bring attention to them.

And, of course, she didn't have her freedom.

Beckham had offered that to her with a ten-million-dollar check in a brown leather folder. She hadn't taken it, because she'd thought it was a trap. A way for Beckham to keep her indebted to him for life. She couldn't have been more wrong.

She knew what real freedom looked like. It wasn't that check, and it certainly wasn't a well-maintained prison cell, no matter what the dickbag who had imprisoned her thought.

Reyna turned on the shower and peeled the sweaty layers off her body while she waited for it to heat up. She stuck the clothes in a chute and grabbed another white T-shirt and a pair of loose cotton shorts, which she dropped on a stool before entering the steaming shower.

Her closet was nothing compared to what it had been at Beckham's apartment. At first, she'd resented the silk and satin and lace. All the little unmentionables. The mile-high heels she'd only just begun to get used to.

No one cared for her to dress up now. She was just a blood bag.

An actual fucking blood bag to the most powerful vampire in the world—William Harrington, the president and CEO of Visage Incorporated and Beckham's boss.

He was the ruthless ruler who had brought vampires out of the darkness. After the economy had collapsed, Visage had emerged as if they were a benevolent organization dedicated to helping humanity. What they'd actually done was instate the blood type cure. It wasn't so much a cure for vampirism as a bandage over the real issue: vampires who drank blood from a human who matched their blood type became less animalistic. Instead of bloodthirsty monsters lurking in dark alleys, they became bloodthirsty monsters in two-thousand-dollar suits, taking over the world.

The newspapers proclaimed that Visage had brought the world back from the brink. They registered the vampires. They paid humans—*blood escorts*—to allow vampires to drink from them. Killed two birds with one stone.

Except Reyna knew that Harrington would never be satisfied with his current status. He would never rest until all the power was his to control. But first he needed a match, which was where she came in.

Harrington had kidnapped her for her specific and very rare blood type: Rh null negative. She had none of the Rh antigens that were found in 99.9% of people in the world. A true universal donor. And unluckily, she matched Harrington.

As if that wasn't bad enough, he'd convinced her only friend in the city, Everett, to betray her. She didn't even know if he had ever been her friend or if he had been conning her from the beginning. She'd been so naive. Worst of all, she had no idea what Harrington had told Beckham, or whether he'd been left without answers about why she'd disappeared.

And knowing her blood type made everything feel worse. That she wasn't officially a match for Beckham. That as a true universal donor she shouldn't have made him turn into a monster. Terrifyingly, anyone could drink from her. So had he only lost control because of…her?

She slammed her hand onto the tile wall. She hated thinking about this. But the shower was her only solace, one of the few places without cameras. She couldn't appear helpless anywhere else.

Even waking up with screams irritated her. It ruined the mask she had carefully constructed these long eight weeks. She needed to get a grip. That dream had gotten to her. It wasn't the first she'd had, and it wouldn't be the last, but it was certainly the most vivid one so far. It made her ache for him, and she couldn't do that anywhere else. Beckham belonged in a compartmentalized shelf in her brain where he could keep her alive and make her stronger but didn't interfere with the person she had to be to survive.

With new resolve, she got out of the shower, dressed, and slicked her still-wet hair back into a ponytail. Time to get this day over with.

When she walked back into the one-room cell, the human nurse was already waiting for her. She was a white woman with nondescript features—dark hair, dark eyes, wan expression.

"Miss Reyna," the woman said.

She wore the crisp white Visage nurse uniform. That uniform

had made Reyna cringe the first time she saw one, at the Visage hospital all those months ago on her first day as a blood escort. The only color on the outfit was the bloodred V logo. The sight still made her feel sick.

"I'm ready."

"You should eat first. You know that you get dizzy if you don't eat breakfast," she admonished.

Reyna wanted to snap at her to stop mothering her. Her mother had died just over a dozen years ago, when Reyna was eight years old. Her deadbeat uncle had taken her and her brothers in for three years before the economy had gone to hell in a handbasket. Then it was ten years alone with her brothers before desperation had pushed her straight to Visage.

But she didn't voice any of her thoughts. She kept her face blank. "Sure."

She sat down and ate the food that had been carefully selected for optimal nutrition. A perfectly balanced diet and a healthy amount of exercise was forced down her throat. No one cared how much iron she pumped; there was no chance of her overpowering a vampire.

"Ready," she said, pushing the tray aside.

"Don't forget your water."

Reyna snatched it off the table as she headed to the door. "Let's get this over with."

"Of course," the woman said with a bland smile.

She'd been the same nurse twice a week for eight weeks. Not a single change in all that time. Reyna didn't know a thing about her. They spent an hour together every Monday and Thursday for one of the most unpleasant experiences of her life, and she didn't even know the woman's name.

The door to the room slid open silently, and Reyna held her breath. Every time it opened, she envisioned herself slipping out and running away undetected. It was a pipe dream. Still she clung to it.

She followed the nurse out of the bedroom and took a right down the hallway. When she'd first arrived, she'd tried the exact thing she still fantasized about. She'd made it three feet before a shock wave ran up her arm and she fell forward flat on her face. Some hugely muscled vampire had picked her up with one arm and deposited her back in her cell.

He'd laughed as he told her about the device they'd implanted into her arm to prevent escape, then shut the door in her face. As if it wasn't enough to have vampires guarding her. They had an invasive *thing* put into her arm.

So, no running away for her.

When they arrived, the hospital room was white and sterile. The sight of it still made Reyna shake with fear. Needles. This room meant needles.

Reyna knew intuitively that it was stupid to still be afraid of needles at this point. Two IVs twice a week to draw blood and two needles twice a week for infusions for eight weeks equaled thirty-two needles. She shuddered as she sank into the plush chair that had replaced the hospital-style bed she'd woken up in. Thirty-two needles in fifty-six days, and she still felt like crawling under the table at the thought. She'd pleaded with Beckham to bite her, but needles made her want to vomit.

The nurse gestured to the chair. Instead, Reyna walked to the chessboard against the wall. William Harrington liked chess, and their board was still up from Monday when she had last given blood. She'd resented the fact that he wanted her to play chess with him, but it was better than hearing him talk. So she played. And lost…regularly.

Knight to C6. She captured another pawn. How ironic.

"Are you ready?" the nurse asked.

Reyna sighed and went to sit in the chair. "As I'll ever be."

"You know I'm quite skilled at this. There's no reason to be afraid."

Reyna nearly laughed, but the nurse was holding the IV needle in her hand, and if Reyna opened her mouth, she might actually throw up. She turned her face away. A tourniquet, a swab of alcohol, and a prick. She squeezed her eyes shut and waited for the sensation to be over.

"There we have it," the nurse assured her.

Needle number one accomplished. The second was always worse, though.

Harrington didn't drink directly from her. Reyna had never asked why, because she didn't want him to change his mind. Donating blood was preferable to him sinking his fangs into her. A hundred and fifty percent better. Even with the needles.

But since he wasn't biting her, she had to be hooked up to a second IV that passed some form of vamp saliva into her system. She'd dubbed it *vamp venom*, though there was some fancy technical term that she didn't remember.

She hadn't had to ask *why* she needed the venom, though. Harrington loved the sound of his own voice, and on the occasions when he graced her with his presence, he told her all about how the venom activated red blood cell regeneration and blah blah blah. Normal humans regenerated a pint of blood every fifty-six days. So, under normal circumstances, today would have been the first day that she could've given blood again after Beckham had drunk from her eight weeks ago. With the vamp venom, usually acquired from a bite, she regenerated a pint of blood every three to four days.

She truly hated science right about now.

Reyna braced herself as the second needle went in without a hitch.

"Measure your breathing. This should be over soon," the nurse said as she prepped to turn on the machine.

Then the latch clicked and Reyna's eyes shot to the sliding door as it whizzed open. In walked her nightmare—Harrington.

"Ah, my little queen," Harrington said in a chipper voice.

Reyna remained blank-faced at the stupid nickname. Reyna. Reign. Queen. Get it? So fucking original.

The days that Harrington showed up were the worst. The absolute worst. Her eyes flicked to the machine. The nurse still hadn't turned it on. Once the machine turned on, she had about ten minutes before the diluted venom would activate in her blood, making her as high as a kite. Nothing as strong as the bite from Beckham, but it still hit her like a freight train before it ebbed off. And she *really* wanted to be high and not have to deal with Harrington today.

"I heard that we had another nightmare," he said, settling into the seat next to the chessboard. His eyes were on the game, but he spoke to her. "Want to talk about it?"

Ah, therapy. Just what the doctor ordered. Of course all she wanted to do was spill her deep, dark secrets to a murderous, psychopathic dictator.

"I forgot where I was," she lied. It was her default answer.

He laughed and moved a piece into position. "It's about time you remember where you are. So forgetful."

His voice was light, but when she glanced up into his blue eyes, she saw the wicked evil underneath. The reason Harrington was on top was because he was both ruthless and a genius businessman. It was hard to forget it when he looked at her like that.

It didn't help that her blood had changed him. Gone was the frail, sickly man she had first met. Harrington had had to walk with a cane he was so thin, pasty, and weak. Now he stood tall, back straight, eyes taking in the room. He still carried the cane, but she knew he didn't need it.

"Now, on to why I'm here," Harrington said. "I wanted to check in on my favorite resident." Read: prisoner. "See how you're doing and ensure you're adjusting well to the new diet."

"It's fine," she said. The machine was still off. "Are you going to turn that on?"

"In a minute," Harrington said before he started rambling on about the latest articles on nutrition coming out of the scientific community and how it affected blood supply. Reyna stared at the machine with a longing she hadn't known she could feel. It was in the moments when she had to hear Harrington's voice that she wished suicide were an option.

If she didn't value her own survival, she would have found a way to end her life long ago. It would have made sense. Ending Harrington's blood supply would endanger him. It would hurt Visage. But when it came down to it, she hadn't been able to do it. Though if he said one more thing about fucking açaí berries, she might reconsider smashing her brain in with a free weight.

"Reyna, you seem absent today," Harrington said. It was a warning.

"You haven't turned on the machine."

"It can wait a few minutes."

"Whenever you're ready, sir," the nurse said.

Reyna shot her a look that said *Whose side are you on?* But it was a stupid question. The nurse worked for Visage. That's whose side she was on.

"Explain to me where your head is."

"Not caring about my diet," she got out.

"And why not? I think it's very important that you—"

"Stop," Reyna told him. "Just stop it."

He arched an eyebrow. She should have seen the warning in it, but she was beyond that. Between the dream and her isolation and the needles, she was losing it. She couldn't hold it together today. She couldn't sit here and have this murderous jackass lecture her on proper nutrition.

"What is this?" he asked, gesturing to her as if she were a strange specimen he couldn't figure out.

"*This* is a human being. An actual human being. I'm not your science project. I'm not even your blood bag. I am a human. I live and breathe and feel, and right now I'm feeling pretty pissed. So turn the machine on, because I'd like to get high in peace without you fucking ruining everything with your stupid fucking speeches."

"Reyna," he growled low.

But she wasn't finished. "And you know what, I can't seem to care about anything. Definitely not about you and your goddamn diet or this fucking place or this fucking prison cell. I'm concentrating on surviving. On dealing with these fucking needles and not wanting to smash your fucking face in."

"Sir, maybe we should give her the venom now," the nurse said quickly.

"Leave it off," Harrington snapped at the nurse.

The edge to his voice and the lethal cut of his eyes said that she'd gone too far. The nurse retreated. The machine stayed off.

Harrington stood, towering over her, and she shrank back in her seat. She knew a predator when she saw one. His physical presence was demanding enough, but it was the sadistic brain behind that mask that terrified her. That made her literally quake in her seat.

He reached forward and without preamble ripped out both of her IVs.

CHAPTER THREE

Reyna screamed.

From the pain and the shock and the needles that had been in her arms…and the blood. She gagged at the sight of it.

Harrington's hand closed over her throat as he pushed her roughly back against the chair. Her eyes locked onto his, and she remembered exactly who was standing over her. Exactly how much she had fucked up.

"You are not invincible here, Reyna. You are not actually a queen of this domain. You are here at my whim, and you will find that if you do not cooperate, your life could become much more unpleasant. Do you understand?"

She choked out a garbled, "Yes."

He removed the pressure from her throat, and she coughed and sputtered as air filled her lungs again. That was going to bruise.

Harrington swiped a finger over one of her open wounds, then brought it to his lips, tasting her openly. For a clinical man who saw a scientific process in all their interactions and treated her more like a treasured pet than anything, she had never seen him so…wild. It was the only way to put it. Even when she had been furious and screamed and cried in the beginning, he had sat calmly by and watched it all as if it were a television show. Some melodrama he could dissect later.

But this was the monster behind the facade. His true nature. The vampire.

"You may be a very rare match, Reyna, but that does not mean you are irreplaceable. Right this moment, the Blood Census is registering people all over this nation. The city is already complete, and soon it will cover the nation, then the world," he said menacingly. "I will find more of you yet."

Harrington sneered down at the wounds he'd created. "Clean her up."

The nurse hurried forward to clean and bandage the wounds. She elevated Reyna's arms to help clotting, but Reyna ignored her, still staring after Harrington. He'd moved to the sink and was sterilizing his hands as if that one drop of blood he'd gotten on his finger was contagious in some way. He was adamant in his cleanliness.

Her arms throbbed. She couldn't believe she'd lost her cool. This meant that she'd probably need to have another venom IV to replenish the blood. Reyna had to close her eyes and breathe deeply at that thought. She couldn't handle this another time. She couldn't handle being here another day. She was clinging to survival, and she felt like she was finally cracking under the weight of it all.

"Let's go," Harrington said.

"Go?" Reyna asked, opening her dark eyes to stare up at him.

"Yes. Now. I have something to show you."

Reyna stood on shaky legs. She hated to let Harrington see her fear, but it was all over her. Oozing out of her pores and filling the room.

She straightened her spine and forced herself to walk toward him. She might fear him, but she wouldn't cower. She only had her defiance left to hold on to.

“I’m ready,” she said with all the power still left in her body.

Harrington opened the sliding door. She took one last look over her shoulder. The nurse’s face was a mask, but Reyna saw her own terror mirrored in the nurse’s eyes. It was reassuring in a way she hadn’t expected. Maybe she didn’t want to be working here any more than Reyna did.

Reyna had decided to work for Visage out of necessity. Her brothers had been working doubles at the factory in the Warehouse District an hour outside of the city. She couldn’t get a job without a college degree, and she couldn’t go to college because they didn’t have any money. So, she had been just another helpless mouth to feed. In desperation, she had joined Visage to help her brothers.

When she had started, she’d expected it to be more like…well, this. Degrading, humiliating work that she should be ashamed of. Instead, she’d gotten Beckham.

She closed her eyes for a second as the name crushed her heart. No, she couldn’t think about him right now. She needed to be on. Harrington was offering her an opportunity. He just didn’t know it yet.

With her head held high, Reyna exited the sterile room and followed on Harrington’s heels. She marked every turn they made through the winding corridors. She had no clue where she was exactly. Until now, she’d only seen the two rooms in the entire facility, and she couldn’t have even guessed that it was this sprawling. But the space must have been the size of several large warehouses. What else did he keep here?

Harrington stopped in front of a giant steel door. He held one hand behind his back as he swung that insufferable cane in a circle with the other. His suit was crisp and presentable—he had taken some care with his appearance today. What could be happening in the outside world to have him dress up?

“Here we are,” he said, clomping the cane down noisily. “This is a special ward. I like to keep interesting projects here.”

Interesting. Projects. Oh no. This wasn’t going to be good.

"Would you like to see my project?"

Of course she didn't want to see his project. But he expected her to say no. So she couldn't.

He laughed when he saw the indecision written on her face. "Ah, my little queen, it's not a trick question." Her nickname was back in the building. "Let's take a look."

Harrington entered a fifteen-digit code in a blur, then put his eye to a retinal scanner, pressed his fingerprint onto a pad, and had to be identified with facial recognition software before the door opened. Talk about secure.

Beyond was a long hallway, and lights flickered on one at a time down the row. Reyna entered after Harrington, and the door closed with a soft metallic *snick* behind them. He stepped up to the first door on the right and typed in a different sequence. The opaque wall suddenly turned into a window.

"Tinted one-way glass," Harrington explained. "We can see in, but she can't see out."

"She?" Reyna whispered.

"Meet B," Harrington said.

Reyna's saw a woman facing the window as she stood in the corner of the room, staring up at the ceiling. She was tall—very tall for a woman. Her hair was short and black, chopped haphazardly with no care for appearance. She wore a black bodysuit that showed off her fit physique. Her hands were at her sides, and she was talking to herself.

"Is…something wrong with her?"

"Why don't we find out?" he asked with that cruel smile of his.

"Oh no…I don't think…"

But he was already pressing a button. "B."

The woman's head snapped forward. Her dark eyes were otherworldly. They didn't scream "fear me" like Harrington's did. They screamed unpredictable and wild and dangerous.

B took three calm steps to put herself in front of the window. She bared her teeth, revealing the sharp fangs. "The sky is green today."

"You can't see the sky, B," Harrington told her.

"The work will burn with you in it. Roses are red and violets are bleeding. Death and destruction taste like your whispers."

Reyna's eyebrows rose dramatically. What the hell had Harrington done to this woman?

"I brought you a friend," Harrington told her.

"A tasty morsel. A pet pet pet. Sometimes the doorknob sings show tunes. Tell it to stop." Then her eyes glazed over and she covered her ears. "Stop! Tell it to stop!"

"Oh my God," Reyna whispered.

"*God* has nothing to do with it." Harrington pushed the door open, dragging Reyna behind him into the room. Harrington wouldn't let her get hurt, right? He needed her. He needed her blood. She was valuable.

But then he shoved her forward so she came face-to-face with B. Fear bit into her stomach, making her queasy. Holy shit, he couldn't do this.

B sniffed the air all around Reyna, assessing her. Then she slowly circled Reyna, prowling as if she were a lion on the savannah about to take down her prey. Reyna stood very still. She didn't even breathe. Her lungs constricted as sweat beaded on her brow.

"You smell familiar," B said. "Have we met before?"

"No," Reyna whispered on an exhale. She couldn't believe she'd even gotten the word out. If she thought she had fears before…they were nothing compared to being next to this erratic, unpredictable predator.

"Oh yes, we've met. Underground and up on high. Beneath and within and deep under your skin." B leaned in and ran her nose up Reyna's arm. Reyna shivered in fear. "You smell wrong."

Reyna swallowed hard. She had never been told that. Usually vampires told her she smelled amazing, like the nectar of the gods. She didn't want to smell wrong to this creature. She wanted to get as far away as possible. She didn't need to be bitten to have fight-or-flight kick in.

"Toy?" B asked Harrington.

Reyna's eyes widened as she faced Harrington. He smirked at her as if to say *This is what your life could be.* Reyna shuddered. Dear God, no. She didn't mask the fear; she let it seep out of her in waves. Oh God, there *was* worse. There was much worse than the life she had been leading.

"Would you like her as a toy?" Harrington asked B.

B grasped both of Reyna's arms, and then she tore off the medical tape and gauze. Reyna cried out as her wounds reopened.

B inspected the wound clinically. "She's broken. You brought me a broken toy."

"B," Harrington said.

"She's broken in here, too," B said, thrusting her hand at Reyna's heart. It landed with a soft thump. Reyna grunted and took an unsteady step backward. "Shattered and empty. Worms and maggots. Festering blistering aching." She tilted her head and then giggled. "Destroyed."

Reyna was repulsed by the words, repulsed by B. Harrington was teaching her a lesson she didn't want to learn.

"Harrington," Reyna said softly.

His smile was deadly. "See?"

"Yes," she croaked.

"Broken!" B yelled and then suddenly shoved Reyna hard.

She collided with the glass, her head smacking against it roughly. She gasped as tears welled in her eyes and she slumped to a heap on the floor. Her head pulsed with pain.

Oh God. Oh God. Oh God. B was going to kill her. The frenzied look in B's eyes revealed how gone she really was. Harrington was holding her back, but Reyna didn't want to wait to find out. Her head felt like it was the size of the room as fear propelled her to escape this nightmare.

"I'll kill her! I'll kill her!" B screamed, trying to claw her way past Harrington. "She can't have it. Doesn't belong to her. I'll take it all back."

Reyna had nearly made it to the door the moment Harrington lost his grip on B. She lunged forward, landing like a cat on all fours above Reyna.

"No. No, stop," she shrieked, clawing at B's face.

B used one hand and held her down, exposing her fangs, and then sank them into Reyna's arm.

It all happened in slow motion. The feeling of adrenaline pumping through her system. The vamp venom she hadn't gotten earlier from the IV flooding her bloodstream and taking over. Tears streaming down her face as B drank her blood. The terror and disbelief and pain.

B was forcing herself on Reyna to drain her blood against her will. At least as an escort she had *chosen* this. She had accepted it as her fate. And Harrington…he took the blood without her consent, but this was…this was worse. This was hell. This was actual hell.

Just when she thought it was over, an electrical shock pulsed through them. She and B screamed. B fell in a heap on the floor, twitching and shaking. Her head cocked to the side, her eyes wide and wild.

Reyna pushed away from B, clutching her arm and shaking from head to toe. It had stopped. He'd stopped it. She had thought that was the end. She didn't care how he had stopped it, just that he had.

Harrington stepped over B. "What a pleasant demonstration."

Reyna curled in on herself. Her body was trembling involuntarily, and her heart stuttered in her chest. Harrington's shadow covered her frame. She skittered farther away from him, pressing her aching head into the glass. She needed to be away from here…far away from here. But Harrington would never let her go. He'd never leave her alone. She was going to be kept like this forever.

He tipped her chin up so she had to meet his keenly intelligent eyes. "You have been living in privilege. You think that there is nothing I could do to you that hasn't already been done, and you are wrong. I need your blood, but only your blood. I don't need your mind. I don't need you happy. I certainly don't need you living in luxury. This is your fate if you continue to displease me."

CHAPTER FOUR

Reyna sank back into her bed with her knees tucked up under her chin. Her tears had finally halted hours after she'd been deposited back in her room. The nurse had stuck around long enough to bandage her up, but vampire bites healed more quickly than average injuries. Usually within a couple of hours, it would fade away to just a thin scar. And sometimes the scars wouldn't even last. She had a feeling this one would. Scar physically, yes, but definitely emotionally. She wasn't soon going to forget the feeling of B biting her and the sheer horror of almost dying.

The rush was already wearing off from the bite, and she was crashing hard. Harrington had lamented the fact that she had never gotten addicted to the venom. A lot of people did. There was an entire group of people who were desperate for their next fix. He couldn't figure out why she wasn't that way.

Reyna didn't say but always suspected it was because her first bite had been from Beckham. He'd told her at the time that emotional connection intensified the reaction. She hadn't thought to wonder if he knew that from personal experience, but as she sat in her bed with a massive headache coming on, she let herself go to that dark place.

All the maybes and what-ifs flew through her mind. What if Beckham was better off without her? Maybe he'd loved someone else. What if biting Penelope had been like this? Reyna shuddered at the thought of Penelope. She was the mayor's daughter and had all the privilege and entitlement that came with that life. She and Beckham had pretended to be romantically involved as a cover for his involvement with the rebellion, a group known as Elle. But knowing it hadn't been real didn't make it any easier to think about them together, or about the fact that he had drunk Penelope's blood. Maybe he really did have feelings for Penny, even though he'd claimed he didn't. Maybe he didn't want to find Reyna. What if he'd orchestrated this whole thing?

She squeezed her eyes shut and rocked back and forth. No. She couldn't think these things. This was what Harrington wanted. He had broken her. He'd put her in a situation that had been beyond anything she'd ever had to handle, and the trauma was coloring all of her thoughts. He wanted her to lose it. He wanted her to turn into a complacent little pet.

She didn't feel complacent after Harrington's demonstration today. She knew now what he would do to her if she acted out: he would shatter her mind.

She could take pain if she had to. She could survive whatever he threw at her. But she would not fall. She would not be broken.

She'd rather die than succumb to Harrington.

• • •

Reyna woke up the next day with a clear head.

She hadn't even realized how depressed she had been until the fog lifted. Trapped in a world with no answers and no hope, she'd been lost. Floating along a river of self-doubt and not even looking for a way to dock. Then it all came back to her—she needed to get out of here. She needed to find a way back to her life.

It started today.

With renewed zeal, Reyna spent the next couple of days plotting. She wouldn't be let out of the room again until Monday. The nurse would come and get her. She usually had all of breakfast and then uninterrupted conversation with the nurse, not that she'd ever taken advantage of it. Maybe Reyna could get some information out of her or at least try to appeal to her sympathies. The woman had looked afraid when Reyna was dragged off after having her IVs ripped out. There was no time like the present to use that to her advantage.

She had a mental map of the corridors she'd traversed in the building, but she didn't know what to do about the little device embedded in her arm. She could feel it right under the skin when she ran her hand over her left forearm. It was about a centimeter long and roughly the width of a grain of rice. If she'd had something sharp, she probably could have cut it out.

Reyna didn't know how long this escape plot would take. Collecting enough information to find an exit was already a big enough challenge. Removing a device with a blunt object was another thing altogether. She was done being complacent, though. She would get out of here.

With a huff, she threw on the provided white workout clothes, walked into the adjoining exercise room, and turned on the treadmill. She had never been someone who worked out before this, but the cardio would come in handy later. Even if she couldn't outrun a vampire, she'd take any edge she could get.

She was sweating and panting by the time she finished her workout. She was leaning over with her hands on her knees, trying not to fall flat on her face, when she heard the distinctive sound of the door clicking.

"Who's there?" she asked.

No one answered. When she walked back into the bedroom, no one was inside. Just a black garment bag was laid out on the bed, along with a handwritten note.

Be ready in an hour.

"Be ready," she whispered. "Be ready for *what*?"

In eight weeks, she'd worn nothing other than the standard-issue white uniform. She hadn't gone anywhere. She hadn't done anything. What game was Harrington playing?

Eventually, curiosity won out. She unzipped the black bag to reveal a long-sleeve black ball gown in her size. She shoved the bag away from her. Why would Harrington want her to go to a ball? After his warnings and introducing her to B, why would he feel the need to extend an olive branch?

With a frustrated sigh, she relented and headed to the bathroom to get ready. She didn't want to play into his hands, and she knew that she needed to be on guard, but she was too curious not to go.

With only five minutes left before she was supposed to be picked up, she slid into the dress and zipped it up the back. It rested just off her shoulders and had lace sleeves that hooked around her middle fingers, but while the black satin material plunged to a deep V in the back, the front covered her collarbones with a surprisingly prudish neckline. In the bottom of the garment bag, there was a box containing black heels with red soles. Everything fit her like a dream.

If only she weren't living a nightmare.

Promptly an hour after the dress had been left on her bed, the same vampire guard who'd been there when she'd tried to escape arrived. He stood in the doorway looking imposing. He handed her a blindfold.

She took it without a word and slid it over her eyes. Maybe Harrington wasn't letting up on her after all.

Once secure, the guy grabbed her by her upper arm and marched her out of the room. This guy must have been ex-military, because his pace was bruising and it wasn't a short trek. She didn't know if he was taking her the long way on purpose, but she wouldn't have been able to find her way back.

Finally, the guard escorted Reyna up a flight of stairs and then opened a door and pushed her through ahead of him. The door closed and locked behind her.

She ripped off her blindfold and found herself in a small conference room. A buffet of delicious-smelling food was laid out against the back wall. A television hung suspended to her right and a projector on the left. A table for one was set up against the wall across from the television with an unopened bottle of champagne chilling in an ice bucket, two empty glasses, and a single lit candle. She was surprised to find it had an actual flame.

But what was the point?

She was circling the room, searching for clues, when the door sprang open. She stumbled back a step and then straightened her spine. No matter what, she had to remember this was a con. It had to be.

Harrington entered, dressed in a crisp tuxedo. His cane was tucked under his arm, and his eyes flashed brightly. She'd never noticed how crystal blue they were. She usually only saw his inhumanity, but today he seemed almost human. It unnerved her.

The door slid closed behind him, and he smiled. This unbelievably powerful vampire smiled at her. This was bad…very bad.

"What is this?" she asked.

"Ah, I knew that dress would suit you. You look like the queen you shall be."

Okayyyy.

"Have you tasted the buffet? I had it prepared with your favorites in mind."

She didn't answer. How would he know what her favorites were? And since when did he care?

He laughed when she didn't answer and walked across the room. She followed him with her eyes. He reached for the champagne and looked down at the label. "Champagne is also your favorite, no?"

Still she said nothing.

"This is my favorite vintage. It's a rosé from this little vineyard in Reims I used to frequent in the early years after I was turned."

Oh God, he just wanted to hear himself talk again. He made her get all dressed up for this?

"I purchased the property when it was clear that the French Revolution was going to destroy everything good about France."

Reyna's eyes widened slightly. The French Revolution. He was born *before* the French Revolution?

"America's fault, of course," he said as he popped the top of the champagne. He poured two full champagne flutes. "If it hadn't rebelled, where would France be now?"

"Are you French?" she couldn't help but ask. Even when he droned on, he never talked about himself.

"Certainly not," he said. He walked back to Reyna and handed her a flute. "Taste it for yourself."

She swallowed in fear. She didn't know that she liked this new Harrington any better than the old one. She couldn't figure out his ploy, and that made it scarier, but nonetheless, she tilted back the champagne.

The bubbles exploded in her mouth and down her throat. It was crisp and dry and the most delicious champagne she had ever had in her life. Something about it popped, and it had the perfect bite.

"You like it," he said with another candid smile.

"Yes," she said carefully.

"Good." He brought his own flute to his lips and took a long swallow. "Ah, as good as I remember."

Reyna knew that vampires could technically eat food, but they didn't do it often. They drank, too, but she had never been forward enough to ask if alcohol tasted the same. If anything tasted as good as blood. She wasn't about to ask now.

"You are probably wondering why you're here." He poured himself another glass of champagne and then set the bottle back in the ice. "Come closer."

She moved an inch. He touched a small control panel she hadn't even noticed, and once again the wall turned transparent, as it had outside B's cell, to reveal an enormous ballroom filled to the brim with people.

Without meaning to, she moved forward and put her hand on the glass. "What…?"

"Another one-way mirror, and a soundproof room. No one can see or hear us. They will never know that you're spying on them."

She deflated. "Then why am I here? What is all of this?" She gestured around the room—the buffet, the candlelight, the champagne, the dress, the heels. "You want to show me the ball, but I can't be part of it?"

"I realized," he said, leaning casually back against the window, "that I showed you only one side of the coin."

"What coin?"

"Your life does not have to be like B's, Reyna. Your life could be just like this."

"I'm still trapped."

"Either you can be trapped," he told her, "or you can *choose* to be here, living this life. It's a choice. I thought you'd like to know that you could choose this."

She stared at him, trying to mask the disbelief she felt. He thought that shoving her into a pretty dress and feeding her fancy food would make her realize that she should be grateful to him for kidnapping her?

"Is it really so different than your life with Beckham?"

Reyna recoiled. Harrington didn't mention Beckham anymore. After a week or two of questions, he had presumably given up on getting any information out of her about him. Since

Harrington never brought Beckham up again, she'd figured that was that.

"Did he not feed you and clothe you and offer you everything your heart desired?"

"He also paid me and allowed me out of his house," she ground out.

"I could pay you," he said dismissively. "And you are, of sorts, out of the house."

"Alone and unsupervised."

Harrington barked out a short laugh. "Do not think for a moment that Beckham Anderson allowed you out alone or unsupervised any more than I have."

Reyna ground her teeth together. It was kind of true. Had she ever really been alone?

"I have known him much longer than you have. Believe me when I say that the man you think you knew does not exist. There is no one more ruthless than he. No one more willing to tear the world apart with his bare hands to get ahead. He treated you like a well-maintained pet. What freedom he allowed you to believe you had was nothing more than an illusion. At least I am not playing games."

No games. That was laughable. Every word out of his mouth was a game. She wouldn't listen to his babble about Beckham. Harrington might've known him longer, but she knew him better. She knew him to his core. She may have doubted Beckham in the darkest corners of her mind, but still she knew how he felt about her. Harrington's words only solidified her resolve.

"Think on it. You could be a guest. Things could be better for you here than they are currently," Harrington said. "Enjoy the view of the guests."

"What's the party for?" she couldn't help but ask.

"We have a new mayor."

"A new mayor?" she asked, whipping around.

As soon as she did, she knew that she'd walked right into his hands.

“Mayor Sky recently passed away.”

She knew what that meant. He was murdered.

“Who is the new mayor?”

He smiled, and she saw his lethal look return. “I believe you’re acquainted with his daughter: Penelope Sky.”

Chapter Five

Penny was the mayor.

Reyna couldn't wrap her head around it. Penelope Sky, the mayor's beautiful daughter who was in her last year of college, had been elected mayor? The human girl who was in love with Beckham, who had been the cover for his involvement in the underground rebellion, who was everything Reyna was not. Penelope, who had been severely burned in the Vault sex club fire a little over eight weeks ago, was somehow mayor.

How the hell had that happened?

Harrington finished his second glass of champagne and waited expectantly. He wanted her to ask more. He knew she was starved for information. Even this little amount made her want to crawl out of her skin to get to the bottom of it.

But that look on his face—that slimy, manipulative grin—said it all. If she gave him an inch, he'd take a mile.

"Interesting," she said instead. Then she returned her eyes to the party below.

"I have to mingle with the guests and congratulate our new mayor. In the meantime, feel free to partake in the food and drinks provided. If you need anything, there is a speaker by the door. You can request it from the man I positioned outside, and he will bring you what you need."

Then he was gone.

She released a long sigh of frustration.

She didn't know what to think about Harrington's plan. Of course, logically, she would much rather live in a prison that looked more like paradise than a hospital. But giving in had as many consequences as resisting did. It would mean she'd given up on any chance of escape. It would mean she was okay living the life Harrington had forced on her. It would mean she was a willing captive, and she was so fucking far from willing in any of this.

She scanned the party as her mind continued to process. Despite the conversation she'd had with Harrington, she was mesmerized by the ball. All the glittering dresses and sharp suits. The drinking, mingling, celebrating. She hadn't seen this many people in weeks. It was all so much. Nearly overwhelming in its intensity, after such a stark, dreary eight weeks.

Amazing to think that she had lived this life with Beckham, before being kidnapped. They had shown up at a ball just like this to celebrate Congress's passage of the Blood Census. That felt like a lifetime ago.

Everyone's attention drifted up to the stage as Harrington walked onto it. He was leaning more heavily on his cane than she had seen him do in weeks. Another of the games he insisted he didn't play. She wondered how many people actually knew that he'd found a blood type match. If she knew him at all—and it was scary that she felt she was getting to—very few. Probably even fewer knew the match was Reyna.

If he was putting on an act as the feeble old man she had first met, then he was doing it for a reason. Harrington always had a motive.

He finally made it to the microphone. She couldn't hear what he was saying due to this wretched soundproof room, but whatever it was, he had everyone's rapt attention. After a few minutes, the audience enthusiastically applauded and Harrington held out his hand to the back of the stage.

Out walked none other than Penelope Sky herself.

She wore a sleek sky-blue ball gown that was both alluring and demure. Her dark mane was piled up high on her head. Known for her perfect heart-shaped face, cute little button nose, and matching dimples, Penelope was one of the most beautiful humans Reyna had ever seen. And even from a distance, she could recognize that Penny looked gorgeous. Yet…different.

Something had definitely changed in her appearance. The burns, even if they were no longer immediately visible, had irrevocably shaped her. Technology was a miracle worker, but even skin grafts couldn't completely remake Penelope into what she had once been.

Not that her beauty was her only asset. She was already rich and educated, two things that were nearly impossible for humans at this point. The income gap between the rich and poor was at an astronomical, unprecedented high; money and privilege went a long way. Her looks were merely a bonus. Still, Reyna couldn't help, despite everything, thinking that she pitied Penny. She felt bad that Penny had been left in the fires. That Beckham had had to go into the club to retrieve her and found her so marred.

Penelope wasn't even supposed to be there that night. Whatever else had happened, she didn't deserve that pain. No one did.

As Penelope delivered her speech, Reyna's eyes crawled the rest of the room, searching out familiar faces. It only took her a minute to find one of Harrington's most trusted advisors, Roland, in the crowd. She shuddered at the sight of him. The man who had tried to force himself on her, who had been determined to have her no matter what Beckham thought. He'd almost succeeded, too. If Beckham hadn't shown up, Reyna didn't know how she ever would have come back from that.

Roland's blood escort, Sophie, was standing at his side, clad in virginal white as always. Sophie was a willing subject to vampires, but Reyna couldn't hate her. Every escort in the system had a story, and Sophie's reasons for joining were her own.

Next to Roland and Sophie was the fiery redhead, Cassandra. She completed Harrington's treasured trio—Beckham, Roland, and Cassandra. She was unpredictable and treated humans as if they were simply a food source. Her last escort, Felix, had been killed in the underground club fires, but it looked as if she had a new play toy beside her.

Reyna kept searching.

Searching, searching, searching.

She didn't want to admit who she was really looking for. She didn't want to hope that he might be here. Or face what it might mean if he wasn't. Her heart couldn't take the desire to see him, just to have it dashed. Hope was the death of the oppressed. It made you hunger, only to be crushed inevitably under the oppressor's boots.

More applause brought her attention back to Penelope, and she gasped. Her hand flew to her mouth.

There he was. *Beckham*.

Draped head to toe in a fuckable black suit. His dark hair, his obsidian eyes, scruff evident on his sharp jawline. She didn't know if it was her mind conjuring every minute detail, but it was all there just the same. Right before her. Fifty feet and a soundproof glass window separated them. It might as well have been a mile.

She couldn't tear her eyes away. She drank him in like a person lost in the desert, seeing a mirage and drinking the sand to satisfy an impossible, unquenchable thirst.

Beckham was even *more* than she had remembered. Her dreams, though tempting, didn't even come close to doing him justice.

He took over the space. Overshadowed the entire ballroom. He was menacing and terrifying and threatening in one glance, and in the next, he was devastatingly handsome. He could snap a neck in the blink of an eye and then cradle her in his arms in a loving embrace.

She didn't deny that he was vicious, that he may have done horrible things before her, before the rebellion, but she could see through the terror and past his mask to the tortured soul beneath.

She wanted to reach out and end this atrocity. But he couldn't see her. He couldn't hear her. He couldn't feel her. He didn't even know she was here.

He wrapped an arm around Penelope's waist. He was there… with her.

Reyna felt like vomiting. This couldn't be real. This couldn't possibly be what he had been doing while she had been suffering all these weeks. Parading around with Penelope and playing their parts for the crowd as the Saint and the Martyr, the nicknames the press had given them when Beckham had carried Penelope out of the fires. He couldn't be at her side. He just couldn't be.

Reyna closed her eyes against the blurry vision before her. This was a trick. It was a plot, a con, a setup.

Harrington had done this on purpose. He knew. He fucking knew.

She had been able to hold a lot back from Harrington. The real reason Becks had never drunk from her for almost all their time together—that he had still been drinking from Penelope. The extent of their relationship. Everything that Beckham had told her about the rebellion and his involvement with it. She had never betrayed him. But she couldn't hide her feelings for him.

Harrington wanted her to see Beckham tonight. He wanted her to see that Beckham looked happy and prosperous, that he had moved on. Harrington wanted her doubt and her unease. If he had those things, then he could use them against her. He could make her realize that she was better off with him than Beckham. She'd be better living a life of luxury rather than miserable waiting around for something that could never be.

She forced herself to look back at the stage. To see Beckham there with Penelope. To see the truth of his happiness. To know what was really happening.

This was a mask. The one he had shown her over and over and

over again while she had lived with him. He was presenting this version of himself to Visage and his colleagues and the entire city. Showing them exactly what they wanted to see.

This meant one very important thing: his cover wasn't blown.

No one knew that he was secretly part of Elle, the rebellion surge against Visage. No one knew that Penelope had gotten him involved with it in the first place. No one knew that he had been complicit in the underground fires or secretly working with Elle to take down the company he worked for from the inside out. When Everett had turned Reyna over to Harrington, he hadn't ruined everything Beckham had been working toward. Even if it meant losing her.

Logically, Reyna knew all of this. She saw it for what it was. She trusted and believed in Beckham beyond reason, beyond thought, beyond her very existence. That didn't mean it didn't hurt to see him down there.

Even if, miraculously, she was able to escape, she could never be with him like *that*.

Down there, he and Penelope looked like the perfect couple. A power couple. A blending of Visage and the government. How could Reyna compare? Reyna would never be able to provide him the sort of power that a Sky had or the cover that she had given him these last few years. If the goal for the rebellion was a better world, he was better off down there, on the arm of the most powerful woman in the city.

Not to mention the fact that Reyna was a warehouse rat from the wrong side of the tracks who had stumbled into all of this. She was nothing and no one. She never had been. She valued her own life and the life she had created with her brothers, the one she had just started to create with Beckham, but she would never belong. Not like Penny. Not even like Becks.

Even though she saw Harrington's trick, it still broke her heart.

She was about to look away and say enough was enough when something miraculous happened. Beckham tilted his head and looked directly at her.

It was impossible.

Beyond impossible.

His head turned. His eyes lifted. His body tensed. A muscle in his jaw twitched. He was staring up, straight into her eyes.

He couldn't see her. He had no way of knowing she was there. Nothing about it made sense. And yet…it happened.

She was lost. Utterly lost to him, as she had always been in his presence. For a moment, everything slipped away. There was no longer glass between them, no longer a room full of people, no longer Roland or Harrington or Penelope. Just the two of them, standing in a ballroom, besotted.

She couldn't tear herself away. She was awash with all the memories of their time together. Her moment of terror when she had first seen him at the Visage hospital. The time when he had saved her life from a rogue vampire and carried her back to safety. Their first kiss in his apartment when she had finally seen his bravado thaw and the real Beckham shine through. She had been a goner from the beginning, but definitely from that moment on. She wanted to relive every kiss and every touch and every smile. She wanted him so much it hurt.

She reached her hand out toward him, wanting nothing more than to believe that this moment was real. That this wasn't all her warped imagination. She didn't want to wake up drenched in sweat again with his face burned into the backs of her eyelids. She'd dream this again and again to know if this one moment was real.

Her heart fluttered, and her stomach lodged in her throat. She waited on bated breath for the moment to end. But it lingered. It could have been a minute or an hour; she didn't care.

Then Penelope tugged on his suit jacket. His concentration broke, and he belonged to Penelope Sky.

Reyna's heart shattered. For a breath, he had been hers once more. She didn't know if she could ever come to terms with knowing he never would be again.

CHAPTER SIX

After Harrington's guard returned her to her cell, Reyna tossed and turned all night long. Sleep didn't come easily the next night, either. Worse yet, when Monday morning dawned, it was time to give blood again. She was worried that Harrington might show up again to their session. He might lay on his charm and try to be the gentleman he most certainly was not. If he did, he'd want an answer to the absurd dichotomy he'd presented her with.

She pulled herself out of bed, delirious from sleep deprivation and even more irritated than normal. Reyna was fighting to keep her eyes open when the nurse walked in pushing the breakfast cart. Except…it wasn't the nurse.

"Morning," the woman said with a smile.

She had on the same crisp white nursing outfit, but this woman was in her late twenties. She had brown skin with lush hair dyed bright red, and she seemed…friendly?

"You're not the normal nurse."

"No, I'm not. Nancy is sick today."

Nancy. So that was her name.

"I'm Meghan with an h. I'm filling in for today. Nancy came down with something. This bug has been going around, and we're attempting to contain it. We'd hate for it to get to our Specialty Residents."

Specialty. Residents.

"Are you ready to go?"

"Pretty much never," she admitted.

"Well, we should probably get the show on the road." Meghan glanced down at the watch on her wrist.

"Aren't you going to force me to eat?"

"Are you hungry?"

Reyna eyed her skeptically. Nancy must not have prepped this nurse on the rundown. "I get dizzy if I don't eat before I get my blood drawn…"

"Grab a banana. You can eat as we go," Meghan said, brooking no further response.

Okay, new girl. Whatever you say.

Reyna did take a banana off the tray and start to eat it as she followed Meghan out of the room. Instead of walking in front of her like Nancy always had, Meghan stood at her side. Her strides were long and confident, mirroring her features—shoulders pushed back, chin raised, red hair in a crisp ponytail, just a hint of mascara to accent her brown eyes, and a secretive grin that said everything and nothing at all.

They entered the sterile hospital room a few short minutes later, and Meghan gestured for her to take a seat in the chair. Reyna frowned. God, she hated this part.

At least she had a minute to stare at the chessboard before she had to sit. She studied it for longer than normal. After B and the ball, she felt like there had to be a clue on this chessboard. She needed a way to beat Harrington. She turned the subject over and over again in her mind, and she still didn't see a way to end this. Eventually, she moved a pawn forward and relented.

"You ready?" Meghan asked.

"Never."

"I had a needle phobia once." She swabbed Reyna's arm and prepped her for the IV.

"You did?"

"Oh yeah. Just the thought of them going into my vein gave me the creeps. I'd throw up before donating blood. I was awful. Anything to get out of it."

Reyna glanced up at her face. At how animated she was as she talked.

"Then one day I said to myself, why do I fear this tiny little thing? It helps millions of people and saves lives and prevents diseases and keeps the population healthy. For some people, it even gets them high."

Reyna laughed unexpectedly, then winced. Meghan had put the needle in, and Reyna hadn't even been paying attention. She'd been so focused on Meghan's story that she hadn't noticed the prick.

"See, that wasn't so bad."

"Well, it's the second needle that gets me high," Reyna said. "Have another story up your sleeve?"

"Why don't you tell me one?" Meghan suggested, moving to the other arm.

Reyna clammed up. What the hell could she tell her? Nothing about Beckham or her life before. Nothing Visage could use. Nothing incriminating.

She shrugged. "No story."

"Guess we do it the old-fashioned way."

Meghan started to count to three but stuck her with the needle when she got to two. Reyna winced, but it hadn't been the worst she'd ever experienced.

They were almost finished with the blood when the door clicked. Reyna shuddered, but when Meghan raised an eyebrow, she straightened her spine and prepared herself for what was to come.

Harrington stepped into the room. His cane was under his arm again, and he surveyed Reyna in the same manner he'd looked at the crowd at the ball. Reyna could practically feel Meghan tense next to her. Well, at least she wasn't immune to his presence. Reyna didn't want her to do anything stupid to jeopardize herself.

"My little queen," Harrington said with a feral grin, "how are we this morning?"

Reyna washed the glare from her face. "I'm being stuck with needles."

"Ah, yes. Occupational hazard," he said, sliding effortlessly into the chair. He crossed his legs and laced his fingers together in front of him. His eyes drifted to the chessboard, and then he tsked. "You exposed your queen."

"I... What?"

Harrington moved a piece and collected her queen. He grinned. "Never leave your queen unguarded," he said pointedly. "Check."

Reyna gnashed her teeth together and focused on what Meghan was doing. It was better than seeing Harrington's triumphant face *again*.

"Well, what did you think of the rest of the ball?" Harrington asked, smoothly changing the subject. "I regret that I wasn't able to see you afterward."

"If you've been to one, you've been to them all," Reyna said with nonchalance.

Harrington shot her an amused expression. His lips quirked up at the corners. "I'm certain that's true. I wondered if you had thought more about my proposition."

Reyna swallowed. "I thought about it."

"And?"

"I don't know."

Lie. She definitely knew. She knew that she couldn't stay here. That she wasn't ready to give up all hope. Not when Beckham was still out there. Not when she could still work out a way to escape.

"My indecisive mouse," he teased. She tried to ignore the bite in his voice. Her eyes flicked over to Meghan, who was dutifully ignoring the entire exchange. At least she'd gotten that part of the job correct.

"I need more time," she finally blurted out.

"Was I not convincing enough?" He leaned his chin into his hand. A dangerous glint appeared in his eyes, and his next words cut deep. "Perhaps there was something Beckham was providing that I am not offering."

Reyna refused to think about what Beckham had offered her. She cared for him so desperately, and his absence was horrific.

"I could probably provide you sexual satisfaction, too," he said so casually she nearly choked.

Oh God. Disgust crawled through her stomach. Somehow, he had made it worse.

"Um…no."

"Not me, of course. Sometimes I partake with women, but usually only because my lovers like it."

Reyna wanted a black hole to open up underneath her and enclose her body. She never, ever wanted to have this conversation with Harrington. Not in this lifetime or the next.

"That's a…generous offer," she made herself say. She feared him enough to keep herself from unleashing on him again.

"But not enough to sway you?"

"I need more time."

"I don't like to be kept waiting," he growled.

No. She wanted to scream it in his face. She wanted to rage. She wanted to fight until her last breath. It felt like a betrayal to even consider his offer. But could anyone fault her for wanting to survive? She didn't think so. Her prison cell was cushy but painfully boring. She didn't want it to get worse, and she didn't want it to get better. She wanted to get out.

He must have read the indecision on her face. "It is either this or B. Those are your choices. I will have your decision."

Reyna opened her mouth, and her throat closed up. She couldn't do it. She had no answer.

"Now, Reyna," he barked.

"No," she gasped out.

He stared at her in shock. His expression said that he never in a million years thought she would utter that word. Not after what he had put her through. Not after what she had endured.

"You would prefer this to indulging in luxury?"

"No," she repeated, her voice wavering. "I'd prefer my own freedom."

"You should disillusion yourself of that notion," he said, standing abruptly. "You will never leave here. You signed your own prison sentence. I was willing to work with you. To give you a wonderful life. Remember that you were the one who tossed it aside so easily. This offer will not come again."

Reyna raised her chin defiantly. She'd made her decision. Consequences be damned.

Harrington backhanded her hard across the face, and she reeled in shock and pain. Her vision went blurry, ears ringing at the sheer force of the hit. "You are a very stupid girl…and I *will* break you."

Reyna blinked away tears. She hated that she cowered away from him. Hated that same fear deep in the pit of her stomach from her encounter with B. She'd thought she was already broken. Yet, somehow, she had found the resolve to still deny him what he wanted.

Harrington stormed from the room, and she watched his retreating form with tears running down her face. His threat was a promise. She just hoped she survived it.

"That was incredibly stupid," Meghan whispered.

"What do you know?" Reyna snapped. "I'd rather die than live that life."

Meghan's smile only grew. "Time to go back."

"We haven't done the venom."

"The machine isn't working. We'll have to come at a later time."

"Fucking great," Reyna muttered under her breath as Meghan removed the IVs and cleaned her up. She was stuck with a chatty, incompetent nurse. And she'd thought Nancy was bad.

Meghan walked her back to her room and followed her inside.

"You don't have to be in here. Go fix the machine or whatever," Reyna grumbled. All she wanted to do was flop back down on her bed and sleep away the rest of the day.

Meghan glanced down at her watch. She was muttering something to herself. "Three, two, one," she barely breathed. Then her eyes jumped back to Reyna and she produced a small metal gun.

"What the hell?" Reyna cried.

"Give me your arm."

"Don't shoot me!"

"Reyna, we don't have time."

"I swear, no matter what I said, I don't want to die. Please."

"I'm not here to kill you," Meghan said, waving the little gun around.

"Then why do you have *that*?"

Meghan grabbed Reyna's arm forcefully in her hand, her gentle nursing skills forgotten. She pressed the tip of the gun to Reyna's forearm and then pulled the trigger. A little buzz shot across Reyna's arm, and she gasped.

"What the hell was that?"

"I deactivated the tracker in your arm. We have ten minutes," Meghan glanced down at her watch again. "Nine minutes and twenty-seven seconds to get you the hell out of here."

Chapter Seven

"You're…rescuing me?" Reyna asked in complete disbelief.

"Trying to." Meghan rushed over to the breakfast cart she had wheeled in earlier and pulled a bag out from the bottom. She opened it and threw clothes at Reyna. "Change into these and hurry. We're running out of time with the cameras down."

"Are you with Elle?" she asked hesitantly.

"Yes," Meghan groaned. "Now hurry!"

Reyna had a million questions, but the look of urgency on Meghan's face said everything. There wasn't time.

She stripped shamelessly and pulled on a matching nurse's outfit. Meghan adjusted Reyna's hair so that it covered some of her face, shouldered the bag, and then nodded. They moved to the door as one. Meghan checked the hallway and, after finding it empty, hurried her out of the room.

"The cameras are down all the way to our destination," Meghan whispered. "The feed should loop for another seven minutes. If all goes as planned, we'll have you out of here before anyone even notices that you're gone. Are you ready?"

Reyna gave her a curt nod. She was ready to get out of here. Abso-fucking-lutely.

Meghan didn't waste any time. They were all but sprinting as they moved together. All she could do was hope that Meghan knew what she was doing and they wouldn't run into anyone. If this was a hoax or Harrington's doing, she didn't know how she would survive.

They kept moving through the maze of hallways. Down to the end, around the corner, another hallway, left turn, right turn, left turn, right. She had thought it was confusing when Harrington took her to see B and then the ballroom, but this was so much worse. She would have had no chance of getting out on her own. None at all.

At least she'd prepared herself in other ways. She'd never been happier that she had taken up running. Her muscles ached, but her breathing was measured. She felt good. Energized, even.

It was probably the adrenaline fueling her body, but she would take any benefit at this point.

They turned another corner, and still there was no one. She'd never seen anyone on either of her two previous trips out of her room, but she'd figured Harrington had engineered that. It seemed too lucky that the long white hallways of closed doors and bright overhead lights were all empty. Reyna caught sight of a camera in a corner. It wasn't blinking red like the ones in her room always had. Meghan must be telling the truth—the cameras were really down.

As they came to another corner, Meghan stuck out her hand and they both skidded to a stop. Reyna stood there with wide eyes as she waited for her breathing to even out.

"We have to get to the stairwell—it's only a couple more hallways. But this area is busier than your sector. Act like a nurse, and if we're stopped, let me do the talking."

Reyna gave her a quick nod to show she understood.

With a deep breath, Meghan directed them into the new sector. They passed a series of glass rooms. Most of them were empty, but a few held scientists and doctors and nurses working in lab gear, wearing the crisp white lab coats she'd associated with the nurses of Visage. A few wore button-ups and ties underneath their coats. Goggles hung around their necks or were perched on their noses as they looked down into microscopes or at little petri dishes. Blood bags hung on racks behind their heads.

Experiments.

They were doing experiments with the blood. She shuddered and wondered if her blood was being used for this, too.

An irrational anger suffused her. No amount of medical advancement would ever make up for the horrors she'd endured. She hoped all these people rotted.

"Smile," Meghan ground out.

Reyna shoved her fierce anger down deep. Then she smiled. It took real effort not to bare her teeth and shoot savage glares at the people they passed. She had to appear placid, bland. She had to be like nurse Nancy to get through this.

They were about to clear the corridor when a doctor stepped out of one of the rooms.

"Hello there," the man said, snapping his fingers at them. "You must be the nurses we sent for."

Reyna shot Meghan a worried glance, but Meghan only nodded. "Yes, sir."

It startled Reyna to realize that this man was a vampire. He didn't have the usual magnetism or terrifying lethal threat. It wasn't until he flashed his fangs at them that she even realized she *should* be afraid. Had she grown so accustomed to vampires that she didn't see them for what they were anymore? Or were Beckham and Harrington that much more formidable?

"Wonderful. Please bring patient X13276 from her room." He handed Meghan a tablet.

"Yes, sir," Meghan said again.

"She's here for her final. Pity," he said with real remorse.

"Her final, sir?" Reyna choked out.

Meghan gave her a sharp look.

"X13276 is the first to be responsive to our testing. We're going to put her through final paces to see if we can duplicate her blood to make the treasured blood antidote." He beamed as if he were giving her great news.

"So, vampires wouldn't have to have blood matches?" Reyna asked in horror. Meghan's answering glare said she didn't mask it well enough.

"Precisely. It's a huge leap for vamp-kind," he said, laughing at his poor joke.

"Great news, doctor. We'll get her and deliver her promptly," Meghan said. She practically tugged Reyna down the hall and away from the doctor.

When they were out of earshot, Meghan shoved her. "What the hell were you thinking? We don't have time to stand around and debate the benefits or consequences of a blood antidote."

Reyna chewed on her lip as a plan formed in her mind. Her eyes darted from the doctor who had just disappeared to the tablet in Meghan's hand and back. "We need to get that girl."

"Reyna, we don't have time."

"Think about it for a second. We can rescue this girl. We can get her out of this place. You saw what my life was like; now imagine what it must be like for this girl. Didn't you hear what he said? She's the key to a blood antidote. I don't want that to happen any more than you do. If we can save someone else, don't you think we should?"

Meghan puffed out a breath. "Yes, of course I think we should save someone. But we're on limited time here. If we miss our rendezvous, we're done for."

"How much more time will it take to extract her?"

Meghan dug through the tablet, pulling up the information on the subject. "Fuck, her name is Jodie and she's just around the corner." Reyna could see the resolve in Meghan's eyes. "Fine. We'll grab her. Stay close and do exactly what I say. This way."

They hurried down the hallway and around a corner, stopping

before a blank door. Meghan was right. Jodie's room only added a minute onto their timeline. Meghan tapped a code into a pad at the door, and it slid open. Reyna reeled back at the sight before her. This room was a true prison cell. A real one, nothing like the lush accommodations Reyna had been given. She really had been lucky these past weeks.

It was a ten-by-ten box with a metal bed in one corner supporting a thin, lumpy mattress and an off-white sheet. A pail sat in another corner for waste, and a drain opened in the middle of the floor. There were no windows. One incandescent lightbulb hung from a string in the ceiling. Otherwise it was just a box—a horrible fucking box.

It took a moment for Reyna to come to terms with the state of the room and focus in on the Black woman who had jumped up from the bed at their approach. She was no older than Reyna, wearing a threadbare version of the standard-issue white uniform to which Reyna had grown accustomed. The woman was tall and rail-thin, with unruly curly hair. She took one look at Meghan and Reyna in the doorway and skittered backward into the corner.

"It's not time."

"It's Jodie, right?"

The girl reared back in alarm at the sound of her name. As if she hadn't heard it in a long time. "Yeah?"

"I'm Reyna." Reyna beckoned to her. "We're here to get you out. Come with us."

Jodie's eyes widened in shock. "I don't know who the hell you are, but—"

"Oh, for fuck's sake," Meghan breathed under her breath. "We're breaking you out, and we're on a tight schedule. Do you want to come with us or stay here?"

Jodie's eyes darted back and forth between them quickly. "How do I know you're not lying?"

Meghan retrieved her little gun from the bag on her shoulder. Jodie looked at her with alarm. "It'll deactivate the tracking device in your arm."

"You're serious?"

Reyna nodded. "Just let her do it and then we'll be out of here. I swear."

Jodie narrowed her eyes before extending her arm to them. "If this is a trick…"

Meghan pressed the gun against the device, and it buzzed once. "Done. Now let's move."

Jodie ran her hand over the tiny knot in her arm. "Y'all are for real?"

"No one deserves this." Reyna gestured to the prison cell.

"We have to go," Meghan said. "We have less than three minutes to get out of this building while the cameras are down. I don't have extra clothes for you. You'll have to pretend to be our patient. Act docile—or better yet, pretend to be drugged on a vamp bite."

Meghan ushered them out of the room. They backtracked through the corridors until they finally hit a stairwell. Up they went. Around and around and around. Reyna lost count of how many flights they climbed. Jodie stayed close between them. Her labored breaths made it clear that she hadn't been exercising like Reyna had. Even with her exercises, Reyna was still panting as they climbed the stairs.

"Where…are…we?" Reyna gasped out between breaths.

"Visage headquarters. I'll explain later," Meghan told her.

Visage.

This whole time, she had been in the building where Beckham worked. She'd been living, eating, breathing, surviving, and also slowly dying, and she'd been doing it in this fucking place. Practically in plain sight. How could Harrington get away with this? How the hell was it even possible?

"I'm going to kill him" was her only response.

"We'd all appreciate that, but right now, keep it down," Meghan said.

Reyna gave a tight nod and kept filing up the stairs.

"Two more flights," Meghan said. So close.

Just as they reached the next landing, an alarm blared overhead.

Reyna skidded to a halt, colliding with Jodie. Both of their eyes widened with fear as they turned to Meghan.

"What the hell is that?" Jodie asked.

"Meghan?" Reyna asked.

Meghan turned frightened eyes toward Reyna. "Shit."

"What?" Reyna asked.

"Control your breathing. Get it under control. Both of you." Meghan fixed Reyna's hair, brushing more in front of her face. It was clear that she was trying to look confident, but her hands were shaking.

"Meghan, what is happening?" Reyna hissed.

"Someone knows you're gone," she whispered. "Our window just closed."

Chapter Eight

"What do we do now?" Reyna asked. "What's plan B?"

Meghan shook her head. "There is no plan B."

"What the hell kind of plan is this?" Jodie asked.

"Look, I don't know what happened, but we still have time to get to our rendezvous spot. We have two more flights of stairs and an exit to get to. We can do it. We have to."

"Then let's move," Reyna said.

The other woman agreed, "No way am I going back."

The stairwell door burst open beside them. A flood of people filled the staircase, responding to the alarm. Meghan grabbed Jodie, and Reyna followed suit as they hauled her up the flight of stairs. Reyna tucked her chin to her chest. She didn't know how many people knew that she had been held captive below Visage, or if any of them would even recognize her face, but she'd rather be safe than sorry.

"Christ, I hate these drills," one woman said at Reyna's shoulder.

"Tell me about it," the man next to her agreed.

"Someone said this isn't a drill," another man added. Reyna tensed, waiting for someone to blow their cover. "That the boss himself is going to be waiting to speak with all of us and give us all permanents."

Reyna blew out a breath. They didn't know what the alarm was for. They thought that, instead of rotating blood escorts every couple of months, they were all going to get permanent live-in blood escorts—what she had been to Beckham.

"I thought only senior officials were getting them," the woman said.

"Now that the Census is finished in the city, they can begin to transition the humans to us."

"I don't want a human to live with me permanently," the first man grumbled. "How invasive."

"Don't you miss the good old days?" the woman intoned.

Reyna bit her lip and tuned out the rest of their conversation.

After the second floor, Meghan maneuvered them through the crowd and toward the door. When they reached the door, however, a guard stood there, impassable.

"No exit, ladies," the vampire said with a smile and a discreet look at her chest.

Meghan leaned in and fluttered her eyelashes. "Look, I don't want to take this girl through all these people. She has that pesky illness that's going around. Can't we pop out the door and take her the long way?"

"Sorry. Boss's orders. Everyone up to the top level for assessment."

"I know. I know," Meghan said, biting her lips. "But do you really want me to bring her up there? She's not an employee. And she's *sick*." She emphasized the last word until he glanced down at the "sick patient."

The vampire narrowed his eyes. "The blood thing?"

Meghan agreed. "Yeah. Severe case."

He took a step back. "It's contagious. What is she even doing in the stairwell?"

"It was supposed to be cleared for us. It's already ravished her body. Look at her." Meghan pointed at the woman's skinny arms and narrow waist. "I don't want this to continue to happen. It'd be easier if we could avoid all of this entirely."

"Maybe I should radio down…" He trailed off as Meghan stepped closer.

"Plus…the sooner I'm finished, the sooner I'll be free for lunch."

His eyebrows rose. "Lunch?"

She was shameless. She tilted her neck sideways as if in invitation. "I know a great place."

He laughed. "Okay. Go on ahead. But be quick. I'll meet you up front at noon."

"Can't wait," Meghan said with a girly giggle before shoving both of them through the open door.

She blew out a heavy breath as their trio tried to seem unhurried. When they turned the next corner and disappeared from the guard's view, they took off at a faster clip.

"That took forever," Reyna said.

"We're late," Meghan said. "I can't think about it."

The rest of the trek was tense. None of them knew if the cameras were working or if they were being followed already. They kept expecting someone to jump out at them and steal them back to the basement…back to hell.

None of them dared to speak. Reyna found she was even holding her breath, as if one exhale would threaten everything they'd worked for. Her gut was twisted up in panic and anticipation. She never stopped hoping they'd make it out, but she couldn't think beyond that. There was only this one moment and then the next. Putting one foot in front of the other and facing down the dark alley.

"We're here," Meghan whispered as they approached a giant black double door. She whispered a silent prayer and then entered her code. It flashed red. "No. No. No." She typed it in again. Again…red.

"Meghan," Reyna hissed.

"It won't open." Her eyes darted around the hallway wildly.

"Try one more time."

Meghan swallowed and input the code a third time. Red. A fourth time. Red.

"We need to get out of here," Jodie said. "Entering the password that many times is going to be a red flag. We can't get out this way. We need to find another."

"There isn't another way," Meghan said.

"Then we fucking find one."

"Hey!" Reyna cried, shutting them both up. This couldn't all be for nothing. "This isn't helping anything. Let's try one more time, and then we'll find a different exit."

"You try it," Meghan said, pushing Reyna toward the keypad. Reyna poised her finger over it and nodded. "0-7-1-5-0-1-1-0-9-2-1-5-2-1-7."

Reyna's finger moved to press the enter key, praying that the code would work this time, when the door suddenly slid open on its own. All three women jumped back. Then an Asian human man with thick dark hair peeked his head around the corner.

"Tye," Meghan said, launching herself into his arms. "I have never been happier to see you."

"You took too long," he told her, pulling back and opening the door farther. He was about average height, wearing a black uniform similar to a delivery driver. "Xavier didn't want me to come look for you."

"Bastard," she hissed. Then she collected herself. "We need to get moving."

Meghan ushered Reyna and Jodie forward, and Tye took stock of the fact that there was an additional person. "Pick up a stray?"

"That a problem?" their stray asked.

"Not at all," he said with a bold smile.

They all passed through the door and into a giant loading dock that was empty save for an enormous delivery truck.

"Get in," Tye said, opening the doors. "Xavier is driving."

All three vaulted into the back of the truck, which was freezing and chock-full of blood.

"What the…" Reyna whispered.

"Move to the front," Meghan directed them without explanation.

Bypassing all the blood and supplies, they reached the front and found two sets of dark coveralls bearing the same logo as the truck waiting for them.

"What do I wear?" Jodie asked.

Meghan frowned and then grabbed a bag. "Sorry to do this."

"You're putting me in a body bag?"

"Temporarily." Then Meghan turned to Reyna. "I think it might be safer if you're in one, too. I'm sorry."

Both of them looked at her in horror, but Tye yelled, "Meghan?"

"Coming," she called. She stripped out of her nurse uniform and pulled on the coveralls as Reyna and Jodie unzipped the body bags and shimmied inside. Meghan jumped out the back, and the truck doors slammed shut behind them, casting them into total darkness. Reyna took a deep breath and closed the bag over her head. She heard Jodie grunt as she slid into the bag next to her. Only their breathing could be heard before the rumble of the truck's engine roaring to life drowned it out.

Reyna's heart began to pound. A body bag. She was being transported out of here in a body bag. She wasn't usually afraid of small spaces or the dark, but these weren't usual circumstances. She couldn't believe they'd even made it this far.

"Hey," Jodie whispered.

"Hey."

"Thank you for doing this."

"Don't thank me yet," Reyna whispered. "We still have to get out of here."

"But still…thanks."

Reyna smiled, even though Jodie couldn't see it. "You're welcome."

The truck rumbled forward. Reyna clenched her hands at her sides and tried to breathe slowly. This would all be over soon.

Only it was *much* too soon for the truck to stop again.

"Why are we stopping?" Jodie asked.

Reyna had no idea, and she strained to listen to what was happening in the front cab.

"We're right on schedule," a male voice said from the driver's seat. That must be Xavier. The one who'd wanted to leave them.

Someone must have responded, because Meghan piped up. "We're all set here, boys," she said in the flirtatious tone she'd used with the guard. "Have all the samples secure."

Another voice entered the mix. "You're going to need to open up the back. We're on a high-security breach."

"Oh no!" Meghan gasped. "And you think somehow we're part of the breach? Aren't we on your schedule?"

A rustling noise and then a grunt. Maybe that meant yes.

"Open the back."

Reyna could practically feel the tension rolling off their rescuers. Of course they couldn't deny them access to the back of the vehicle. That would raise more flags than complying. But if they complied, would the guards open up the body bags?

A door opened up front, and someone got out. Reyna didn't so much as breathe. Jodie had gone completely still beside her.

This was it. This was life or death. This was freedom or captivity. This was the end.

The back door opened.

She could hear voices at the far end of the truck. A foot stomped on the bumper, and a body hoisted into the cavity. The truck rocked at the extra weight.

Reyna balled her hands into fists to keep from trembling.

"What's in that?" a gruff voice asked.

"What do you think?" Tye asked in an easy, joking tone.

"Didn't have bodies on the report."

"They were on ours."

"Blood illness," Meghan said, joining them. "It's going around and extremely contagious. We're taking them to be disposed of. Too dangerous to do it on-site."

A foot stepped right by Reyna's head.

The bag rustled as he reached down to take a look.

The zipper dragged down, and cold air hit her face. She remained perfectly still and tried to look like death. Her eyes were closed. She could see the light from his flashlight through her eyelids. Her lungs constricted as they demanded air, but she held on longer. They were so close. So damn close.

"Didn't you hear me?" Meghan asked. The zipper stopped moving, leaving her shoulders exposed. "It's a blood illness. If you get any closer, you could catch it. Vampires aren't immune. It's killing them off, too."

"Fine," he spat. The zipper snapped back into place, covering her once more, but still she didn't dare move. Her blood pounded in her ears, demanding oxygen. "But let me double-check your report. Everything else looks in place."

"Of course," Tye said.

A rustling of papers, and then the doors were slammed shut once more. Reyna released a breath at the same time as Jodie. Neither of them said a word, but Reyna was glad that Jodie was with her. Even though she couldn't see her, she still felt less alone.

It was a few minutes before the truck came to life again.

"All good to go," someone said from the front.

Xavier put the car in gear, but a voice stopped them in their tracks again.

The gruff vampire said, "Wait!"

Reyna closed her eyes. No. They were so close. So close.

"You forgot to sign for it."

"Of course," Xavier said.

A final, interminable pause. A garage opened noisily before them, and then they were out. Reyna couldn't see it for herself, but she knew. She could tell by the truck's acceleration and Meghan's whoop of excitement.

They were finally free.

Chapter Nine

Reyna and Jodie still didn't move. Not while they waited to see if anyone would follow. Then the front door slid open. A sliver of light shot over the body bags, and Meghan's voice rang out. "We're in the clear, ladies. Come out of there."

They both yanked down the zippers and tossed the bags aside with eager excitement. It was done. It was over. Finally.

"We're free," Reyna whispered. Her eyes moved to Jodie's equally dark ones. "We're really free."

"I can't believe it," Jodie said. "When y'all said you were getting me out, I thought you were full of shit. But it really worked. We're really gone."

"I dreamed of getting out. I even plotted for it. But I never knew if it was really possible."

"I didn't even dream," Jodie whispered.

Reyna frowned at that statement. She wondered how long Jodie had been inside Visage. How long a person had to be held captive before they gave up any hope of being rescued or escaping.

Meghan came forward with a switchblade. "This isn't going to be pleasant."

"What..." Meghan snatched up Reyna's arm without warning and dug into her forearm. Reyna howled and tried to pull her arm away, but Meghan held Reyna steady. Meghan stuck the tip of the knife into the wound she'd created, and out popped a tiny piece of metal.

"Sorry," Meghan said. She held the little tracker in her hand. "We can't take any chances."

"A little warning next time."

"You don't like needles or blood. I wasn't going to take my chances with you being squeamish," Meghan told her. She was already bandaging up the wound with the efficiency of a real nurse. Reyna wondered which parts of her personality were an act and which parts were reality.

"I'm not squeamish," Jodie said, offering Meghan her arm. "Get this sucker out of me."

Meghan made quick work of removing Jodie's tracker as well. After Jodie was patched up, Meghan dropped both devices into a plastic bag and sealed it shut.

"What are you going to do with them?" Reyna asked. She was applying pressure to her arm in the way that Nancy had shown her dozens of times with the IVs. She was practically a pro at blood loss.

"Decoy. They already know that you're missing." Her eyes darted between Reyna and Jodie. "One of you, at least, if not both by now. We're going to need to get rid of these."

"So like...who the hell are you people?" Jodie asked.

"Elle," Reyna answered for Meghan.

"What the fuck is an *L*? Like a capital letter?"

Meghan sighed. "Elle, like the name, is the underground rebellion organization working against Visage. It was started by a human named Elle who opposed Visage's rise to power. She was killed in Elle's Rebellion a decade ago, and we've been working as a rebel group ever since. Our goal is for vampire and human autonomy and equality."

Jodie snorted. "Good luck with that."

"We broke you out of prison," Meghan said. "We're doing good work here."

"I'm a realist. I appreciate y'all saving my ass back there, but no one is taking down Visage."

Meghan blew out a frustrated breath. "Whether you believe that or not is up to you. Some of us are risking our necks to try to make it a reality."

"All right."

Reyna could see the tough-girl routine for what it was: Jodie was scared. This behavior was bulletproof armor against the world. Reyna knew what that was like—had endured situations where she had needed her own armor. It was necessary. Shedding it would be hard.

"Just leave it," Reyna told Meghan.

"Okay. Be ready to move when I tell you to. Tye is going to give us the signal, and then I need both of you on me. We have another short drop window. Hopefully we haven't already missed it."

Everyone fell silent at that. They weren't at headquarters yet, which meant everything could still fall apart. As the truck bumped along, the three women stood tensely in the back, waiting.

Finally, the vehicle slowed and rolled to a stop in a gravel parking lot that sent the women and all the equipment bouncing. Reyna reached for the side of the truck to steady herself, but Meghan was already launching herself to the back of their getaway car.

"Are you coming or what?"

They darted after her, and as soon as they jumped down out of the back, they received no reprieve from the outside temperatures, which were also frigid. Reyna did the math in her head. She'd been kidnapped in September. The leaves hadn't yet started changing in the park outside of Beckham's penthouse. The colder temperatures had barely graced the evenings. Now, it was November...after Thanksgiving. It was a bitterly cold morning, with thick dark clouds overhead and a slow drizzle. Not quite cold enough to freeze, but cold and wet enough to be annoying.

She hustled out into the rain and sprinted with Meghan over to a nondescript pickup truck and a dilapidated sedan. Meghan handed off a baggie with the trackers to Xavier, a large Black man with short, coiled hair and a menacing glare. Vampire. It was written all over him. She knew that vampires worked with Elle—Beckham did, after all—but it was still surprising to see a vampire running a prison break detail or getting into a piece-of-shit, rusted-out car.

"Thank you," Reyna managed.

Xavier shot her a swift smile that barely touched his lips before speeding off into the distance with the trackers.

Tye hopped into the front seat of the pickup truck. "Over here."

Reyna followed Jodie into the back seat of the extended cab while Meghan took the passenger seat. As soon as the door was closed, Tye took off like a bullet.

The ride was tense and silent. At one point, sirens blared in the distance. Meghan chewed on her lip and kept glancing out the window. Only when they were far enough away that the sirens were just a distant ringing did Meghan straighten once more and exude all the confidence Reyna had already grown accustomed to.

"Sorry about this," she said, tossing Reyna a black mask. She dug around in a bag for another second and then passed a black strip of fabric to Jodie. "It'll be safer, in case something happens, if you don't know where the entrance to headquarters is. We blindfold all newbies."

Jodie grumbled something vulgar under her breath and held up the blindfold. "You think this will fit around my hair?"

"We'll switch," Reyna said, offering her the mask.

Jodie grumbled again, wrestling the fabric over her voluminous hair. "Congrats. I can't see shit."

Reyna stared down at the blindfold in her hands. It was basically just a black tie. Her hands shook as she thought of all the times she'd been forced to wear a blindfold. When Beckham had led her down to the Vault before the fires wiped out the club, when she'd been kidnapped from Everett's apartment, on her way to the ball where Harrington had forced her to watch Beckham with Penny.

"Reyna," Meghan said softly in her nurse voice. "Everything okay?"

"Yeah," she said unconvincingly.

Nothing was okay. As she slid the blindfold over her eyes, she didn't know if anything would ever be okay again.

• • •

As soon as their truck came to a stop, Reyna yanked the blindfold off as quickly as she could. Her heart had hammered and her hands had shaken the entire way. She hadn't removed the blindfold before it was time, but only with great effort.

They were in some sort of underground garage. Before them was a solid, steel door. They hadn't driven very far since she'd been blindfolded, and still she had no idea where they were or what was on the other side of that door.

"Honey, we're home," Tye singsonged with a wide grin.

It had been so long since Reyna had seen anyone this genuinely happy. She honestly couldn't remember ever seeing a smile that vibrant before. Had his life been that pleasant? Joy was not something that came naturally to her, even before the kidnapping. Now...well, let's just say the glass was half empty.

Jodie pursed her lips at his enthusiasm, which made Reyna feel marginally better. Meghan and Tye got out of the front seats and corralled her and Jodie out of the back.

Trepidation bit at Reyna. What *was* Elle, anyway? What would they expect of her? Had she traded one prison for another?

One thought propelled her forward: Beckham. He was part of this organization. If he trusted them, then she would give it a shot.

Then her heart fluttered. *Beckham.*

All those weeks, she'd had to lock him away in a far-off place. He helped her through the tough moments, but she couldn't think of him without breaking. Through all of that…she'd worried that she would never see him again. Be in a room with him, hold him, touch him, love him once more. She'd left that part of her life for her dreams. Those sweet, toxic dreams.

But now she was here. He was here. She would see him. They could be together again. Her heart expanded with hope. It was all right behind that door.

Tye entered a security password and looked into a retinal scanner before the door hissed open on silent hinges. Meghan looped her arm through Reyna's and strode inside behind Tye and a fearless Jodie. It opened to a sky-blue room with wooden floors and paintings hanging from the walls. It was clear and light and even comforting. No whitewashed walls or white-tiled floor. No antiseptic or hospital smell. No bright light overhead. Just a room. An empty room.

She didn't know what she had been expecting. A welcome party, maybe? Beckham standing there with open arms? Anything would have been better than nothing.

"Welcome to Elle," Meghan whispered to Reyna. "Welcome home."

Home.

Chapter Ten

The room was empty. Beckham was supposed to be here. He was supposed to be waiting for her. She'd been anticipating this moment for eight long weeks. Her chest ached at the thought that he wasn't here.

"Where is he?" Reyna asked.

"Beckham?" Meghan asked warily.

"Who else?"

"He's not here." Meghan swallowed. "He hasn't been here in weeks."

"What?" Reyna nearly shouted.

"Or at least, I haven't seen him in weeks. Tye and I are a step down from high command. From what I know, he's been trying to keep a low profile. He was under investigation after your disappearance. He went to Harrington himself and told him that you'd run away once he found out what had happened to you."

"How long have you known?"

"We knew you'd been kidnapped almost right away, but it took weeks for us to find out where he'd taken you. We thought we'd lose Beckham and the information he provided, but he stayed on. He has to play it off like nothing happened."

Reyna winced. Nothing happened. He must have been convincing for Harrington to allow him to stay in his position as a senior vice president of Visage. Because the alternative wasn't possible. She couldn't believe that he actually *didn't* care about her.

"So when is he coming back?"

Meghan shrugged sadly. "I really don't know. I'm sorry. Why don't I show you around in the meantime?"

"Okay," Reyna said hollowly.

Reyna followed Meghan and Jodie down the hallway and through Elle headquarters. They moved into a larger corridor, which Reyna was surprised to find full of people. Some stopped to say hi to Meghan. Others high-fived Tye as they passed. But everyone was busy and engaged and happy. Reyna and Jodie received a few strange looks, but overall, most people waved or smiled. They must be so used to strangers in their midst it didn't even faze them.

Their group turned the first corner, and Reyna froze.

"Surprise," Meghan called, holding her hands out.

Her brothers stood before her. Brian and Drew were standing in Elle headquarters. She blinked and blinked again, but it was *real*.

"Reyna," Brian whispered in shock.

Drew couldn't even get words out. He was sputtering.

Then she was running. She couldn't hear or see anything else going on around her. She collided with her brothers, throwing her arms wide around them. They tightened their grip on her, and she breathed them in. They weren't in the warehouses anymore, laboring away. They were here in Elle. Safe and sound.

Tears streamed down her face. She didn't even care that she was soaking through Brian's T-shirt as she buried her face in it.

"Oh my God, I missed you," she gasped.

"I can't believe you're here," Brian said, brushing her hair back.

"We were so worried, Rey," Drew added.

"You're alive. God, we pushed for your escape every single day."

She pulled back with a sniffle. "How are you guys here?"

"The day after you were kidnapped, a group of Elle agents showed up at our apartment," Brian told her. "They told us what happened to you and that we needed to leave with them. There was a fear that Harrington would try to kidnap us as well and torture us to use against you. We didn't believe them at first, but then we spoke to Beckham and we went along with what he said. They brought us in, and it's been great so far."

"We're so glad you're home," Drew said.

Reyna wiped her tears with the back of her hand. "It's so good to see you."

"What did they do…" Drew trailed off when she shook her head. She wasn't ready to discuss what had happened in that basement in Visage.

"Hey, guys," Meghan said, jumping into the conversation.

"Hey, Meghan," Brian said with an easy smile.

She nodded at him. "How's Laura?"

"Laura is here?" Reyna gasped.

"Yeah. It was one of my stipulations for leaving. And well…" Brian scratched the back of his head as if he were embarrassed.

"They're engaged," Drew filled in.

Reyna's jaw dropped. Her brother was engaged. "Brian, congratulations! That makes me so happy."

"Yeah. We're engaged," Brian said. "We can go back to our rooms and you can see her until they have a room worked out for you."

"She already has a room," Meghan said. She threw her thumb back at Jodie. "It's this one we have to figure out accommodations for."

"I don't care about a room," Jodie said. "And I'm all for what appears to be a happy reunion. But first, food."

Reyna's stomach grumbled as if on command. She remembered that she'd only had that banana all day. It was the first day in more than eight weeks that she'd gone without a full meal. Before she was hired by Visage, it had been irregular for her to eat *more* than one full meal a day. Things changed quickly.

"Food it is, then," Meghan chirped.

Reyna introduced Jodie to her two brothers as they followed Meghan and Tye to the cafeteria. It was in between mealtimes, so the place was deserted, which was a relief. She wanted to talk and hear about their experience at Elle so far.

When Jodie went with Meghan and Tye to rummage through the pantry, she turned back to her brothers. "I'm really, really, really glad that you're safe. I tried not to wonder what would happen to you after I was taken."

"You're happy *we're* safe?" Drew gasped out. "Reyna, you were kidnapped."

"What happened to you in there?" Brian asked.

Reyna chewed on her lip. "I'm alive and healthy. That's all that matters right now, okay?"

"That's no..." Brian started, but Drew cut him off: "You can tell us when you're ready."

She gave them an appreciative smile. "Can you fill me in on what's been going on since I was taken? I feel like I've missed so much."

"Well, Elle HQ is an enormous operation," Brian told her. "We weren't sure of it when we first got here, but they really are working for vampire and human equality. That isn't just a line that they feed you. Everyone here has a job. The inner circle of command delegates tasks, and it trickles down through the ranks. Drew and I are both working in security."

"Security?" Fear crept through her.

"Yeah," Brian said as if it were no big deal. "It's hard to find guys around here with any fighting skills."

"Is the job dangerous?" Her brothers exchanged a look she knew all too well. "Don't you dare shield me from this."

"It's not a walk in the park," Drew said. "We have pretty grueling training, fighting techniques, strategy classes, weapons…"

"I've been locked up, and you two have been training to get yourselves killed."

"It's not like that," Drew said, reaching out for her.

Brian straightened up. "We had to do our part. After you were kidnapped, we had no idea what was going to happen. We spent every day feeling utterly helpless. We did the only thing we could—we trained. We bought into the cause, and we're going to keep fighting for what's right if it keeps you safe," Brian said passionately. "The leader of Elle is ex-military, and she's doing a great job. We're happy to be working for her. Happy to have a purpose in all of this."

Reyna sighed. She might not like her brothers working on a security detail where they could be harmed, but she understood the idea of needing purpose. It was something that she had so desperately needed while living with Beckham. Something Harrington could never give her. She didn't want to think about Harrington, and her heart hurt too badly to think about Becks.

"Okay." Meghan's cheery tone rang out as she exited the kitchen.

Tye held up brown paper bags. "The goods."

"Here you go." Meghan passed Reyna a bag filled with a sandwich, a bag of potato chips, and a chocolate chip cookie. "Best we can do until next shift comes in to cook."

They ate in a hurried silence. It was the least nutritious meal she'd had in weeks. It filled a hole that she didn't even know needed to be filled. The food made her happy. It didn't just fill her stomach.

Once they were done, Meghan's gaze found Reyna. "How about I show you to your room? You look exhausted."

"Sure." She was both exhausted and wired. All of her emotions roiled through her at lightning speed.

"Great. Jodie is going to tag along with us. Tye will take Brian and Drew back to their command." Reyna opened her mouth to protest, but Meghan barreled forward. "They'll come see you after their shift is finished. You could use some rest."

"It's fine," Brian said, kissing her forehead. "We'll be fine. You're in good hands. You're safe here. We'll find you later."

"Love you, Rey," Drew said. He dragged her into another hug, and then all the guys disappeared.

Jodie trotted out of the kitchen with her mouth full of a second sandwich. "The iiii ta da fer."

Reyna's eyebrows rose. "What?"

Jodie chewed and swallowed. Then she repeated, "This is to die for."

"PB&J, baby," Meghan said.

"Peanut butter," she groaned. "I missed peanut butter." She took another huge bite.

"Let's get out of here. I think a tour can wait for tomorrow when you're both fed, rested, and have begun to acclimate." Meghan was already storming out of the cafeteria.

Reyna and Jodie shared a look. It said everything that neither of them could speak aloud. They weren't going to acclimate. Not now… maybe not ever.

Still, they followed Meghan. They took an elevator up two levels and exited onto a floor labeled RESIDENCE.

"We only have so much space for housing right now. That's the main room where the girls bunk, but the outer walls are all private or shared rooms. Hard to come by." Meghan grinned devilishly. "But this one is yours."

Reyna twisted the knob and pushed the door open. She gaped at her surroundings when she entered. "Wow."

"Cushy," Jodie said. "Enough room in here for two. Don't you think?"

"Up to Reyna," Meghan said. "I've got extra space if you want to crash with me until we find something else."

She could hear Meghan and Jodie making arrangements, but she was lost taking in this room. The bed was enormous and high off the ground with a white comforter. Photographs lined the walls. In his apartment, the photos had all been Beckham's; now she was amazed to find her own images staring back at her in frames and on canvas.

Black-and-white photographs straight from the website *Perspective* that she had used to showcase her art. Visage had worried that it was an Elle sympathizer website. Turned out they were right.

She walked in a hazy dream to the closet and laughed. None of the silky doll outfits awaited her. Just practical jeans, fit T-shirts, and a whole rack of Converse to choose from. There was also an olive-green military-issue jacket, two ball caps, and her backpack. She pulled open the first drawer and grinned from ear to ear. Lace bras and silk thongs and satin matching sets and corsets and lingerie galore. Drawer after drawer after drawer.

"He did this," she said, shutting the drawer with reddening cheeks.

"Yeah. He set this room up for you before we even began to work on your extraction."

"Thanks, Meghan," Reyna said softly, facing her at the door. "For everything."

"Of course. I'll just…" She gestured down the hallway. "If you need anything, take the elevator down two floors and someone will find me."

Reyna nodded and listened for the click of the door closing behind her. The rest of the day caught up with her in a rush, and she sank into the pillow-top mattress. Adrenaline wore off, and exhaustion hit her. Without warning, tears sprang to her eyes. She was free. She was finally free. She couldn't believe it.

And yet, Beckham wasn't here. After everything she'd gone through, she'd thought he would be here waiting for her. Her eyes moved around the room that had been created for her. She saw it for what it was—a slice of a once-wonderful life. Beckham had done this for her. He'd wanted it to feel like home when he brought her here. Which meant that he'd always intended for her to show up.

But if that was the case, then where was he?

Chapter Eleven

The next three days passed in a blur. Reyna slept off and on the entire time, only waking up long enough to eat. Even then, sometimes she couldn't be bothered. She could hear her brothers come in and out of her room with Meghan and occasionally Tye on their heels. She knew they were worried about her sleeping so much. She knew that she should get up and act like a human again, but she had never been more exhausted.

On the fourth day, Meghan went about checking Reyna's vitals. "We're going to have to dose you with vampire saliva."

"What?" Reyna asked groggily.

"Or we could have someone bite you if you prefer."

"No!"

"I didn't give you the saliva after I drew your blood, and I took a lot of blood from you at Visage. Harrington was taking *more* than the recommended amount each time, Reyna. Then he was giving you extra-large doses of his saliva to make up for the blood he was taking.

You didn't get any this time. The first time in *weeks*," Meghan said with a weighted frown. "I thought you were tired and that I should let you rest. I should have known better. Your body is trying to make up for the loss of blood, and I suspect it's going through withdrawal."

"I'm not an addict," Reyna countered.

"I didn't accuse you of anything. You just went through a traumatic experience. Sleeping is perfectly normal, but I'd prefer to check you out before I let you live the rest of your life in that bed."

"All right," Reyna relented. "How's Jodie?"

"Incredibly resilient. She won't let me check her out, but at least she's not still sleeping."

"And Beckham?" she whispered.

Meghan shook her head once solemnly.

"Okay." She shucked the covers off her. "Where to?"

"Medical center," Meghan said.

"A hospital?" Reyna shuddered at the thought.

"It's a safe place. I'll be there with you the entire time."

Reyna didn't reply. It was bad enough that she had to get dosed one more time or that Meghan thought she was jonesing for her next hit. Back to hospital rooms. More hospital rooms. She hated that her body was reacting this way. She just wanted it to be over.

Meghan brought Reyna to the mess hall to eat breakfast. She wasn't hungry, but she ate anyway. Jodie showed up as they were finishing and agreed to join them, with the caveat that she was in no way agreeing to any invasive medical procedures.

Reyna would have liked to tell Meghan the same thing. She understood why Jodie wouldn't want another person near her. Reyna didn't particularly want it, either, but she really felt like shit. And while she didn't want the venom, if it helped, then she'd do it.

"No time for the official tour, but this is the workout room."

Meghan pointed out rooms as they passed. "Here we have a weight room." She gestured to a large lifting area. "And this is everyone's favorite: the rec room."

Reyna peeked her head inside to find a large room containing everything from Ping-Pong to air hockey to cards to Monopoly. A projector took up one wall, displaying six different shows at once. Someone was arguing which one should have sound for the room, though it looked like a couple people were wearing headphones for the show they wanted to watch. Everyone looked so happy and carefree.

"Wow," Jodie breathed behind Reyna.

"Yeah. It's…something."

"Overwhelming?" she suggested.

"Loud?"

"It's a lot," Jodie said.

Someone must have finally won the remote to change the sound to a different program in the center left of the screen.

"The news," Reyna said.

"Ugh, don't watch it. They're in Visage's pocket," Meghan grumbled. "All they do is lie."

"Well, at least nothing has really changed," Jodie said.

"I'd like to know what I've missed, though."

"You won't get it from there. Harrington bought out most of the news stations. If you want to hear the truth, you have to tune in to the underground networks and listen on the radio frequencies. This bullshit runs twenty-four seven, and it's all nonsense. They focus on celebrity gossip in the midst of the world falling apart. Anything to deflect from reality."

"I bet," Reyna said.

Reyna was about to turn away from the rec room when her eyes narrowed in on the figures in the news frame. She gasped.

"What?" Meghan asked, then went pale when she looked up at the screen.

"What am I missing?" Jodie asked.

Reyna took a few steps into the room, ignoring the now blatant stares from the other people inside. The screen was filled with Beckham and Penelope's smiling faces. Underneath it read, "The Engagement We've All Been Waiting For."

Reyna's hand flew to her mouth. Engagement.

Beckham and Penelope were engaged.

Her stomach heaved. Her eyes went blurry, and she couldn't hear a word the news reporter was saying. All she could see was the fuzzy picture of Beckham and Penny. What the fuck?

"Reyna, come on. Don't look at that," Meghan said.

"He's engaged," she whispered.

"Let's get out of here, okay?" Meghan said, using her nurse voice.

"He's…he's engaged."

Reyna wasn't seeing or hearing a thing. Her world was spinning. She was upside down.

Meghan reached for Reyna's arm and tugged her toward the entrance. Reyna took one last look at the glowing faces on the screen and then forced herself to turn away. She didn't know what she was feeling right now. Sick and twisted up in disbelief. But also…angry. Beckham and Penelope were engaged? It wasn't even possible. She had seen them together at the ball and known that was his cover. She had said in her mind that she was letting him go. But that was before she had escaped and seen all that he had done for her. That he had been planning to get her out all along. But an engagement was a whole other thing. She ground her teeth together and followed the girls to the medical center.

"Look, it's a trash news network," Meghan said. "I told you from the start that everything they say is a lie."

"You think they're not together?" Reyna asked her pointedly.

Jodie snorted next to her as they finally came to a stop.

"What's your problem?" Meghan asked.

"I'm just saying that I got a good look at that girl. No one is forcing a man to be with her."

"Can we just get this over with? I don't want to talk about him anymore."

"Great. Thanks for that." Meghan shook her head at Jodie, who shrugged.

Reyna needed to pull herself together. After everything she had been through and everything she'd endured, she wouldn't fall apart now. She was finally free. Right now she needed to concentrate on getting better and trying to acclimate.

"You know," Meghan said as they walked away, "we have a therapist who works here, too. It might help if you two talk about what happened with someone."

"We don't want to talk about it," Jodie cut in.

Reyna wasn't even upset that Jodie spoke for her.

"I understand," Meghan said at once. "I was just offering so you knew you had the option."

Reyna wasn't about to talk to a therapist about anything. Not about Beckham or Harrington or Roland or the needles or the venom or the prison cell. Or…or B. Revealing what had happened at Visage meant reliving it, and she definitely wasn't prepared for that.

She'd do better trying to move on and find a new place for herself in Elle. Her brothers had already done it. She might not like their path, but at least they had one. She hadn't been content in Beckham's penthouse as a cooped-up doll, and she wouldn't be useless here, either. After everything she'd gone through, it would be nice to have something to do again.

Reyna sat in an all-too-familiar chair inside a sterile white medical facility. Jodie paced relentlessly around the room like a caged animal. Reyna's own fear should have spiked at the setting, but the only thing she really felt was numb.

She had been here before. Not this building, of course, but it was set up much the same as the Visage rooms. The chair was less comfortable, straight-backed and forbidding. Harrington wasn't going to walk through the door, but the equipment was the same. The gentle beeping of the machinery was the same. The sounds and sights and smells… It was all the same.

Meghan trotted around the room as if her two patients weren't ranging between feral and catatonic. "Let me get the saliva and we'll be good to go."

"Venom," Reyna corrected.

"What?"

"I call it vamp venom."

"Fitting," Jodie chimed in.

"Vamp venom it is, then."

Jodie was opening drawers and picking up various scalpels and syringes and then putting them back. Over and over.

Meghan put her hand over Jodie's. "Leave it."

Jodie threw her hands up and stalked into the corner.

Meghan sighed softly before disappearing into a giant walk-in refrigerator.

"This place is the same, huh?" Jodie asked.

Reyna nodded. "Same company probably built and outfitted it."

"Probably so." Jodie poked the heart-rate monitor. "You okay about your boy?"

Boy. Reyna almost laughed at that. She didn't think anyone had referred to Beckham as a boy in a very, very long time. He was a hulking, brooding, vicious vampire. He'd earned his reputation with fear and intimidation and murder. The innocence of childhood was long gone.

"I don't even know what I expected," she confessed.

"Obviously that he wouldn't propose to some chick behind your back."

Reyna couldn't help her laugh then. "Yeah. That. I mean, I was only gone eight weeks."

Jodie's eyes widened. "Eight weeks is a lifetime in there."

It was.

"How long were you there?"

"Doesn't matter." Jodie turned her back on Reyna. "He was pretty and all, but maybe you could hook up with a human this time. Find one who doesn't want to eat you for breakfast."

Jodie was probably right. Things would be easier if Reyna wanted someone other than Beckham. The problem was that she had never wanted anyone like she wanted Beckham.

Meghan returned, fit the venom to the IV, and prepped Reyna's arm. Reyna tensed as she waited for the inevitable needle. Jodie blanched at the sight and disappeared from the room.

"I am so glad that I was working that day you came in for testing," Meghan said, drawing Reyna's attention back to her face. "I was the nurse who ran the test on your blood and found out how special you are. I changed your file from Rh null to O negative. We'd been looking for you for so long. It was perfect timing, too, since Beckham had to take a permanent escort and he'd been putting it off. It was the first day I learned he worked for Elle."

Reyna's mind was whirring to life with the new information. A sharp prick jolted her back to reality.

"Needles," she groaned.

"Don't worry. The worst is over." She glanced at Reyna. "So, I don't know all the details about what's up with you and Beckham. Only that Elle placed you in his custody for protection."

Reyna's eyes swept to Meghan's. "So, the whole thing was a setup? Beckham knew about my blood type?"

"Well, yeah. Otherwise you would have ended up with Harrington right away. We would have brought you straight to headquarters, but we hadn't vetted you yet. We wanted Beckham to vet you and then bring you in. Perfect, really."

"So that's why he didn't drink from me," she said.

"In theory, all vampires can drink from you, but no one wanted to test that theory, either. It doesn't always work for vampires to drink other blood types. Like even if O negative can be used for transfusions for other blood types, that doesn't mean vampires can drink it. A lot of times it makes them more animalistic still. It was safer for him not to try."

"Oh." Reyna bit her lip. "But he did."

"I know," Meghan said softly. "And then you were kidnapped."

Reyna sank back in the chair as Meghan turned on the machine to filter the venom into her system. All this time, she had wondered why Beckham wouldn't drink from her. She'd assumed for so long it had been because he didn't approve of the new permanent escort program, and in rebellion he'd continued to drink from Penny, who was also his blood type match, instead. Beckham had known all along that they didn't match. Though she was a true universal donor, he hadn't wanted to risk her. Only he *had* risked her.

Her mind muddled as the venom took ahold of her. She wanted to think the best of Beckham. Yes, he was a good actor. He had to be to play double agent. But she didn't want to think that their relationship had been a ploy, too.

Her heart raced. Her stomach clenched. Her eyes drooped.

And she was floating away.

Voices broke through her subconscious. She couldn't figure out who it was or what was happening. All she could do was giggle.

"How is she?"

"How would you be?"

"That bad?"

"Worse. She saw the news."

"So soon?"

"Unfortunately."

A hand touched her forehead and brushed her hair off her face. She didn't know where the hand had come from or why it was touching her. She didn't know if she should even care.

"We'll have to take it easy with her."

"I don't think anything we do is going to help."

A sigh. *"I told Beckham to be gentle with her heart."*

"As if he listens to anyone."

"As if he's ever gentle."

No, Beckham wasn't gentle. Definitely not with her heart.

• • •

Reyna awoke with a start. Her hand flew to her chest, which was heaving up and down. Her eyes flew around the room, taking in the bed and the closet and the pictures.

Elle.

She was at Elle. She wasn't back at Visage. She wasn't with Harrington. She wasn't being turned into B. She'd had a nightmare. That was all. Just a nightmare.

Tension released from her shoulders. A headache was blossoming pretty spectacularly in her temples, though. The venom always left her with a headache. She'd forgotten all about it. Someone must have gotten her back to her rooms after she was dosed.

Her hand moved to the nightstand. She flicked on the lamp, ready to get out of bed and try to find something to curb the pounding in her head—but then she felt it. A prickling at the back of her neck. As if she wasn't completely alone.

She pressed herself against the headboard as fear crawled through her. A figure sat in a darkened corner. All she could see were long fingers steepled in front of the person's face and shiny black shoes. Her eyes drifted over the mysterious figure as fear turned to awareness.

"Hello, Little One," Beckham finally said.

Chapter Twelve

"Beckham?" Reyna whispered into the stillness.

He stood from the chair, dusted off his black suit jacket, and buttoned the front button. She swallowed at his immense size. Tall and broad and foreboding. His very presence screamed run. Run far away.

His face was a mask carved out of granite. He revealed nothing of his thoughts. Nothing about why he was here or what he was doing or where he had been. He simply stood there in all his terrifying beauty and waited.

"What are you doing here?" Reyna hastily got out of the bed. She didn't like being on unequal footing with him. It didn't help that she was only wearing a T-shirt and one of the lacy undergarments left in her drawers. His gaze dropped to her bare legs, and she saw desire flicker in his irises. She grabbed sweats off the floor and tugged them on.

"Would you prefer I hadn't come?" His tone was dark and laced with aggression.

"I didn't say that."

A muscle in his jaw twitched. He paced away from her to the other side of the room and then back. When he looked at her again, his stare held all the force of a freight train.

Reyna tried again. "I meant why are you here in my room in the middle of the night?"

"Vampires enjoy the darkness, Reyna. Did you forget?" He smirked at her, his mask firmly in place. This was the man she had first met at Visage, not her Beckham. Not the man she had gotten to know.

She swallowed back anger at the bite in his tone. This wasn't what she had pictured. All those times she had dreamed of their reunion, she had envisioned heartfelt words, love and devotion and apologies broken by enough vigorous sex to make up for all those lost weeks. Not crisp conversation and words that danced around the issue.

"You didn't answer the question," she pointed out.

"You were sleeping. So, I didn't wake you," he said simply.

She suspected that was only part of the truth. Once again, she was left in the dark. She'd thought they had gotten over that, but what the fuck did she know? Clearly, everything had changed.

"I thought you would be here when I was brought back."

"Did you?"

Was that actual surprise, or was he mocking her? His eyes were empty, blank in his expressionless face. He was stoic and reserved and in control. Perfect control. He had mastered it over the years, and now he was using it on *her*. She hated it.

"You should have been here."

He arched an eyebrow. What the hell was he thinking?

"What are you even doing here if you can't answer a simple question?"

"I am perfectly capable of answering a simple question."

"Well, where were you?" she ground out.

"Busy."

Her frustration mounted, and a chasm opened up between them

the longer he stalled. If she walked any closer, she'd fall into that bottomless pit forever.

"Busy doing what?"

"Working."

Her anger overloaded, and she broke. "With Penelope? Are you two back together?"

His nostrils flared, and his eyes hardened. "I don't want to talk about Penelope."

"Oh, what else is new?"

Some of his facade slipped away, his own anger finally clear. "You cannot expect everything to be the same now that you've returned."

"You make it sound like I *chose* to leave," she said, her voice rising. "That I decided to go to Visage and work with Harrington. That this was what I wanted."

"How could I possibly know if that was true or not?"

Reyna gaped at him. "Because I'm not suicidal!"

"He wouldn't kill you. He needs you."

"Don't I know it."

Her breathing was uneven as she remembered all the things Harrington had said he would do to her if she didn't comply. But she didn't tell him. She hadn't told anyone.

"You left that night," Beckham said, reminding her all over again of the night he bit her, when she ran and this nightmare started. "How am I supposed to react now that you're back?"

"Something other than this. I didn't *want* to leave that night. It was just instinct. I never would have left permanently." She bit her lip. "Tell me what's going on."

All she wanted was the truth, even if it hurt. Or, at the very least, she could try to pick up the broken pieces of her heart.

"Are you ready to speak about your experiences at Visage?" he asked, sliding his hands into his pockets nonchalantly.

She clammed up. No. No, she definitely wasn't.

"Are you engaged?" she shot back.

"I said I don't want to talk about Penny."

"Oh God," she said, backing slowly away from him. "You *are* engaged. You actually are."

"Reyna…"

"Don't." She held up her hand.

"Reyna," he said, his voice harsher, trying to fight for control. She didn't care that it was slipping away from him.

"I don't want to hear you evading my questions." She held her head high as she faced him down. She'd had to be strong with him from the start. It was only fitting that she had to be strong while he was breaking her. "I don't want to be treated with kid gloves. You said once that you would tell me all your secrets."

"That was nine weeks ago."

She shook her head. "Harrington told me the truth. Even the truths I didn't want to hear."

Beckham didn't so much as blink at her slap in the face. She saw him straighten, however. She could see the tension build in his shoulders, could see the damage her words had inflicted. She'd meant them. Harrington was at least an honest monster.

"I have told you before and I will tell you again, Reyna: I am a ruthless vampire. I am not a man. I would not have gotten to my current position without doing things that would make your blood run cold."

"Harrington is a vampire, too."

"Would you like me to act like him?" he asked as he bridged the gap between them. His body was so near she could reach out and touch him.

"No," she said through clenched teeth as she balled her hands into fists to keep from doing just that.

Beckham's finger moved to her chin, tilting her head up to look at him. "You called me a monster," he said, his voice low. "You were not wrong. That is what I am."

Understanding hit her at last. He thought those words she spoke in fear and the first dizzying side effects of the bite were her truth, but she'd never meant them. "You're not."

"Yes, I am. You were right when you ran. You trusted me to stop, and I didn't. You trusted me, and I failed."

Remorse shone bright in his eyes, those obsidian orbs splintering to finally reveal the man she had known. Deep self-loathing radiated from him. She could see painted across his face as if it were a canvas that he felt he was nothing more than the beast within.

"I did not deserve your trust," he said. "I do not deserve it now."

"Please," she whispered. She didn't know if she was begging for him to stop or to continue. For him to slip just a bit closer. For his lips to graze hers. For this distance to shatter into oblivion.

He used the hand still on her chin to move her head and bare her neck to him. Her breathing hitched as memories assaulted her: Beckham buried deep inside of her. His fangs grazing the artery on her inner thigh. The pleasure mingling with pain as he sank his fangs into her neck. The shudder of adrenaline as she came.

She was so angry with him. So uncertain about their future. And yet she still wanted this. She wanted all of him, if he would open himself up to her.

"There are no bite marks," he finally said.

"No," she breathed, swallowing.

"No scars."

"No."

"All this time…"

Their eyes met. "He never…"

Her body pulsed at his nearness. No matter that she was still uncertain about everything. Having the sole attention of Beckham Anderson was like being a mouse caught in a trap. And yet her mind went blank at his touch. The lacy panties stood no chance.

"Your smell…" His voice was indulgent.

Her body only ached more, bowing toward him, her insides taut like a nocked arrow.

"Becks," she breathed.

"…is different," he finished.

Her eyes locked on his. "Different?"

"If there was no bite, then he's been giving you an injection?"

She nodded mutely.

Beckham growled low. "Then he has owned you."

"No one owns me," she said defiantly.

"The bite is possession," he told her. "The saliva in the injection says just as much: that you are his. That you belong to him."

"I belong to no one. Least of all William Harrington."

His eyes searched out the meaning in her words. She wanted to tell him everything that had happened. Lay her soul bare. But it was so fresh, and there was this gap between them. She'd thought they had finally torn it down, but the wall was back, bigger and taller than ever. She had broken it down once, but it seemed impossible now.

Whatever he saw in her gaze made him shift forward. His lips landed on her forehead, and she shivered from head to toe. This was what she wanted. This man. Even if this wasn't the reunion she had wanted. But it just wasn't enough. She lifted her hands, and instead of twining them in his suit coat, she pushed him backward. It didn't budge him more than an inch, but it was enough.

Any warmth in his eyes shuttered and dissipated.

"I can't do this again. I spent eight weeks in hell wanting nothing more than to escape, to be rescued. For you to storm into the room and carry me out of this nightmare. I dreamed of our reunion, Beckham, and it wasn't this," she said, her voice hollow. "I won't… no, I can't live in a world where Penelope stands between us again."

Beckham took a step backward. "She's… It's complicated."

"Then you should go."

"Go," he growled at the dismissal.

"Come back when you can talk to me like you once did. When we don't have to play games. Because I'm through with the games."

"Fine."

She watched as he moved toward her closet. She followed him, wondering what he was doing. Then she saw it: a doorknob. He had come in through a secret doorway in her closet. Of course he wouldn't want anyone to see him.

His hand rested on the doorknob. "Sydney will want to see you. You're important to the organization. This was where you should have been all along. Not with me."

Then he strode out of the bedroom and became a shadow, disappearing into the darkness as the door closed behind him.

She couldn't believe that after all this time and everything she had dreamed about this day, he was going to walk out…walk away from her. No. She couldn't have that. She didn't want him to walk away. She wanted to make things right.

Her heart thudded as she rushed toward the door, back toward Beckham. She could right these wrongs. They could make this work.

She closed her hand over the doorknob, ready to rush after him—but as she twisted it, there was no give. It was locked from the outside. A way for Beckham to get in but not for her to get out.

Reyna's knees hit the carpeted floor as her heart cracked open wide. What had they done? This wasn't how any of it was supposed to happen. She wanted a do-over. She'd stood her ground and refused to give in to him when he'd evaded all her questions. She'd made him go even though she'd wanted nothing more than for him to stay.

And now he was gone…maybe forever.

Chapter Thirteen

"Let me get this straight," Jodie said later that day. She fluffed the coils that she had spent several hours fixing after being at Visage without appropriate products. "He shows up in your room to see you, and you flip?"

"Sort of," Reyna said.

"You've been mooning over him for however long you were in that hellhole. You get out of said hellhole. Then your dream man shows up for you. And what do you do? Turn him away?"

"It's not that simple."

"Seems that simple to me," she said, lounging back on Meghan's bed. They'd dragged a cot in for Jodie to sleep on until they got her a more permanent place. "You know what you should have done?"

"What?"

"Fucked him."

Reyna choked on her laughter. It felt nice. Waking up in the middle of the night from a nightmare and confronting Beckham hadn't been her best move, but his choice to completely avoid her questions and act like a total stranger hadn't been that great, either.

"I'm for real," Jodie said when Reyna didn't respond.

"I know you are, but…I don't know. It wouldn't fix everything."

"It would sure as hell fix the lack of orgasms."

"I can't argue with that."

"'Course you can't."

"But come on, wouldn't you argue with a guy who was possibly *engaged* to someone else before sleeping with him again?" Reyna asked.

Jodie tapped her finger on her lips. "If I'd just gotten out of prison and been on a dry spell, I'd probably have to think about it for a second."

Reyna stared up at the white spackled ceiling. "What do I do?"

"If you want sage advice from a girl who has been locked up for longer than you, I'd say find him and fix things. We both know that time is fickle and we might not make it out of this."

Reyna knew that Jodie had been in Visage a *lot* longer than Reyna had, but she had never come out and asked about it. She figured there was a lot that Jodie wasn't ready to talk about.

"I know," she finally said. "I just want the truth."

"And you're willing to give it, too?"

"I don't know."

"Going to have to give to get," Jodie said, flicking a lock out of her eye. "You want him to be open, you have to be prepared to open up about what happened."

Reyna hated that she was right. Couldn't she forget Visage and move on?

"I could tell him, but he's not going to be happy."

"Are you happy about the little you know about what he was doing those eight weeks? No. And you know what…it's simple. If you open up and he still doesn't, you dump his ass."

As if it were that simple.

"I probably should have done things differently," Reyna said.

"Well, that's obvious."

"I was just so upset. It didn't help that I was coming down from the venom and had a massive headache."

"Yeah, plus probably PTSD," Jodie said flippantly. As if it wasn't something they both might never heal from.

"I hadn't thought of that."

"Meghan mentioned it. That's why we're both sleeping so much. It's why she wants us to go to a therapist." Jodie rolled her eyes. "As if I'm going to spill my guts to some stranger."

"I'm spilling mine to you."

"Yeah. What's with that, huh?"

"I don't know," Reyna said. "You were there, too."

Jodie shrugged. "I guess."

Then Meghan entered the room.

Jodie gasped and rose to her feet. "Who did your box braids? They're perfect."

Meghan's bright-red hair had been carefully braided nearly to her waist, and she smiled at the pair of them. "I had them done by the same woman who got me the products for your hair. You like?"

"Love," Jodie confirmed.

"Definitely," Reyna agreed.

"Good. Now let's get going," she told Reyna. "Sydney requested your presence."

"Really?" Reyna asked.

"Yes, Sydney authorized your rescue. She's the reason you're here and not still with Harrington. I'm sure you have a lot of questions for her."

"Okay. I'll see you later," Reyna said to Jodie.

"Good luck," Jodie said before falling back on Meghan's bed.

Reyna followed Meghan out the door. "So, what's Sydney like?"

"She's amazing. Ex-military and a brilliant strategist. She expects and commands respect from everyone. Mouthing off to her is not something that I'd suggest."

"How do you talk to her, then?"

"Carefully," she said with a quick grin. "But really...be careful."

"Why do I feel like I should be afraid of walking in there?"

"Not afraid. Cautious. She's gotten ahead for a reason. Everyone who succeeds gets ahead for a reason," she told her. "She's not the kind of person that you want to have on your bad side."

"Anything else I should know?"

"Sydney is the only reason we've survived this long, but don't let her see any weaknesses. Be strong and confident. You've got this."

Reyna didn't respond. All she could think was that Sydney sounded a hell of a lot like Harrington. The tactics were the same: Lock down your emotions. Show no weakness. Control your reactions. Don't get on her bad side. It all felt too familiar. Uneasiness settled in her bones.

Meghan stopped in front of a steel door.

"Situation room." Meghan tapped in a code and then did a retinal scan. The door popped open. "Good to go."

"Aren't you coming in with me?"

Meghan shook her head. "Just you, but don't worry. Everything will be fine. Chin up."

Reyna took her advice before stepping into the situation room. It was about the size of a large conference room with a table taking up the center and a wall of television screens showing a loop of all the major news networks.

Her eyes landed on three figures standing on a platform on the other side of the room. She recognized the two men immediately, though she knew them from completely different worlds. One wore a white doctor's coat. He was pale, tall, and disheveled in his middle years—though she knew he was a vampire and thus likely much, much older. He had been the doctor on duty who'd handed her over to Beckham that fateful first day at Visage.

The other was a white human male with red hair and a slight but fit build—a fighter's body. Someone who had crawled their way up from the streets to make something of himself. His green eyes were haunted, but his smile was light, almost inviting when he noticed her standing in the open doorway. She had once photographed him when he was in an underground fighting ring at Five Points.

The last person was dressed in a sharp charcoal gray suit. This must be Sydney. She had her back to the door—a bold move. All Reyna could see was that she was tall, though not as tall as the doctor, and had light-brown skin and dark hair slicked back into a low bun.

"This must be Reyna," the fighter said. He whistled low. "Everything suddenly makes sense."

Sydney slowly turned around to face Reyna. She was imposing. Everything about her was sharp and hard and controlled.

Reyna took a half step backward. She should have known—should have prepared herself for this—but she had asked the wrong questions. So how could she possibly have known in advance?

The leader of Elle was a vampire?

"Gabe, go see Tony about this. See if we can get eyes on the subject," she said in a crisp, clear voice. A commanding tone that said she was in charge and if she ever had to raise her voice, you were done for.

"Sure thing, boss," he said with the cocky grin Reyna had seen in the ring. He winked at Reyna as he slipped past her. "See you around."

She sincerely hoped not. He had bad news written all over him.

Gabe shut the door behind him, leaving Reyna alone with two very keen, very intelligent, very domineering vampires.

"Miss Carpenter," Sydney said, straightening her already impeccable suit and taking the stairs down the platform. "Please come in. It is a pleasure to finally meet you."

"Hi," Reyna said. She took one step forward and then another.

Sydney stuck her hand out. Reyna looked at it a beat too long before placing her hand in Sydney's. It was cold to the touch and clearly strong. Very strong. Calloused in a way that said she knew hard labor and was skilled in her work. You didn't get hands like this without years of rigorous training.

"You have met Dr. Washington before, I believe," Sydney said.

She gestured the doctor forward; he nodded at Reyna.

"Yes. We've met."

Washington had saved her from Harrington the first time. Sydney had saved her from him a second time.

"Thank you," she said immediately. "Both of you, actually, for what you did to help me."

Sydney had a severe face, but her lips quirked up at her comment. "We're glad that our mission was successful and that you were able to be brought back safely. The cost could have been greater. It's fortunate that we only lost four sleeper agents to retrieve you."

Reyna's mind whirred. "Sleeper agents?"

"Meghan, Tye, and Xavier were all in key positions in Visage. Washington had been working in the Visage hospitals from the beginning. All were scrubbed from Visage after their work for you. Luckily, we have other people working there, so it's not a total loss."

"But most unfortunate," Washington said.

"You know Harrington wouldn't have let you live," Sydney said to him.

"William and I have a complicated history. I do not know if he would have killed me, had he gotten the chance."

"You knew Harrington?" Reyna blurted out in surprise.

"My dear girl," he said with a flash of fang, "I was his closest friend. His only friend for most of his wretched years looking for a match such as yourself."

Reyna's mind spun. "But…you work in opposition to him."

"Penance."

For what?

Sydney seemed to read her mind. "You must not be aware that Dr. Washington here discovered the blood type cure."

Reyna nearly fell over. "*You* discovered the cure?"

She was standing before the man who had found out that pairing a vampire with a human of the same blood type "cured" their baser tendencies. This was how Visage had become an enormous company that employed humans. This was how Harrington had taken over.

"Quite by chance, really. I was a scientist before I was turned. When I met William, only sheer force of will kept him from catapulting into the animal so many of our kind succumb to. He has always been…" He stopped, considering. "A sanitary type of man. A germaphobe—before the word existed, of course. It set him on the path to asking why this happened to him. A question so few had the mental capabilities to ask. And then when we connected, he had a means to figure out how to change it."

"Enough of a history lesson for the day, Roger," Sydney said.

"So…this is your fault?" Reyna couldn't help but ask.

Washington frowned. "I suppose it is."

"But he is working to right the wrongs of his past," Sydney said. She gestured for them to take a seat at the end of the conference table. "Which is where you come in."

"How do I fit into this?"

"You are the key to Harrington's blood. There is something special about you."

"It's chance that our blood types match."

Sydney met her gaze for a long moment. "Why don't you let us determine that? In the meantime, I would like to debrief you. Tell me everything that happened in the eight weeks of your disappearance. Nothing is too big or too small."

Reyna gulped. This was not going to be pleasant.

"That's it. That's all I know. That's everything," Reyna ground out a few hours later.

They'd made her tell and retell and retell all her stories. It was like they kept expecting her to trip up and prove that she was lying.

There were a few things she kept back for herself—seeing Beckham and Penelope together at the ball, meeting B, and her dreams. She knew that she should tell them about all of this—

especially B—but everything was still so agonizing to remember, her fear so acute, she couldn't dredge it up.

"Are you sure?" Sydney asked for what felt like the thousandth time.

"Yes. I'm sure." Reyna glanced down at her hands and then straightened. "I actually did have one question for you, though."

"Oh?"

"You have all the information that I have. You have a complete picture now. I want to help the rebellion. I could be valuable on your team."

"Valuable how?" Sydney asked.

"Whatever you need. I could do security with my brothers. Or learn to be a double agent. I could be a part of this."

"Perhaps I could offer you a job in the medical wing with me," Washington said with a cheery smile.

Reyna balked. That was the absolute last place she wanted to work. She turned pleading eyes on Sydney. "Anything but that."

Sydney shuffled the papers in front of her and stood. "You asked for a job, and Washington is offering you one. Take it or leave it."

"I understand. I appreciate the offer. But I am *really* bad with hospitals after what I went through. I don't think that I can handle that kind of position. Don't you think I could work with my brothers on security?"

"You are important here, Reyna. You are not important dead," Sydney said bluntly. "Do you understand?"

Reyna nodded solemnly.

"Good. You're dismissed."

CHAPTER FOURTEEN

It was a week of doing absolutely nothing that finally did Reyna in. She hated sitting around. Had always hated it. Between Meghan's insistence that she needed to rest and Sydney's insistence that she couldn't do anything she truly wanted to do, she was restless. Not to mention the fact that she hadn't heard from Beckham.

Eventually, she got so tired of resting that she threw on workout clothes and headed downstairs. She was already through her fifth mile on the treadmill when her brothers showed up. It took little convincing to get them to start training with her in their spare time. Since her cardio was already on point, they started her on weights and high-intensity workouts.

Four days later, Tye strolled into the room and said with a nod to Brian and Drew, "Tonight."

They straightened and said in unison, "Yes, sir."

"What's that about?" she asked as Tye left.

"Work detail," Brian said.

"It's stuff we do every day," Drew said with a smile. "It'll be fine."

"Can I come with you?" she asked hopefully, even though she already knew the answer.

"No," they said as one.

"Come on. You're training me. I want to be useful."

"It's not about being useful," Brian said. "It's about keeping you safe."

"I know. I totally get that. I don't want to be kidnapped again or anything. Trust me. But I can't sit around and do nothing."

"I heard Meghan say that you could work in medical with her," Drew said.

"No. I don't want to work with blood and needles." She shuddered. The absolute last thing she wanted to do was work in a hospital. Why did no one understand that? "I want to make a difference and take down the bad guys."

She fake-punched Drew's arm. Brian shook his head and adjusted her hand so that her thumb wasn't covering her knuckles.

"If you punch like that, you're going to break your thumb."

"I can be taught," she said with a reassuring smile.

They just shook their heads with a laugh and got back to teaching her some basics. She acted like it was fine, but it wasn't fine. She was sure there was something else she could do for Elle besides work in that insufferable lab.

"I'm sure something else will open up and you won't be stuck in this limbo for long," Brian reassured her. "When we get back, why don't we do something with you and Laura? It'll be great."

Reyna grinned. "That'd be good. Now, show me that flip thing again."

Drew stepped forward into her space, showing her how to flip him over her shoulder.

"That was good, but your best option is to run, Rey," Brian said, looking her square in the eyes. "Run as fast and as far as you can."

"I know," she told him.

Except that hadn't helped her last time. It hadn't helped her against anything she had ever encountered; she'd always been caught, eventually. She wanted to know how to defend herself. Better yet, how to stop any of this from ever happening to her again.

Reyna tore off her workout clothes and stepped into the scalding shower. Her muscles ached in the best way, but her mind never seemed to shut off.

Sometimes, when she closed her eyes at night, she still remembered the person who had reached for her in Everett's apartment. She could feel their hand clamp down on her arm. She could see their masked face. Smell the fear in the air. Sense the disaster unfolding around her. Sometimes that hand dragged her under and the nightmares started. Sometimes she was lucky and it was only the needles that blurred her sleep. But usually, it was B.

She shuddered at the images that unfolded behind her closed eyes. The water hit her in a fierce spray. She didn't think these memories would ever leave her alone. When something traumatic happened, there were only two choices: sink into the pain or grow around it. It never went away. It became a part of her.

Reyna shut off the water with a sigh. She wasn't going to sink into that pain. She would have to rise above. Take back control of her life. One step at a time.

She toweled off and wrapped her long dark hair up on the top of her head before exiting the bathroom. She screamed when she saw someone was standing by her bed.

"Some warning next time, Jodie."

"Sorry. Thought you were going to move into the shower, you were in there for so damn long."

"What are you doing here?" Reyna asked as she yanked jeans and a T-shirt out of her closet.

"I hate this place. I mean, I don't hate it as much as Visage, but I still hate it. How can you stand to stay cooped up like this? I can't keep breathing recycled oxygen. I need to be free."

"We are free."

Jodie snorted. "Then try to walk out the front door and see if they stop you."

They would. Reyna knew they would. Sydney had made it clear that she was too valuable to leave. Her and Jodie's blood unlocked the answers to questions everyone had long been asking. No one was going to let them out to do whatever they wanted. On some level, she understood it, but she'd been a prisoner once before and she didn't relish being one here a second time.

"Maybe we can try to get out of here?" Jodie suggested.

Reyna stepped out of the closet. "There's no way out of here other than the heavily guarded way we entered."

Jodie sighed. "There has to be another way in and out. We've never seen Sydney walking around this building, but we know she's here. How does she get around? How is she so secretive? Plus, aren't there other sleeper agents? They wouldn't want to be seen if they're playing spy, right? No one is supposed to know who they are. Which means we can find another way out."

Reyna sighed. "I know how they're getting around."

Reyna stepped back into the closet and jiggled the all-but-invisible doorknob.

"Is that a secret door? Tell me it's a secret door."

"Beckham used it." She'd been trying not to think of him or the fact that he hadn't been back. "It's locked from the outside, though. I don't know what security is on the door."

"Fuck yes." Jodie jumped up and rushed over to where Reyna was standing. Jodie slid a bobby pin out of her lush black curls and began digging around in the lock. Reyna knew how to pick a lock in theory, but she had only ever tried it on the shitty ones back in the warehouses. She couldn't imagine Elle would be stupid enough to have locks that could be easily picked.

Click.

The door swung outward soundlessly. Reyna stared at it in both shock and awe. "I can't believe you did that."

"Hell yeah. My best friend taught me before..." Jodie trailed off, then held her hand out to Reyna. "Now, are you ready to go?"

Reyna knew she shouldn't go. It was reckless and potentially dangerous. She should stay where she was and wait for someone to give her an assignment she could stomach. But God, she didn't want to live that life. She didn't want to stay on a leash and sit down when she was told and bark on command. She'd only seen the sun for a few scant minutes. She needed more.

"All right. I'm in, but only for a minute, Jodie. I don't want to get caught and be in trouble. I just want to see the sun for a bit."

"Excellent. Whatever you say," Jodie cheered as she rushed out the door.

Reyna took a tentative step forward, glancing over her shoulder. She kept expecting someone to burst into the room and tell them not to leave, but no one came.

She took one step out of the bedroom closet and then another. No alarms blared. Nothing happened at all. She just walked into a neatly maintained corridor.

"Let me look at the door," Jodie said. She messed with the doorknob a few times. After another minute, she had the door rigged so the lock never fully clicked into place. "Easy peasy." She opened and closed the door to show Reyna. "This is going to be fun. I swear."

Reyna tried to relax as she and Jodie walked down the innocuous corridor. There were other doors along the way. Jodie tried a few of the knobs, but they were all locked like Reyna's. She had thought maybe the secret passageways would conceal an underground airplane, or at least secret rooms that only top-level Elle members could access, but all she got were more blank hallways and a stairwell. They went up five floors before the stairs abruptly ended.

Jodie pushed through the doorway first into a tightly sealed vestibule. The doors were steel with heavy plated armor and a series of security measures to keep anyone from coming in...or out.

Reyna sighed. "Guess this is the end of the road."

"We didn't even get outside," Jodie grumbled. "Maybe we can get through the security."

"It'll probably alert someone that we're here."

"Probably," Jodie grumbled. "Fuck, we were so close."

Reyna knew this whole thing had been too easy. Elle wasn't worried about anyone getting out of their room, because there was no way out of the bunker. They were as good as trapped.

She tried to breathe in through her nose and out through her mouth. She felt sick at the very thought. She couldn't be trapped again. She needed to get out. She needed a moment to live again. Reyna put her arms around her stomach and backed away from the door. Her back hit the wall. She was still trying to get herself under control when the door behind them opened.

Shit! She hadn't anticipated getting caught before they even made it outside.

Then the person walked into the room and she nearly groaned. Trouble was in the building.

Gabe smiled. "What do we have here?"

"Who the hell are you?" Jodie asked.

Reyna cringed. "This is Gabe. We met at my meeting with Sydney."

"And you must be Jodie," Gabe said, offering her his hand.

Jodie stared down at it and crossed her arms. "We weren't doing anything."

"That so?" His eyes crawled back over to Reyna's, and he arched an eyebrow. "Tired of being cooped up?"

"Amen to that," Jodie said.

Gabe grinned at them both. "How did you get up here, anyway?"

Neither of them responded. He just laughed.

"Pick the lock in your room? Yeah, I did that, too, when I first got here. Got me in some real trouble with the higher-ups, but they kept me around. They need people like me." He eyed them both. "Like you two, as far as I can tell."

"I don't want to be used," Reyna said.

"That's all life does. Chews you up and spits you out. Get used to it."

"Not something I plan to get used to," Jodie told him.

"How about this," Gabe said, holding a hand up. "I have somewhere I need to be. I'll be gone two, maybe three hours tops. Why don't you two come with me? Then when you come back, we can talk about how *you* can benefit from Elle by working with them. How does that sound?"

"Did someone send you to do this?" Jodie demanded. "Because if this is a trick…"

"It's no trick. I'm doing you a favor."

"No one does favors for free," Reyna told him.

"And I'm not doing it for free. It's a deal. I help you out for a bit, and you come back and try to help our rebellion. Deal?"

Reyna's eyes swept to Jodie. She lifted one shoulder. They probably shouldn't be leaving the premises for a couple of hours, but they would be with Gabe. He was probably lying about this not being sanctioned by the higher-ups, but she might as well take advantage of the opportunity if she could.

"Deal."

Chapter Fifteen

Piled into Gabe's heavily tinted black SUV, they zipped out of an underground garage and onto the road leading into the city. Reyna drank in the sights around her. It had been so long since she had seen much of anything of interest. The sensation was like being dunked into a cold pool.

Her eyes flitted over the large building they had just exited from, and she nearly choked when she realized where she was. Her hand flew to her chest as she all but craned her head out the window to get a better look.

Gabe glanced at her. "What's up?"

"That building," she breathed.

"Yeah? Didn't you see it on your way in?"

Reyna shook her head, but it was Jodie who spoke. "They blindfolded us."

"Oh yeah. Shit," he muttered as if he'd forgotten protocol. "Well, if either of you is a Visage spy, then I'm fucked."

"What is that building?" Reyna asked.

"That's our front. The building is home to a popular real estate company, but we live underneath it. Gives us cover to move above during the day if we have to, and no one looks too closely at what's below, since the place is legit."

Reyna sat back heavily in her seat. That building was the front for Elle. She couldn't believe it. And yet, it made perfect sense.

It was the very building that Beckham had taken Reyna to the night they'd snapped photographs of Visage from the rooftop. After they'd had a long talk about the two factions of vampires—those who thought of humans as equals and those who thought of humans as food. Even then, he had been showing her this other world, trying to draw her into it, and she had never suspected.

Her heart panged at the memory. Where was he now? And how had their relationship disintegrated so completely, like sand through her fingers?

She faced forward, putting the Elle headquarters and longing for Beckham behind her.

Gabe drove through the city until he came to a stop in an open spot next to a graffitied park. Reyna rolled her shoulders and hopped out of the car, looking cautiously out into the darkness. They were not in the best part of town, and she was glad for her casual jeans-and-T-shirt combo, but it was also fucking freezing.

Gabe popped the trunk. He tossed Jodie a long-sleeve flannel shirt. "This is the best I can do."

Jodie wrapped it tightly around herself. Gabe passed Reyna the leather jacket off his back. She slid into it, and it seemed to swallow her whole.

"What about you?" she asked. He was in just a white T-shirt.

"I'll live." He handed both of them a baseball cap. "Put this on, too."

"This is never going to fit over my hair." Jodie pointed at the mass of curls on her head.

"Best I can do."

Jodie muttered obscenities under her breath before trying to mash her curls down to get the cap on her head.

"You'll need these, too." He produced two dull black bracelets.

"What the fuck is that?" Jodie asked.

But Reyna knew. "ID bracelets."

"Yeah. They're required in the city now for basically everything. These aren't programmed to you, and there shouldn't be any cops nearby, but it's for appearances."

Reyna slipped hers on and felt the weight like a shackle. Jodie irritably added hers to her wrist.

"What happened to curfew?" Reyna asked. There had been one citywide after the fires. The curfew and the bracelets had both come with the start of the Blood Census.

"The old mayor lifted it. Said it was only temporary, but the bracelets stayed. So, we're straight." Gabe nodded his head toward the stairs, and they followed. "Now this place, it's a vamp-free zone. So you should be safe, but stick close to me at all times, and remember, don't be seen. The last thing we want is for Harrington's people to swoop back in and try to abduct you, okay? I can protect you from a lot, but I don't know what I'd do if that happened. So let's not let it."

"We don't want to go back. Don't worry. We'll stay close," Reyna said.

It was only when they turned the corner and Reyna got a good look at the building they were about to enter that she started to sweat.

"We're going to Five Points?"

Gabe's eyebrows shot up his forehead. "You've been here before?"

"Yeah. I saw you fight once."

"Yeah?" he asked, beaming.

"You're a fighter?" Jodie asked, eyeing his body corded with muscle. He was only about average height, but he looked scrappy.

"Yeah. I dabble here and there."

"Why are you bringing us here?" Reyna groaned.

"I have some business. Plus, this place is as safe as it gets as far as you're concerned."

"The last time I was here, there was a riot."

"That almost never happens."

Reyna tried to calm her racing heart. Just because there had been a riot the first time she came to Five Points didn't mean it was going to happen again. Except she couldn't shake the feeling that she usually found trouble wherever it was lurking.

An enormous bouncer loaded with weapons grunted at them as they approached. "Gabe."

"Brought some strays," Gabe said with a fierce grin.

"They're not your usual."

"Nah. Have to keep them fresh."

"No fangs, right?"

"No guns. No fangs. No trouble." Gabe quoted the motto for Five Points back at the bouncer. The guy nodded, and the door popped open for them. He gestured for Jodie and Reyna to go in first.

"You frequently bring girls here?" Jodie asked.

"Easy cover."

"I'm sure," Jodie drawled.

Reyna stopped short in the doorway. When she was last at Five Points, it had been a fighting ring. Now it was completely bedecked in flashing red lights, grinding on the dance floor, and club music.

"What the hell," she muttered.

"You like?" Gabe asked, running a hand back through his russet hair.

"I thought it was a fighting house."

"Yeah. It cleans up pretty nicely when it wants to." He reached out for her hand, and she pulled back hastily. "Just to get us through the crowd."

Reyna took his hand. Jodie slapped her palm into Reyna's, and as a trio they snaked across the room. She kept her head low, but it didn't seem to matter much anyway. The room was dark enough that

Reyna could hardly make out more than a couple of feet in front of her. She didn't think anyone was going to be checking under her baseball cap.

"This is amazing," Jodie cried behind her. "I cannot wait to get out on that dance floor!"

"Jodie, we shouldn't."

"This is our one night of freedom. I am not squandering it. Plus I'm an excellent dancer. I took ballet classes back…before."

She could imagine Jodie with her long, lean limbs being a graceful dancer. Reyna loved to dance, too, and hated that Visage was making her scared of her own shadow.

Gabe spoke to the bartender, a blond woman who seemed to be familiar with him. Jodie lifted her arms in the air and swung her hips to the rhythm. Reyna waited for Gabe's interaction to be over.

Gabe slipped an arm around Reyna's waist, drew her close, and said into her ear, "I have to meet up with a contact. You two can dance. Just stay near the bar and out of the lights. I need to be able to find you. I'll be back in ten minutes. Sonya is the bartender. She can locate me if you need me before then."

"Okay."

"Chin up, babe." He knocked her chin playfully with his fist and then winked before he disappeared again.

Jodie had found a group to dance with and reached her hand out to Reyna, who obediently moved toward her friend. They danced and tried to forget everything but this moment. Jodie turned to face a sexy Latino man with biceps that popped out of his shirt. Reyna closed her eyes and melded into the crowd. Jodie tugged her close, and their bodies moved in perfect harmony.

Hips against hips. Gyrating movements. Heated skin. The temperature spiked, and Reyna slid Gabe's leather jacket off her shoulders. She tied it low around her waist while Jodie threw his long-sleeve shirt around Reyna's shoulders and used it to drag her in closer.

"This is the best," Jodie cried.

And it was. Now that her limbs had awakened and her brain had quieted to the techno beat, she remembered what it was like to be young and carefree.

One of the guys Jodie had been dancing with disappeared for a minute and returned with a tray of shots. He tried to pass one to Reyna, but she shook her head. No way was she going to drink during all of this madness.

"Oh, come on, Rey," Jodie grumbled, shoving the shot into her hand. "What's the worst that could happen?"

"We already know the answer to that." Reyna placed her shot back on the tray.

Jodie tipped her own shot back and shook out her curls. "Phew, that's the stuff." Then she grabbed Reyna's shot and hit that one back, too.

The guys around her cheered. She flashed them her teeth as she took in their hungry expressions. Maybe one drink wouldn't kill her. Reyna reached for the tray of shots, but then Jodie tilted wildly into Reyna. She dropped the shot, and it splashed on her feet, but Reyna was beyond caring.

"Hey. Hey," Reyna said, reaching out for her. "Are you okay?"

"I feel fucking amazing."

But when Reyna looked into her friend's eyes, her pupils were dilated and she sure didn't look fine. "What was that shot?" Reyna asked the nearest guy.

"It's a new shot. Like a Hot Damn, but we call it an Oh Shit," the guy said.

"What the hell was in it?"

"Whiskey, rum, vodka, and orange juice," the guy said.

"And a dropper of that new vamp drug," another guy said with a laugh.

Reyna's stomach dropped out. "What vamp drug?"

"Don't worry, baby. It's not dangerous. It comes from their bite or something. It loosens you right up."

Venom. Fucking fantastic.

Venom was addictive in most people. The more a person had, the worse it got. Reyna may not have succumbed to it completely, but Jodie, it seemed, definitely had.

"We need to get you home," Reyna said.

Just a touch of venom made you feel like you were on cloud nine. Like the whole world was at your feet. It lowered inhibitions and boosted the endorphins in the body. It was supposed to kick the fight-or-flight signals in your body into gear, telling you to get the fuck out of there. Right now, it was clear all Jodie wanted to do was live up the night.

Fuck.

Reyna reached for Jodie, frantic. Where the hell was Gabe? This was bad. The guys were still leering at them. They'd known what they were doing when they gave them those shots.

"Come on, baby," one of the guys said.

Reyna shot him a threatening glare. "No."

Adrenaline flooded her system for all new reasons as she held her ground. She latched onto Jodie's arm and all but dragged her back toward the bar.

Luckily, the guys didn't follow. Maybe they were really just out here to have a good time; they *had* said that drink was on the regular menu. She had reacted on instinct—save Jodie, get the hell out of there.

She shoved Jodie onto the first available bar stool and flagged down Sonya. She sauntered down to them. "What'll ya have?" she asked in a thick northern accent.

"She needs a water. Have you heard from Gabe?"

"Here you go, honey." Sonya filled a glass with ice water and then slid it over to Jodie. "He's still upstairs. You can go on up with your friend if she can walk."

Reyna looked Jodie over. She couldn't.

Jodie brought the water to her lips. Reyna wanted to go upstairs and find out what was taking Gabe so long, but she wouldn't leave Jodie's side. She would just have to wait.

When Gabe finally returned, he found Jodie's head down on the bar. "Come on. Got to go."

"I need your help. Some guys dosed Jodie with vamp venom."

"Venom?" Gabe asked.

"Vampire saliva. They're using it as a drug that they drop in drinks," Reyna explained.

"Here?" he asked.

"The guys said it was on the menu."

"Not in my fucking club."

Reyna blinked at him. "Five Points is *your* bar?"

Gabe shot her a smirk. "Forgot to mention that, huh?" He snapped his fingers at Sonya, and after a heated conversation, the word got out that vamp venom was a no go. It didn't fix what had happened with Jodie, but at least some other girl wasn't going to get dosed.

Gabe slipped an arm around Jodie's shoulders. She sagged into him, and he nodded his head at the exit for Reyna to follow.

They staggered together through the crowd. About halfway through, Gabe gritted his teeth and lifted Jodie into his arms as if she weighed nothing at all. Reyna kept glancing over her shoulder, tilting her baseball cap up a smidge so that she could check her surroundings one more time before they left the dance floor.

No one.

She couldn't shake the feeling that they were being followed, but no one was there. She breathed a sigh of relief. Maybe she was just acting paranoid.

When she turned around to catch up with Gabe, she careened right into a guy. She put her hands out to stop herself from falling.

"Sorry," she said. She tried to move around him, but his hand was still on the leather jacket she'd slipped back onto her shoulders.

"I thought that was you."

Reyna's eyes slowly dragged up to the guy's face. Her stomach hit the floor.

"Everett?"

CHAPTER SIXTEEN

"Reyna!" His expression was a mixture of shock and confusion.

Reyna was shaking. She had to get away. She had to run. This was bad.

Everett had turned her in. Everett had lied. Everett had betrayed her. If he was here, then Visage would know *she* was here.

No, no, no. This couldn't be happening.

"Hey, can we talk?"

He reached for her, but she scurried backward, knocking into people. She heard their furious shouts but couldn't process them. All she saw was Everett's face, the people in masks bursting through the door, the darkness, the needles. She saw prison in his eyes.

"Stay away from me," she said.

His face crumpled. "Reyna, listen to me. I didn't know."

"How could you not know?"

He reached for her again, and she fell backward into a girl.

"I said stay away from me," Reyna yelled.

They were drawing a crowd. Eyes were turning to them. People were memorizing their faces. She tugged the baseball cap down. Fuck.

"Please, you have to understand. I never wanted to hurt you," Everett pleaded with her. "They had someone I cared about. I didn't have a choice."

"There's always a choice." Then she pushed people out of her way, looking over her shoulder, as she ran from Everett.

Her heart was in her throat. She suddenly remembered all too clearly why she was forever stuck inside, why she kept being passed from one prison to another. The outside world was dangerous, and she had treated danger like a lost companion beckoning her in from the cold.

A hand grasped her arm, and she screamed. Then another covered her mouth. She tried to protest, clawing at the hand and kicking at the assailant.

"Hey! Hey!" the person was yelling at her. "What are you doing?"

She twisted her head and realized her attacker was Gabe. He saw her recognition and dropped his hands.

"He's here. He's here," Reyna gasped.

"Who? Who is here?"

Reyna whipped back around to accuse Everett—but no one was there. Her head swam as she craned her neck around to see where he'd run off to.

"Reyna," Gabe said, drawing her attention back to him. "Are you sure you didn't get dosed, too?"

"He was *here*," she said again. She hadn't imagined it. He'd touched her. He'd tried to apologize.

"Who?"

"Everett."

"The guy who turned you in?" Gabe asked.

She nodded. "He found me. He was trying to talk to me."

"Shit. We need to get out of here. If a Visage plant is in my club, then it's not safe. We have to get back to Jodie. I'll have some guys scour the place for him and they'll report back to me if they see him."

"I'm screwed. I'm so screwed," she muttered as she followed him to the entrance. "He saw me. He could tell someone. He might have seen you. We could all be compromised. This whole place could be."

"Reyna, slow down. We don't know what's going to happen. Let's take it a step at a time. Just focus on helping Jodie. Let me handle the rest."

Reyna's eyes continued to flit around the room. She wondered if her mind had conjured Everett out of thin air or if he had really been there. It seemed impossible. Even during all those weeks in isolation, she had never done something so outrageous as to picture him in front of her. Beckham, of course. But Everett? No.

Gabe hauled her out of the club and deposited her on the sidewalk next to Jodie, who was being held up by the bouncer.

"Another one?" the man grunted.

Gabe held up two fingers, and the man straightened and nodded. Reyna tried to follow the exchange but lost track of it when she bent over to catch Jodie again. Already the effects of the venom were wearing off, but the alcohol was holding on strong. Who even knew when Jodie had last had a drink?

"We should stay longer," Jodie said, holding on to the brick wall for dear life. "I could use another drink."

"You could use a kick in the ass."

It was another ten minutes before Gabe came back. "Did a quick sweep and didn't see anyone that matched his description. I have my guys on it. Let's get back. I'll have a report within the hour."

They retreated to his SUV in silence with a drunk Jodie between them. Neither spoke on the ride back to Elle headquarters, though the drive took much longer than it had on the way out. Gabe kept checking his rearview mirror, changing directions, backtracking, trying to make sure they weren't being followed. By the time they made it back into the underground parking lot, Reyna was exhausted from both the excitement of the evening and Jodie, who was crashing hard.

Unfortunately, that exhaustion would have to wait. A furious

Meghan met them as soon as they entered through the steel door.

"What the fuck were you thinking?" she screamed, not at Jodie or Reyna…but Gabe.

"Hey, Megs. Good to see you. How you doin'?" Gabe said.

"Oh my God, Gabriel," she shrieked, running a hand down her face. "I've been pissed at you before. Compared to all the shit that you've put me through, that is *nothing* compared to this. This is the most irresponsible and reckless bullshit thing you have ever done in your worthless life."

"Are you done, love?" he purred with a smirk.

"I am not done with you."

"When are you ever?"

"Sydney is going to kill you for this. Literally blow your brains out."

Gabe waved his hand nonchalantly and hoisted Jodie in his arms. "This one needs medical attention. Know any nurses around here?"

"What's wrong with her?"

"Got dosed with vamp saliva, and she's kind of drunk."

Meghan grumbled angrily under her breath. "Let's take her to the medical wing. Tell me exactly what happened."

They entered the stairwell and instead of trekking back down five flights of stairs, Meghan pressed a nearly invisible button for an elevator that dinged open on command.

"Well, that would have been nice to know about earlier," Reyna said.

"Don't think I've forgotten you," Meghan hissed.

Reyna leaned against the elevator wall and kept her mouth shut. It was definitely better when Gabe was the one taking the heat.

"Well?" Meghan asked.

"I had business tonight. I brought them along. Thought we'd be there and back before anyone even noticed," Gabe told her.

"You were so far from right."

"I'm getting that from your visceral anger. But you know it's kind of hot."

"Don't start with me."

The elevator stopped. Reyna looked out to see the same type of plain corridor as the one outside her room, empty and dimly lit with crappy carpet.

"You and Reyna go to Sydney. She's waiting for you. I'll take Jodie the rest of the way to medical," she said in a huff. Gabe had the good sense not to argue with her. He put Jodie on her feet, and Meghan wrapped an arm around her shoulders to keep her steady.

"Is she going to be okay?"

"She'll be fine," Meghan assured her. "And Gabe…"

He turned to face her as he and Reyna exited the elevator. "Yeah, love?"

"Come see me after." Her voice was menacing.

He shot her a two-finger salute as the elevator doors closed.

"This is going to be bad, isn't it?" Reyna asked.

"Not going to be good." He held out his hand and stopped them in front of a closed door. "You ready?"

"As I'll ever be."

Gabe knocked twice on the door, paused, then knocked three more times. The door swung open. Gabe put a reassuring hand on her back as they both entered the same conference room Reyna had been in earlier this week only from the opposite side of the room. Unlike last time, when Sydney and Washington had been the only other people in attendance, the table was nearly full.

Sydney stood with her hands on the back of the chair at the head of the table. Washington sat on her left. There was an open seat next to him, then a handful of unfamiliar men and a few women seated the rest of the way around. Tye sat next to Xavier, who had an open seat next to him.

Reyna's stomach, which was already in knots, nearly dropped out of her body when she saw the person to the left of that empty seat: none other than Penelope Sky herself. She was dressed in a simple black pantsuit with her dark hair falling dramatically around her face. Her makeup was carefully done, and she sat straight-backed and regal.

Even worse was the person on Penelope's left, who was staring daggers at her—Beckham. Her heart lurched in his direction, and she took an involuntary step forward. Their eyes connected, and everything slowed to a crawl. He was here.

"Nice of you to join us." Sydney's crisp voice cut through the tension.

Reyna broke eye contact to glance up at Sydney. She looked formidable as always, in her customary all black with her hair slicked back. Her nails dug into the chair when neither Gabe nor Reyna said anything.

"Care to explain what happened this evening?" she asked.

Reyna turned to look at Gabe.

"Made contact with our supplier," Gabe said. "He gave me a few leads on the shit that's going down. He put our order in for what we need, though. The asshole tried to shortchange me. Didn't know who he was dealing with. Don't worry, I let him know. But his boss showed up. Looks like they're moving their shit now because the big V knows what's going on. He thinks we're to blame."

Sydney tilted her chin up. "That is what you would like to report?"

"That was the job."

"You're right. That was your job tonight. Get us any information you can about the supplier selling diseased blood and make sure we continue to get what we need from the black-market business you somehow manage out of your nightclub. I never could understand how someone so incompetent could be one of the biggest Irish mob bosses in the city."

Gabe grinned as if she hadn't given him a backhanded compliment. "Runs in the family."

Well, at least that explained a lot.

"Do you know how much we invested in getting Miss Carpenter back from Visage?" Sydney asked, dangerously low.

"I remember the meetings. But look, she was fine with me the whole time. You think she's going to get hurt with me in my *own* establishment?"

"You do not get to make decisions where her safety is concerned," Beckham growled dangerously.

"And you did so well?" Gabe spat back.

Beckham flew out of his chair. He moved so fast that he was already across the room in the time it took Reyna to blink. Beckham shoved Gabe back against the wall with his hand around Gabe's throat. Gabe stared back at him in amusement, but Reyna could see fiery hatred buried deep underneath it all.

Beckham hadn't said a word to her, and now he was ready to rip out Gabe's throat for an offhand comment.

"You're a piece of shit, O'Connor. I should end your worthless life for what you risked tonight," he spat in Gabe's face.

"Beckham," Sydney barked.

"No," Reyna whispered.

"Fuck you, Anderson," Gabe shot back.

"Beckham, stop it," Reyna said. "I snuck out. I wanted to get out of here. I was tired of having nothing to do and everyone telling me no. Gabe had nothing to do with it. He happened to be there when I was leaving."

Beckham didn't seem to hear a word she had said. Gabe continued to sneer. He did an incredible job of looking at Beckham as if he wasn't worth the scum on his shoe. Beckham's face was a mask of fury. He channeled all his anger and aggression into that one look. A lesser man would have backed down.

"I am the last person that you want to fuck with," Beckham told Gabe.

Gabe laughed in his face.

Everything and everyone faded away. That laugh sent Beckham over the edge.

She rushed to Beckham's side, heedless of the danger. Reyna put herself between Beckham and Gabe before he did something he couldn't take back. She touched his arm, and he was solid beneath her gentle touch. She didn't try to move him because she knew that would be impossible. She just stood there.

"Hey," she whispered. Her heart was lodged in her throat. "Hey, look at me. Look at me, Becks."

His body tensed at her words. Gabe was frowning at the both of them. She could hear the whispers behind them, but she focused on Beckham. On the anger slipping off of his features and his black eyes shifting back from stone.

Slowly, he turned his attention toward her. He still held Gabe's throat with his hand. She could see the color beginning to drain from Gabe's face. She needed to reach Beckham faster. Her heart stopped beating when their eyes connected.

"Do you see me?" she asked, gently caressing his jaw. "I'm fine. I'm not hurt. I'm here. Come back to me."

He had attacked Gabe for her. He had gone to that dark place within himself for her. She didn't know what that meant about what he felt for her. It didn't erase the errors in their past, but at least he was showing something.

He released a breath and retracted his hand from Gabe's throat. Gabe bent over and coughed as air reached his lungs once more, but Beckham's attention was solely on her. Usually it was a very unnerving position to be in, but he wasn't looking at her like a predator. He was assessing her because he had been worried.

His hand enveloped her own where it rested on his cheek. "You're okay."

"Yes," she uttered on a breath.

"You're prone to danger, Little One."

"It finds me."

"We have much to talk about, you and I," he said just loud enough for only her to hear.

"I'm ready to talk."

A throat cleared from the other side of the room. "As much as we'd all like to continue to witness this reunion," Sydney drawled dramatically. "Everyone take a seat. We'll decide what to do with Mr. O'Connor and Miss Carpenter after we've heard their stories."

Gabe ambled over to the empty seat next to Washington. Reyna figured that left her with the seat next to Penelope, which, under the circumstances—or any circumstances—she'd rather keel over than take. But Beckham didn't give her an option. He took her hand in his and guided her over to the table. He gestured for Penelope to move down a seat. She gave him a wide-eyed expression and then shot one of loathing toward Reyna before moving. Beckham gave up his right-hand seat next to Sydney and offered it to Reyna. Reyna cautiously sank into his vacated seat, and then he sat down between Reyna and Penelope. Cozy.

As soon as they were situated, Gabe launched into everything that happened—including the full details of his meeting, Jodie getting drugged, and then casually mentioning that Reyna had run into Everett.

"What?" Beckham asked, exploding out of his chair all over again. "And you let him get away?"

"I personally searched the premises. I put my guys on it. They're looking, and I'm waiting to hear back about the tapes, but the guy fucking disappeared," Gabe said.

"You compromised her security. He was the person who got Reyna kidnapped, and you let him walk right up to her?"

"I didn't just *let* him," Gabe ground out.

"Did he see you?" Beckham continued, ignoring his response. "Does he know that you work for Elle? Did you check to see if you were tailed?"

"I'm fucking competent, Anderson. Sit your cold, lifeless ass down," Gabe spat. "No one tailed us. No one knows that I work for Elle. He's not going to figure that out."

Beckham looked as if he were about to launch across the table and rip out Gabe's throat this time. Sydney slapped her hands down on the table.

"We'll continue monitoring Everett. Gabriel, you are lucky your reach extends so far and that we have a history, or I'd kill you myself," Sydney said. "Reyna Carpenter is the only known blood match of the most dangerous man in the world. With her, he is invincible.

You know where this Blood Census has led us. You know that he is already rolling out permanent escorts to everyone at headquarters. Do you want to see him take over?"

"No," Gabe ground out.

Sydney continued as if he hadn't spoken. "Now, we find out that he has purchased a huge plot of land, and recent reconnaissance missions have shown that he is building an enormous facility. Can you guess what that would mean, Gabriel?"

"Nothing good."

"Exactly. So next time you decide to compromise the only person who can allow William Harrington to take over the world, maybe think again. Are we clear?"

"Yes," he spat.

"I didn't hear you."

"We're clear," he shot back.

"Good. Now get out of my sight."

Chapter Seventeen

Sydney ordered everyone else's dismissal soon after Gabe's. Reyna was relieved. She'd had quite a night. She knew it wasn't over yet, though—she and Beckham had unfinished business.

Before she could say anything to Becks, Sydney snaked a hand around her wrist. "And you."

Reyna's eyes widened. "What?"

"You and Jodie engineered this little outing. It was foolish and reckless. We put in a lot of effort to free you from Harrington's grasp. Perhaps you should show some more respect around here."

"I know it was reckless, but I never thought it would happen like this. Who would have guessed I'd run into Everett? I'm not going to do it again."

Sydney's anger simmered, and her eyes narrowed. "You have free rein of the facilities. There are no locks or bars on your doors. We keep you in to protect you from the outside world, not to keep you from it. You could be happy here."

"I am a recovering kidnapping victim who found herself in another prison," Reyna spat. "I am a pawn on your chessboard. I already played the first blood game with Harrington."

"This is not the same."

"You may be fighting for the greater good, but I know you'll use me just as fast as he would." Reyna yanked her arm out of Sydney's grip.

Sydney gave her an appreciative look. "You have fire. I'll give you that."

"I appreciate that you got me out of there and that my brothers are safe. But I offered to be of help, and all anyone has told me is no. I want to help this organization, Sydney. So let me help, but I'm not going to be used. Not by you or Harrington or anyone."

Sydney crossed her arms and arched an eyebrow. "I think we understand each other."

"Good," she said and then shoved past Sydney. She knew Sydney had every intention of using her, but wouldn't it be easier if they worked *with* her?

Reyna took a deep breath and prepared herself to walk over to Beckham, who was standing next to Penelope.

"Time for that talk?" she asked Beckham.

"Hello, Reyna," Penelope said.

"Penny." Reyna couldn't help it—her eyes darted to Penny's left hand. Empty. It was empty. Her heart stuttered. There was no ring.

"Good to have you back on board."

"Good to be back." Reyna nearly sighed at the pleasantries. "Sorry to hear about your father."

"Yes, it's dreadful," Penelope said, frowning at the mention of her father's death.

"Congrats on becoming mayor, though. Following in his footsteps."

"Oh, you heard?" Penelope asked.

"I was at your mayoral ball, in fact."

Penny scrunched up her almost perfect face. "Weren't you still with Harrington then?"

"He brought me along."

"I didn't see you," Penny said.

Beckham's attention shifted, his eyes widening slightly. "You were there?"

"In a soundproof room with one-way tinted windows overlooking the festivities." She hated the memory. Beckham's brow furrowed.

"How voyeuristic of you," Penelope said.

"Not my idea of a good time. Trust me." Reyna turned her attention away from Penelope to concentrate on Beckham. He seemed to be piecing something together, and she couldn't read what he was thinking.

"Where was the room?" Beckham asked.

Reyna tilted her head. "I don't know. I guess, from the stage, it was in the upper left corner. Why?"

Beckham straightened, and something dawned on his face. "You're right. We should go talk now."

"But Beckham," Penelope all but whined.

He shot her a look. "Go home, Penny. You shouldn't be absent much longer anyway."

"You're not coming back with me?" Her jaw flexed, but Beckham just pointed to the door.

"No," he flatly refused.

Penny rolled her eyes and then left the room. She glanced back at Beckham one more time, but his gaze was still on Reyna.

In the wake of Penelope's absence, the silence lingered.

Beckham gestured to the door. "Come on. I know the way."

Reyna exited the conference room, and Beckham moved to her side, walking in silence down the hallway. Reyna wanted it to be the comfortable silence they had developed before her kidnapping, but it was more like when he had first been matched with her. Tension crackled between them. She finally spoke just to break the silence.

"Were you always in Sydney's inner circle?"

Beckham glanced her way. "No."

"When did that start?"

"You do love to ask questions, don't you?" He shot her an inquisitive look.

"Yes. And you promised to answer them all."

He slid his hands into his pockets and faced forward once more. "It's more dangerous now."

"It was always dangerous. I just didn't know it. You knew about my blood type and why I was valuable and why you wouldn't drink from me…" Reyna said, cutting off her rambling.

Beckham reached for the stairwell door. "Let's continue this conversation somewhere more private."

They trekked down the stairs, and soon they were back in front of the closet entrance to her room. She sheepishly revealed Jodie's handiwork with the door. Beckham's nostrils flared.

"You want to let anyone have access to your room?" he asked.

"It was Jodie's idea. So we would have a way to get back in."

"Jodie." He seemed to be considering her presence as they entered Reyna's room. "I still can't believe you saved her. Though I understand why."

Reyna shrugged. "Jodie is just like me. She's a broken girl who was taken from her home and forced to work for those monsters."

"Ah," he said, straightening. "At least you're admitting again that we're all monsters."

She shook her head. "Harrington is a monster."

Beckham leaned back against the closet and observed her. "I believe there are more pressing matters to discuss."

Reyna sighed. "Yes, there are. I still can't believe you left."

"You told me to."

"Of course I told you to leave," she said with a wave of her hand. "You wouldn't tell me if something was going on with you and Penny *again*. You wouldn't even tell me whether or not you were engaged."

He looked down at the floor and muttered, "I deserved your hatred."

Reyna reeled back. "What?"

He gave her a look.

"I don't hate you," she gasped. "I could never hate you."

"Oh, Little One," he said, taking a silent step forward, "how do you still have such a heart?"

"When I was gone, the only thing that kept me going was you. Knowing you were on the outside, waiting for me. I'd put all our happy memories in one part of my brain and cornered it off so no one could ever damage them. But then I got out and it was as if I meant nothing to you." Reyna choked out the words that had been haunting her since her release.

"I am a monster. I fed off you. When you realized my true nature, you fled my presence. You left with someone else, you were so desperate to get away from me."

A tear slipped down her cheek as she realized the turmoil he must have been suffering all this time. The turmoil she had inflicted. "When we were together, when you bit me, it was the best moment of my life, Becks. I trusted you. I told you I trusted you, and then I spit it in your face. I was wrong. As soon as I woke up at Everett's, I tried to come back to apologize to you and let you know I didn't mean anything I said. But by then it was too late."

Beckham stepped forward to where she stood before the bed, cupped her face in both his hands, and wiped the tears from her cheeks. "What did I ever do to deserve you?"

"You showed me the real you. The real Beckham underneath this facade."

His obsidian eyes stared deeply into her own, and she was utterly lost. His hands were on her. His mouth mere inches away. This was the moment she had dreamed about.

"I knew you were at the ball," he confided.

"You…what? How?"

He frowned and glanced away. "It sounds outrageous."

"You looked at me."

He dragged his eyes back to her. "I could sense you somehow. It was like something in my veins just knew that you were there."

"My blood?" she asked in confusion.

"No. I don't know. It was as if you were calling out to me and I was the only one who could hear your cries."

"I thought it was impossible. When you looked right at me, I didn't think you actually knew I was there. I thought I'd imagined the whole thing."

"It made no sense to me at the time. Now it feels right. Also, if you saw me that night, then I understand more your frustration with Penelope."

"Yeah," she whispered. She didn't want to talk about Penelope right now. She had just discovered their connection was so acute he could sense her across a crowded ballroom when he couldn't even see her. Her heart lurched at the thought.

"It is complicated, but she does not hold my heart," he said fervently.

"Are you together?" she asked carefully.

He breathed out. "In public. A cover, as we always were."

"And in private?"

"No," he said at once. He reached out and took her hand. "Penelope knows it is for the cameras. That it is our cover to be the Saint and the Martyr after her injuries, and now that she has become mayor."

"*Does* she know that?"

Beckham's eyes slipped over her distraught features. "I will remind her, if that will put your mind at ease."

Reyna swallowed the words she wanted to say—that she would never be at ease with Penelope anywhere near him. She also understood what he *wasn't* saying—that his cover was more important than ever. He couldn't bring suspicion down on himself, which might compromise everything. It was easier to have Penny as part of his public image even if they were not truly together.

"What happened with you and Harrington after I was kidnapped? Obviously, if you retain your cover with Penelope, then he doesn't suspect you?"

"He does suspect me. I was investigated after your disappearance. The penthouse was raided. But after I found out what happened, I knew I would have to go to Harrington and tell him you'd run away. He said he'd heard from one of his contacts—Everett, obviously—that something had gone wrong. I told him that I'd been drinking from Penelope and so I never knew you weren't my blood type match."

"But *can* you drink from me, since I'm a universal donor?"

Beckham's gaze went far away. "I don't know. After the last time…I could barely control myself."

"That might have just been the connection. You said so yourself."

"Perhaps," Beckham said, his eyes dipping to the vein in her neck, then sliding back up. "Anyway, Harrington wanted to pin something on me about your disappearance, but he couldn't exactly tell me he had you in his clutches. And since I came forward immediately, he had to go on as if nothing had happened. The investigation wasn't fruitful." Beckham shrugged. "He might still believe I'm part of Elle, but I have been careful about my involvement. It was the reason I couldn't come to you right away. I needed to be seen out in public when you escaped so I had an alibi. It killed me to wait."

Reyna's heart wrenched at the words. "So, what does this mean for us?"

Beckham responded by moving back into her personal space. His huge frame dwarfed her small body, but he slid his hands into her dark hair, tilting her head up to him. Her body responded instinctually, melding against his. He was hard and solid and strong. Then he brought his mouth down to cover hers and the world slipped away.

As everything with Beckham, he was not gentle or submissive. Once his lips were on hers, he commanded the kiss. His tongue breached the seam of her lips, opening her to him. She gasped as their tongues touched. He was coaxing and delving for more and more, and she gave him all she had.

Her head was light and dizzy. Her heart pounded in her chest. Nothing else existed outside of this moment. Not the rebellion or Penny or the consequences of their actions. She wanted nothing in the world more than this man. He was responding in kind, and she was not going to let him get away this time.

He pulled back, and she reached for him, keeping him close. He growled low in his throat. His hands skimmed down her neck, over her shoulders, down the curve of her waist, and to her hips. He dug his fingers into her skin, pulling her tight against his body. He backed her up into the footboard of the bed, and everything ignited in her core at the thought of how they could use that bed.

"Please," she whispered against his lips shamelessly.

"Reyna," he groaned.

"Becks."

He held her at arm's length. "You make it very difficult to stop."

"Then don't stop."

"I can't lose control with you again."

"You won't."

"You said that last time, and it didn't make it any more true."

"It's been so long, Becks." Reyna reached for the waistband of his pants and tugged him back against her. "I had dreams about us."

"Dreams?"

"Together," she whispered. "Vivid dreams."

Both of his eyebrows rose at that. "*Incredibly* difficult to stop."

Her eyes were wide and desperate when she met his gaze. "I was trapped for eight weeks, Beckham. I dreamed of this moment. Don't you…want me?"

His shoulders relaxed. "Of course I want you." His jaw flexed, and for a moment, she thought that would be all that he would give her. That he'd leave in the night with her heart in her throat, desperate for him. "I always want you."

Then his lips landed on hers, and there was a hurried desire in them, as if the only reason he had ever held himself back from her was out of fear for her safety. It eradicated her doubts. Left everything else they were dealing with by the wayside. She would think of them later. Not now.

"I can't stay," he said, walking her backward toward the bed.

"Okay," she said as she ripped at his tie.

His hands found the edge of her pants and shucked them to the ground. "I have somewhere to be in ten minutes."

"Fine," she said, undoing buttons. "Ten minutes is enough."

"You deserve more than a hurried fuck."

She slammed her lips on his as her fingers touched bare chest. She wouldn't beg again, but she wasn't going to let him go without this. She couldn't.

He groaned deep in the back of his throat, his control splintering as his hands ran along her ass and down between her legs. She was already wet, and the feel of his fingers grazing her through the fabric nearly sent her over the edge. This was real. It was *real.*

"I'm going to make you come for me."

"Yes," she gasped.

He pushed her onto the bed and ripped the fabric of her panties, laying her bare before him. His fangs traveled along the vein in her inner thigh. "I haven't had enough to eat."

She groaned. "We could…"

A finger slid inside of her, and her back arched against the comforter. "I don't trust myself," he admitted. "If I fuck you, I'll drain you."

"I trust you."

"Don't," he said and then buried his face into her pussy.

His tongue ravaged her as if he had been dreaming about eating her pussy as much as she had been dreaming about him all those long weeks apart. Her body hummed under his practiced measures. The rough thrust of his fingers and the even swirl of his tongue and the scrape of his fangs against her sensitive core.

"Please," she begged, unsure if it was for release or for his cock or for those fangs to bury into her. She wanted it all.

As his fingers pushed deeper inside of her, he curved them

upward and then moved his wrist up and down. The curved fingers hit a sensitive spot inside of her over and over and over. Until her legs trembled and she clawed at the mattress and her body shook.

"Oh fuck, that feels..."

"More?" he teased, hitting the spot again as he lapped at her clit.

"Fuck!"

She squirmed as if to get away from the intense feelings crawling through her. She wanted him to bury himself in her, and she wanted it now. She turned feral as the pressure mounted, and then there was nothing to do but to hold on as it hit her full force.

She cried out his name into the silence as wave after wave crashed down against her. Her body shuddered and then fell flat as it all ceased, leaving her drifting among the clouds.

Beckham came back to his feet and carefully righted his shirt and tie as he watched her return to reality.

"Hey," she whispered with bedroom eyes. "You should stay."

"I wish I could, Little One."

"You'll come back?" she asked, rising to a sitting position.

He leaned forward and pressed a kiss to her lips. "I'll come back."

"Soon?"

He nipped her bottom lip. "Very."

She nodded as she went to pull on a fresh pair of underwear and pants. "I hate this," she said with her back still to him.

"I know." He reached for her, pulling her chest against his in an embrace. He pressed his forehead against hers. "I'll be back. This isn't forever."

She swallowed, ignoring that it felt like the end every time he left. Like she was back in her prison and she'd never see him again.

Beckham was to the secret door again when he turned and said, "Reyna, Sydney recorded your conversation about what happened while you were in Visage."

"I know." Reyna bit her lip, her stomach dropping.

"She let me hear it."

Reyna's cheeks warmed. "And?"

He tipped her chin up, and the fierce predator was revealed in his features. “One day I will rip out Harrington’s throat for what he did to you. That is a promise.”

And somehow, that was a relief.

Chapter Eighteen

Reyna hated that Beckham had to leave. That they'd had to cut short the reunion they should have had in the first place. She had so many questions still, and her body ached for more of him.

After a quick shower to wash the remnants of the club off her skin, she changed, grabbed a snack, and headed down to the medical wing. Meghan had said that Jodie was going to be fine, but she wanted to check for herself. When she entered the sterile environment, she shuddered and closed her eyes as memories flooded her mind. She waited for the feeling to pass before opening them again. The medical wing was still there. She wasn't back in Visage. No one was going to force her to do anything she didn't want to do.

"Miss Carpenter," Dr. Washington said, stepping out of a lab with a smile. "Good afternoon."

"Is Jodie here?"

"She was just released with a bill of good health from Meghan. I believe she is likely sleeping off a hangover at the moment."

"I see. Well then, I'll just…" She gestured to the door.

"Could I steal a couple of minutes of your time, since you're here?"

"I'm not going to donate blood," she said hastily.

He waved his hand. "I simply wanted your opinion about something."

"About something medical?" she asked suspiciously.

"Yes, I would like your insight."

Reyna chewed on her bottom lip. This felt like a trick, but she couldn't see what it could be.

"I'll listen, but I don't know if I have any insights."

"Fair enough."

Reyna followed Washington into a lab. It was white and clean, full of medical equipment. It looked like a science experiment gone wrong, with microscopes, petri dishes, blood samples, test tubes, and an assortment of other things she couldn't even put names to.

"As you may remember, last night at the meeting you sat in on, we briefly mentioned the presence of diseased blood in the population," Washington began.

"Okay."

"Some blood illnesses are common, such as anemia, which is usually a result of an iron or vitamin deficiency. Others are not so common, such as sickle-cell anemia or hemophilia. You've heard of all of these cases, yes?"

Reyna nodded. "I did finish high school."

"Of course. I've seen your test scores. You would have gone on to a top university if they would have funded you. Ah, easier times."

"You looked at my high school test scores?"

"Visage has access to everything, and since I was working for them up until you were taken, I had access to whatever I wanted. As I told you, I have known William a rather long time. He trusted me with top-level security."

"So did you already know about the other patients under Visage?"

Washington frowned. "Unfortunately, yes."

"Then why didn't you do something?" Reyna raged.

"I *was* doing something. I still am doing something." He pointed to his lab. "This is what I'm good at. I'm not a fighter. I have never been able to stand up to William or his ambitions. I never could have gone in and retrieved you as bravely as Meghan did. But I gave her all the information she needed to get you out of there, and I worked on the inside for many, many years, as Beckham does now. Do not discredit my service to the organization because it does not align with what you wish it could have been."

Reyna sighed. She understood what he was saying, but she still thought it was shitty that Elle seemed to forgive him for his transgressions against humanity just because he had grown a conscience.

"But as I was saying…blood diseases," he said, returning to his lecture. "Many of these have no impact whatsoever on a vampire's eating habits. Anemia is problematic to the human if they cannot produce enough replacement red blood cells after having been fed on. Or hemophilia would be incredibly problematic for a human if their blood is unable to clot, even with the added clotting components found in vampire saliva."

"Venom," Reyna told him.

"Excuse me?"

"Vamp venom. Saliva sounds way too scientific. I'm really going to make venom a thing."

Washington laughed. "Venom it is," he said, indulging her. "A few new diseases, however, have sprung up in the last hundred years that affect vampires both physiologically and cognitively. The most prevalent is called cogitare anemia. Have you heard of it?"

"No. What is it?"

"Humans are the carriers, like mosquitos carry malaria. It does not affect them except that it appears like they have regular anemia with a deficiency in red blood cells. But in vampires…" Washington tapped the pen in his hand. "Here, take a look. This is what happens to vampire blood that comes in contact with a human host infected with cogitare anemia."

Reyna leaned forward with interest despite herself. She pressed her eye to a microscope and watched the interaction as the two specimens were combined. Her eyes widened with shock as the perfectly normal vampire blood seemed to shake and tremble against the invasion of the new blood.

"Whoa. What kind of reaction is that?" Reyna asked, pulling back.

"What you're witnessing is the deterioration of the antigens on the blood. Antigens are markers on the surface of red blood cells that invoke an immune response; they are also what determines your blood type. There are 342 different known antigens in a person's blood. The most common are the Rh antigen, which you either have or you don't, and the ABO antigens."

Reyna leaned back against the counter. "So, this disease destroys antigens on the blood cell? If a person is A negative or B positive, and it rips that away, what does that mean for the vampire?"

"Excellent question. If a vampire no longer has a blood type, then they can no longer drink from a blood type match."

"Oh God," Reyna whispered as realization dawned on her. "They revert back to how they were?"

"Worse, I'm afraid. Without a blood type match, the disease effectively eliminates the ability for higher thinking and exacerbates the animalistic tendencies of my brethren. But if it goes untreated, the red blood cells can further deteriorate so that *any* blood they ingest will be rejected. It's the same response we see in humans when they receive a non-match blood transfusion and the blood is rejected. And while the vampire is frantic for food, they seek out more people to eat and pass the illness back into the human population."

"It's passed from vampire to human. Does it pass from human to human?"

"Yes. Though we're not entirely sure how, as there are no symptoms in humans, which makes it more difficult for us to track. It is like men who carry the HPV disease with no signs and then spread it to women who can then get cancer. This is the blood disease that has been circulating so effectively throughout the city."

"What does that mean for the population?"

Washington frowned. "There are more rogue vampires on the loose, more humans are getting attacked, and the disease is spreading swiftly. I haven't seen anything so widespread in decades."

Reyna's head swam with all the new information. "And there's a cure?"

"We've found a way to stop the deterioration of the red blood cells. However, new blood cells would have to be created, and a safe blood supply would need to be acquired to keep everyone safe. We've never had an outbreak like this."

"It sounds engineered."

"How so?" he asked.

"It sounds like someone is trying to drum up hysteria in the population. Like when the recession hit ten years ago, it was prime picking for Visage to swoop in like a savior. No one bothered to look more closely because we were in such dire straits. This blood disease sounds like a similar issue."

"That is an interesting theory. It would fit the intensity with which the disease seems to be spreading. Especially considering we have a cure."

"So someone is keeping them from being treated?"

"It's a possibility." Washington drummed his fingers on the counter. "Well, thank you for your insight. It is always nice to have another person to bounce ideas off of."

"You think he's planning something, don't you?" Reyna asked intuitively.

"William is always planning something."

"But it's related, right? Did he engineer this disease for his purposes?"

"I really do not know. Right now, I am hoping to find a cure for those vampires who were not fortunate enough to get treatment early. Also, I would like to find out if there is an indicator I've missed in the human blood so I can begin testing a way to stop it at the source. Maybe if I had a sample of your blood…"

"No," Reyna said immediately.

"It would give me a basis of comparison," he finished.

"Absolutely not."

"Miss Carpenter, you can be of value here."

"While this was all enlightening," she said carefully, "I don't want to be of value in that way. I won't be used for my blood ever again."

"I understand your hesitation."

"I don't think you do. I find the blood diseases interesting. I hope you find a way to stop the cogitare anemia spreading in the city so that nothing else bad happens, but I am *never* going to be anyone's blood bag again. Got it?"

Washington sighed. "I do wish you would reconsider."

"Don't count on it," she said before turning and hurrying out of the medical wing.

When Reyna wandered downstairs, she was hoping to clear her head, which was still full of the blood science talk with Washington. She felt like a hematologist after that one conversation. Antigens and antibodies and red blood cells, oh my!

She shouldn't have been surprised that Washington had asked for her blood. That was the last thing she wanted to do with her life. In that moment, she missed her camera and the freedom to photograph whatever she chose. It wasn't a job, per se, but it gave her purpose. She doubted she'd find anything like that here.

She passed the mess hall only to find her brothers sitting together at a table by the far wall. She angled toward them.

"Reyna," Brian said, jumping up and more or less tackling her.

She laughed. "Um, hey."

Drew was there in another second, pulling her into a hug. "We heard what happened."

"You did?"

"You tried to run away?" Brian asked with a sigh.

"I didn't try to run away."

"Guys, breathing room," Brian's fiancée, Laura, said from her seat.

Reyna waved off both her brothers. She took a seat next to Laura and drew her into a hug. "It's been so long."

"I know. Sorry, I haven't been feeling well or else I would have found you already." Laura truly didn't look too well. She had always been pale, but she looked a little green. Her blond hair at least shone as if she had taken special care with it. She'd even put on makeup. Reyna felt drab in comparison.

"I've been a bore. Let me see your ring."

A smile split Laura's face from ear to ear as she shoved her left hand in Reyna's face. It was an oval-cut ruby with little crusted diamonds around it on a simple band. Nothing too fancy, but still classy, classic, and beautiful. The fact that Brian had been able to purchase anything on a meager warehouse salary was amazing.

"I love it," Reyna gushed. "When is the wedding? Next year?"

She turned from Brian to Laura and back. Brian opened his mouth and then closed it. It wasn't often that he seemed flustered, and he was never lost for words.

Laura's cheeks flushed. "Well, actually, we were just discussing moving it up."

"Oh yeah? To when?"

"Christmas," Laura said with a small giggle.

"Christmas," Reyna cried. "That's two weeks away."

"When did this happen?" Drew asked with wide eyes.

"We decided yesterday," Brian told them.

"That's so soon," Reyna said. "Oh my God, do you have everything planned? Do you need help with anything? I can help."

"We don't have anything planned," Laura said. "It's all happening so suddenly. I don't even know who to ask to get the things we need for a wedding or if we can legally do that here or what."

"I can figure that all out," Reyna told her. "Don't worry. We'll make it a day to remember."

"Thank you, Reyna," Laura said, beaming.

"But why are you moving it up?" Drew asked.

Brian and Laura exchanged a look, and her cheeks turned rosy again.

"Oh my God," Reyna whispered. "Are you…?"

"Pregnant." Laura bit her lip. "Found out yesterday!"

Reyna squealed, drawing the attention of half of the cafeteria with her excitement. Screw everything else in life. This was too incredible not to celebrate.

"A wedding and a baby," Reyna said, clasping Laura's hand.

"Congrats, bro," Drew said. He slapped a sheepish Brian on the back. "Guess this is my cue to move out of the room."

"You don't have to do that," Laura protested.

"Well, actually," Brian said with a laugh.

"It's cool. I think Gregory has extra space," Drew told them, his cheeks flushing again.

"Gregory, your boyfriend?"

"He's not my boyfriend," Drew grumbled. "Yet."

"Ahhh, boyfriend," Reyna said. "You have been holding out all this good info from me. I can't believe this. Good things do come out of horrible circumstances, huh?"

"He's not my boyfriend," Drew repeated under his breath.

Laura laughed. "Can't say I don't agree."

Reyna felt a rightness settle over her as she grilled Laura on all the details about the baby and the future wedding and Drew's maybe new boyfriend. Hanging out with her brothers and her future sister-in-law and just being totally normal reminded her of everything she had been missing since she left home to work for Visage. Brian and Drew were the reason she had gotten the job in the first place. She loved them so fiercely that she wanted to give them a better life. And now they were all living it.

Chapter Nineteen

Jodie still hadn't surfaced the next day, or the day after that. Her hangover had to be long gone. Reyna didn't know why she wouldn't come out of her room. Or, rather, Meghan's room.

Reyna banged on the door. "Jodie, open up! I know you're in there."

She was still banging on the door when it abruptly opened in her face. She tilted forward and had to catch the doorframe to keep from falling over. Jodie stood there in baggy gym clothes, her hair tied back into two buns on the top of her head.

"What do you want, Reyna?"

"I came to check on you. It's been days since the club. Why are you still in here?"

"I don't want to be *here* at all." She closed the door to emphasize her point, but Reyna threw her hand out to stop her.

"What happened to make you feel like this about Elle?"

"Are you serious?" she asked. "I was the one urging you to break us out. I always wanted to get out. I mean, did you ever think about whether I had someone else out there?"

Reyna swallowed at the pain on her friend's face. She had considered a lot about what Jodie must have gone through and how long she had endured it, but she hadn't wondered about her life before Visage. Jodie hadn't wanted to share, but Reyna hadn't pressed. She should have.

"No, I'm sorry. I didn't think you wanted to talk. But if you have people out there you want to see, I'd help you get them here. Elle went out of the way to get my brothers and soon-to-be sister-in-law. I'm sure they'd do the same for you."

Jodie gestured for Reyna to come inside. Reyna slipped the door closed behind her and took a seat on a chair as Jodie dropped onto the bed.

"So who is it that you want to find?"

Jodie shrugged. "My cousin and best friend, June. I was living with her in the capital after the economic collapse. Visage had just taken over, and her neighborhood was a test area for blood type testing before it went nationwide. When my blood type came back abnormal, June and I overheard them tell her parents I was going to have to leave, with *them*. That *they* had a special program for us. They made it sound like a great opportunity, but we could tell right away it wasn't." Jodie glanced away as she fought back tears. "June tried to get me out of there. She promised she'd keep me safe. We didn't even make it across the county line before we were picked up. June was taken from me, and I was taken to Visage. I've been there ever since."

Reyna's hand covered her mouth. "Oh my God, Jodie. How old were you?"

"Twelve."

Reyna had no words. No words for the life that had been stolen from Jodie. It proved all over again that Visage was the villain of this world. One she was more determined than ever to take down.

"I think we can find June," Reyna told her.

"No one is going to help me."

Reyna walked over to the bed and sat down. She placed her hand on Jodie's. "I'll help you."

"Really? And what do you want in return?" Jodie asked in the most jaded way possible.

"Nothing."

"Yeah. Sure."

"Well, one thing," Reyna said with a small smile.

"Oh, here we go."

"I need help planning a wedding."

Jodie's eyes widened. "You're getting married and you're just *now* telling me? Damn, that vamp moves fast. When did he ask you?"

Reyna laughed. "Not me. Though Beckham and I did get back together. But my brother is getting married on Christmas."

"Like in two weeks?"

Reyna nodded. "Bun in the oven. And I promised I'd help. I thought some normal would do me good. Maybe it'll do you good, too?"

"All right. If you help me find June, then I'll help your brother get married in two weeks."

Reyna held out her hand. "Deal?"

"Deal," Jodie said, shaking her hand. "Now, tell me all about you and Beckham getting back together."

• • •

A few days later, the girls had wrangled Meghan into helping them get the supplies they needed and a facility for Laura's wedding. She was still pissed with both Reyna and Jodie for going out with Gabe, but she didn't take it out on Laura. She just sent silent reprimands with her eyes.

"But the dress," Reyna said.

"Seriously, the dress is the last thing on my mind," Laura insisted. "If we can pull this all off by Christmas, I'll be over the moon."

"No, you need a freaking dress," Jodie told her.

"You do," Meghan agreed.

"Where am I going to find a wedding dress?" Laura asked. "I can't go try stuff on anywhere."

"Maybe you could," Reyna said, jumping up and looking around the small office space they'd commandeered for planning purposes.

"What do you mean?" Laura asked.

"Just think about it. We have connections. We could get her somewhere discreet to try on a dress."

Meghan's withering look was enough to say that it was a bad idea. "I don't think so."

"Don't be a party pooper, Meghan," Jodie teased.

"I don't want to cause anyone trouble," Laura said. She scooted back in her chair. "We can make do with what we already have."

"If I could get you out and to a wedding dress shop without anyone the wiser, I would do it. But it's a risk. Visage saw Laura when we got her out with Brian and Drew. Do you really want to risk her being on their radar?" Meghan asked.

"Seriously, don't even worry about it." Laura stood and pushed the notebook she had been writing in away. "I have a dress with me. No one needs to go out of their way for this."

Laura scurried out of the room and to the bathroom. They could hear her heaving into the toilet. She'd had the worst morning sickness already. Well, more like all-day sickness. She was throwing up constantly, but Meghan said everything seemed normal.

Meghan sighed. "I'm going to check on Laura."

As soon as she left, Jodie tilted the front two legs of her chair off the ground and leaned backward. "I hate being so confined."

"Run it off in the gym."

"I hate running."

"Well, you need to find something to let off steam."

Jodie kicked her feet up on the table. "Maybe I just need to get laid."

Reyna laughed. "Maybe you do."

"Maybe I'll see if Tye is interested."

"Tye?" she asked with wide eyes. "Have you even talked to him since the rescue?"

Jodie winked. "I'm about to."

"But you don't even know him."

"Sex is a release, Reyna. Doesn't have to mean anything. If Meghan didn't have such a stick up her ass about this whole Elle thing, I'd see if she'd be down."

Reyna grinned. "I kind of love you."

"You, though," Jodie said, tapping Reyna's nose once, "are *not* my type."

"Well, thank God."

"No hard feelings."

Jodie sauntered from the room. Reyna could do nothing but laugh. At least the wedding planning seemed to have lifted her spirits. Reyna stretched her arms over her head, releasing the tension in her back and shoulders. Laura reappeared from the bathroom, looking pale, Meghan at her back.

"I'm going to go lie down," Laura muttered. "I feel awful."

Reyna hopped up and gave her a hug. "Do you want me to walk you?"

Laura waved her off, already halfway out of the room.

"Is she doing okay?" Reyna asked Meghan. "I know throwing up is normal, but it's a lot."

"She's fine. Baby is fine. I'm giving her some nausea medicine once it comes in, and that should help."

Reyna relaxed. "Good."

"Have you thought any more about working in the lab with Washington and me?" Meghan asked. "I know you got upset when he asked, but your blood could save lives. And we can always use an extra pair of hands."

Reyna sighed and chewed on her lips. "I want to be useful, Meghan, but does it have to be in that way?"

"No. I suppose you could work in the cafeteria or clean or

something. But it seems like a waste."

"You understand why I have an issue with donating my blood and seeing it used in any way?"

"Yes, but this could be for the greater good."

Reyna glanced away and then back. She had an idea. "Look, I'm not sure I'm ready yet, but I'll think about it if you help Jodie."

Meghan groaned. "I've been trying to help Jodie. She's even less receptive than you are."

"Well, she was gone a lot longer than I was. Have you looked into if she has any family left?"

"We did when she first got here, but we couldn't find anything," Meghan admitted. "I would love to bring more people into Elle if it helps Jodie. Loved ones always help."

"After what she went through, she's a cynic. If you could help her find her family, I think it would go a long way."

"All right. I'll look into it again, and you think about the medical wing."

As if she had a choice about where she could be useful.

"I'll think about it."

Meghan tugged her into a hug. "I'm so glad you're here. You and Jodie both."

"Me too," Reyna whispered, finally feeling as if she was starting to have a place here. Maybe not the one she had wanted, but finally something.

Chapter Twenty

Reyna grabbed her planning materials and returned to her room. She hadn't had dinner, just the snacks the girls had smuggled into their planning session, but the thought of trekking back to the cafeteria made her head hurt.

When she entered her room, she was glad she hadn't delayed.

"Becks," she whispered.

He was silhouetted against the light from her closet. He was actually dressed down for once, in dark jeans and a button-up with a jacket. It seemed he hadn't come straight from the office this time. Like he'd planned ahead to be here.

"Little One," he said, his voice deep and seductive.

The sound went straight to her core, igniting her body. She suddenly forgot all about the wedding planning and the fact that she hadn't eaten.

"You're here."

"Yes. I worked it out so I would have the night off."

"Oh," she said as she shut the door behind her. "You got a night off?"

"It didn't go over very well," he said carefully. "I was supposed to be at an event with Penny."

Reyna frowned. She knew it was a part of his cover, but she didn't have to like it. "And you chose to come here instead?"

He nodded. "I chose to see you. I would rather see you."

"She didn't like that?"

"You'll probably see it on the news in the morning," he said blandly.

Reyna's eyebrows lifted. "That bad?"

He shrugged one shoulder. "It doesn't matter."

"But your cover…"

"Don't worry about my cover." He bridged the distance between them. "I've been investigated enough since your disappearance. My cover is solid."

Beckham's hand ran up her arm, over her shoulder, and came to rest on her neck. Her heart beat a tattoo. He pressed a kiss to her forehead, and she breathed him in.

"Why don't you bundle up and I'll tell you all about it?"

"Bundle up?" she asked breathily. Her mind was on his hand on her neck and his lips so near hers…and the bed and the warmth of the room.

"I'm taking you out."

Her eyes snapped up to his. They were dancing in the faint light. "What do you mean?"

He grinned a dark, mischievous smile. Then he planted an achingly soft but commanding kiss on her lips. "I'm breaking you out for the night. That is," he said, offering her his hand, "if you'll have me."

With her heart in her throat, she placed her hand in his. "I'd love that."

He brought her hand up to his lips, staring down at her the whole time. "Then you are going to need more clothes."

Beckham retrieved a bag from the closet and passed it to her. A few minutes later, she was decked out in winter clothes, including a sleek peacoat. She wrapped a dark scarf around her neck and slipped a pair of gloves into her pockets.

Beckham held his hand back out to her. "Are you ready?"

"Yes," she said, a thrill running through her as she put her hand in his and followed him out of the room.

Beckham clicked a new lock into place. They'd added security to her room since her breakout. It did make her feel a little better that not just anyone could get in, but not *so* great, since she could no longer get out if she wanted to.

"They're going to install a hand scanner soon," he told her with a short laugh.

"Great," she grumbled. Talk about overkill.

She followed Beckham down the hall to the elevator and then zipped up the five floors. She could barely keep still as it opened to the antechamber. Beckham drew her closer again.

"You are full of unrelenting energy," he breathed into her hair.

"I'm here with you, and we're going out together. I don't know how you can expect me to be calm."

"Calm is not your natural state of being."

"Where are we going, anyway?"

Beckham laced their fingers together and didn't answer. Of course he didn't answer. She knew asking was futile. Beckham wasn't one for words. When he wanted to keep a secret—well, he'd already proven he was plenty adept at it.

They exited the elevator, Beckham got them through the steel door, and then they were out. It was fucking cold, and she scrambled into her gloves, burying her face into her scarf.

"It's not far," he told her, pulling her in close as they crossed a dark, empty parking lot.

They went up a few flights of stairs, down another corridor, and then up in another elevator before Beckham opened the door to the rooftop.

Her smile was magnetic. "I feel like we've been here before."

"I wanted to create new memories with you."

Reyna braced herself for the chill as she stepped outside and was not disappointed. The temperature was frigid. Snow dusted the rooftop and fell gently from the heavens. The view into the city was stunning with everything coated in a layer of white powder, but it was the rooftop garden that really caught her eye this time. Lights decorated the winter plants, and a fire was crackling in the center of a firepit. Heaters had been added to help with the extreme cold. The bench where they had first been intimate was clear of snow, and it held blankets and a tray of food.

"Is this a date, Mr. Anderson?" she asked coyly.

"And suddenly, I'm no longer Becks." His eyes were teasing, and she was certain she would never be able to get enough of it.

"I didn't even think you liked the nickname."

"I like it when you say it," he admitted.

"My Becks," she said, standing on her tiptoes and dragging him into a kiss.

"My Little One," he said just as fiercely.

"I like that, too."

He flashed her a rare real smile and then escorted her through the rooftop garden. They took a seat in front of the fire. Beckham wrapped blankets around them to keep her warm and put his arm around her shoulders.

"I figured you didn't eat," he said, gesturing to the covered tray.

"How do you know me so well?"

"You lived with me for some time."

"True. I sometimes forget to eat. But then again…so do you."

He laughed softly. "Not anymore. I am more careful now. More careful around you."

Reyna arched an eyebrow at him, but he simply removed the cover from the tray to reveal all her favorite foods from the restaurant they used to go to across from his penthouse.

"Oh my God, this is the best."

"I'm glad I got the order correct," he said. Though he honestly sounded a little…nervous. Beckham could never be nervous.

"It's perfect. Now, while I eat, tell me more about this investigation."

"Harrington redid background checks. The penthouse was raided after they took you and then again when you escaped him. As if I would be stupid enough to bring you back there if I had gotten you out." He fumed at the audacity. "I had to get a new permanent."

"What?" Reyna asked, covering her mouth.

"Yeah. Part of the cover, I'm afraid. I couldn't look like I was disagreeing with Harrington when it might jeopardize finding you. I hate having to keep up appearances."

Reyna could see that he thought it was beneath him to follow all of Harrington's orders. She didn't blame him. She hated following them, too.

"Do you drink from her?" Reyna couldn't help asking.

"Would you rather I drink from Penelope?" he asked, his voice low.

"No," she said slowly. "I hated it the time you did it in the Vault."

"I know. I couldn't drink from you, and I was starving. I no longer drink from Penelope, if that makes you feel better."

"It does," she admitted. "But we could try again."

"I don't know if that's a good idea, Reyna."

"I should be a match for you, though."

"You *should*. But a true blood type match is preferred. At least, that was what I thought before I drank your blood."

Reyna put down her sandwich. "What do you mean?"

"Your blood is preferable to any other," he said, staring directly into her dark eyes. "*You* are preferable to any other."

She flushed. That sent heat straight between her legs, and suddenly she felt very, very toasty. She unwound the scarf from around her neck. Not on purpose. She wasn't enticing him. Or…maybe she was.

"I think Harrington must feel the same way," Beckham added. She could tell the thought infuriated him.

"Why?" she asked.

"The fact that there was a security breach is only known to top-level employees. And even then, we don't know what was breached. Or more importantly, who. No one knew that he had found a match, but we guessed. Well, I knew, but I had to act as if I did not. He tried to pretend he wasn't doing better, feeling stronger, but he was." Beckham turned back to look at her. "And now he's not again."

"Good," she spat. "I hope he shrivels up and dies."

"I'm not sure which scenario makes him more dangerous, though," he said, considering. "When he had you, he could take on the world. Without you, he's much more desperate. Desperate men do desperate things."

"You sound as if you are speaking from experience."

"I am," he said.

But when she waited, he didn't elaborate, so she went back to her meal. When she finished, she snuggled into Beckham's side. His hand wove through her hair absentmindedly. Her side was pressed against his strong body, and he laced their fingers together. They sat there in the stillness of the night as the fire crackled before them. She didn't care about anything else going on outside of this moment. She had everything she wanted right here.

"Becks?"

He kissed the top of her head in response.

"I want to know all there is to know about you." Snow kissed her eyelids as she faced him again. He didn't say anything, and she could see his eyes go distant. "Will you tell me your story?"

"It's not a pleasant tale."

"Please?"

He faced the skyline again with a sigh. She could tell he didn't want to give in to her. That he didn't want to have to tell her about his gruesome past. But she wanted to know all of him. Everything there was to know.

"You do not want to know what I once was…what I am still on the inside."

"I do," she insisted.

He whirled around, his fangs visible. "I am not the hero you have constructed in your story, Little One. I am the villain."

Reyna reached up and gently ran her thumb across the fangs. Not hard enough to break the skin but enough to feel the sharp point. "Someone made you this way."

He took her wrist in his hand, removing the temptation. "And would you believe me if I said I chose this?"

Reyna froze. "Did you?"

"Yes."

"And would you choose it again?" she whispered.

"That hardly matters."

Reyna assessed him. "It makes all the difference in the world."

"That is where you are wrong. We can't change the past. It's futile to even consider it. I am a vampire. I am a murderer. My backstory will not change your mind except to poison you against me."

"Why don't you let me make up my own mind about that?"

"When I tell you, it will be a mercy."

"Mercy?" she whispered.

"Then you will not need another reason to leave me."

Chapter Twenty-One

Arguing with Beckham about it was pointless.

He would never see her point about his past, and she would never see his. She would wait for him to tell her. She wished he could realize that she accepted him for exactly who he was. She was already aware he had done terrible things before joining the rebellion. It wouldn't change her mind about him.

They stayed at the rooftop garden until Reyna could no longer feel her fingers or toes. Then Beckham insisted he return her to her room.

"So," she said, running her hands up the front of his shirt once they returned to her room, "do you have the rest of the night off?"

"A gentleman simply kisses his date good night on the first date."

"It's probably a good thing you aren't a gentleman, then, isn't it?"

"It seems to be your favorite quality about me."

"Oh no, I like the brooding, silent, self-loathing the best."

"Perfect match for your never-ending speech and vibrant

optimism."

"I'd say that I'm leaning more toward realism lately."

She stripped out of the heavy jacket, gloves, scarf, hat, and thick socks, tossing them all haphazardly around her room. She was halfway through pulling the giant sweater over her head when she felt Beckham's hands on her waist. They slipped under the material of her black T-shirt and caressed her stomach. She dropped the sweater to the ground, forgotten.

"Fuck," he growled low.

"I missed you."

"Every day you were gone, I was out of my mind."

"Me too," she whispered.

"I would have burned the city down to get to you."

"I worried you wouldn't." She hated the squeak in her voice at the admission.

"It killed me not to be here when you got back. To not be here doing this." He dropped his mouth onto hers, and the kiss seared through her. "Cover be damned. Visage be damned. I wanted you, and then when I finally had you, I fucked it up again."

"Shhh," she said, pressing a finger to his lips. "It doesn't matter. You have me now."

He relented, placing a kiss on her finger. Then, latching a hand around her wrist, he directed the pad of her finger into his mouth. His tongue caressed her and then gently nipped at her. He repeated this on each finger before turning her palm up and pressing a kiss into her wrist.

"Your heart rate has elevated, Little One."

"Uh-huh," she said desperately.

His nose connected with her wrist, and he dragged it up the length of her arm. Her body tingled at each touch, shivers coursing through her body. When he reached her shoulder, he tugged the material aside and his lips touched her skin, kissing across her collarbone to her neck. She tilted her head for better access and felt as if she were about to float away.

The last time they were in this position, he bit her. Her body was primed and waiting for that moment once again. The kisses weren't enough. She could feel the sharp edges of his fangs and tensed to prepare herself. Her body thrummed—her heart rate ratcheted up and her breathing went ragged. She shivered in his embrace.

"Becks," she groaned.

His thumb moved up to cover the spot he had just been kissing. His eyes stared down at her, the bottomless pits of onyx so dark in the light. There was nothing but darkness in him. Nothing but the pure-blooded dominant vampire he was. And somehow…somehow, he was still stopping.

"Please."

"I want *you*, Reyna. Not your blood. I don't want to want your blood."

"But you do."

"I can feel the ache in my very bones. It sings to me."

"Then why…?"

"Because if I want it like this, I won't stop."

The phrase was final. Delivered with an unparalleled intensity. This was the law. The line he would not cross.

"Okay," Reyna said slowly. "We'll figure it out."

"There is nothing to figure out. I will not jeopardize your safety."

"I mean we'll find out a way to make it safe. I accept you for who you are," she said, threading their fingers together. "I don't want you to hold back when we're together."

He grinned—a feral, primal thing—and dropped her hands, then slipped them down past her waist and over her ass. He grasped the backs of her thighs and hoisted her into the air. "Don't worry. I won't."

She threw her arms around his shoulders. She pushed her hands up into his hair, drawing his lips to hers. Everything slowed down to this moment. To his raw, unbridled passion and the way his lips and hands and entire body claimed her. All she wanted was him. His taste and touch. Purely Beckham. The man she had dreamed about for so, so long in that terrible place. She wanted to forget. Forget everything but skin on skin and breathless panting and sweet release.

Beckham didn't hesitate. He walked them into the nearest wall. Her back collided with the hard surface, and she grunted. She bit her lip from the jarring movement. Blood spilled from the gash.

"Shit," he groaned.

For a second, she thought he was going to drop her. His eyes narrowed to the tinge of red coating her lips. He was pure predator.

"We should stop."

Reyna ignored him. She ran a finger through her sickly sweet blood and pressed it to his lips. "Taste."

He groaned deep in the back of his throat at her command. Then he took her finger into his mouth and tasted her blood. Sweet ecstasy crossed his face. "Reyna…"

She dragged their lips together. His tongue moved across hers before swiping across her busted bottom lip. Fangs scraped across her lips, and she arched into him, wanting more.

He broke their kiss again. "You will be the end of me."

"Aren't I just the beginning?"

"Do not entice me to bite you."

"Taste me, Becks."

He hesitated, restraint in his eyes and the bruising squeeze of his fingers and the pulse where their bodies were connected. Then something broke and he dove back in and captured her lip. He sucked it into his mouth, drinking the small amount of blood that rose from the unexpected cut. He pressed himself even harder against her and sighed deeply with pleasure. The sound of his own excitement sent heat straight between her legs.

He released her lip gingerly, as if the thought of stopping was nearly impossible. She could see the struggle between man and monster, and she knew the man would win out.

"I'll do anything to have you make that sound again."

"Anything?" he asked, raising an eyebrow.

Slowly, she dropped onto her knees. She sneaked a devious glance up at him before reaching for the belt of his jeans and pulling it free. He watched her silently as she popped the button and dragged the zipper down to the base. She ran a finger across the waistband of his black boxer briefs before reaching within and freeing his cock.

Beckham watched her with fascination as she wrapped her hand around his shaft and pumped up and down once, then twice. When he didn't object, she removed his clothes and kneeled. His fingers tangled in her hair as she took him in her hand once more. She hesitated, looking at the length of it. She had never been particularly good at this, but she wanted Beckham to have all the pleasure she had. She wanted to make him squirm.

"That's right," he said, coaxing her head forward. "Open your mouth for me, Little One."

So much for squirming. Somehow, he managed to still be in complete control. It was even fucking hotter, if her soaked panties were any indication.

She did what he said. She opened her lips, allowing him the access he so desired. He pressed his cock forward and entered her mouth with control and precision. Just far enough that she wasn't gagging, but almost to the brink, and still she wasn't even close to taking him all in. She palmed his length in her hand while she sucked on the head. Then he thrust forward into her, forcing her to open her mouth wider and farther to compensate for him.

She moaned against the feel of him. The taste of him. When he next withdrew, she licked a drop of pre-cum off the tip and he jerked in her mouth. A smile spread on her face. Oh yes, he wanted this. He wanted her.

"More," she moaned around his cock.

His hand tightened on her hair nearly to the point of pain before he leaned deeper into her throat. Just when she thought she might not be able to breathe, he withdrew. He did it again and again. Pushing her boundaries. Testing her limits. All the while trying to hold on to that control she felt slipping around the edges.

He fucked her face, and she enjoyed it. She felt intensely erotic. She didn't have to fumble to pleasure him, and his dominance only made her body ache for more.

Once he was buried nearly all the way inside her, he shuddered and removed himself.

"Wait, no…"

"I want you to finish twice before me," he insisted, helping her to her feet.

She was wobbly, and her body betrayed her. If it weren't for Beckham catching her and carrying her to the bed, she would have sunk right back down to her knees.

Beckham slid her shirt over her head and then peeled her jeans down her legs. He inhaled deeply as he spread her out on the bed.

"Fuck," he said. "Your desire is nearly as intoxicating as your blood."

He reached for the silky bra and unhooked it, letting her breasts spill out before him. He caressed one, kneading it in his hand and rolling the nipple across the pad of his finger. He brought the other one into his mouth. She was not half as controlled as he was. Her body writhed as his expert tongue assaulted her nipple until she could barely function. When he dragged a fang across the sensitive nub, she thought she might come right then and there. He played her body like a musical virtuoso. Raw technical prowess met unbridled emotion and dazzling stage presence.

"Beckham, please."

"I want all of your pleasure, Reyna. It belongs to me now. Do you understand?"

"Yes," she said breathlessly.

"These are mine." He fondled her breast as he bit down on the other exposed nipple. He didn't release her until her legs were locked around his back and her body was shaking. "All of this is mine." Then he kissed his way across to the space between her breasts and down, down, down slowly to her navel. His tongue dipped into her belly button.

"This is mine," he growled, slipping under her body, taking her ass in his hands. He lifted her lower half up off the bed and pressed her core into his face. He dragged his nose up her soaked underwear, drawing in a deep breath. "This pussy is all mine."

"Yes. Dear God, fucking yes."

He tore the thin material off her body and buried his face in between her legs. His tongue teased her clit while his hands forced her legs wider apart. He slicked a finger through the wetness already coating her opening and inserted it into her. She was already so primed, he was able to push a second finger into her. It wasn't enough. She wanted more. She was already on the verge of orgasm, and she wanted to feel his cock pulsing inside of her while she let loose.

"Beckham, fuck me. Just fuck me," she said, trying to sit up to pull him toward her.

But he had other plans. He used one arm to weigh down the top of her body. "Put your hands over your head and don't move them until I tell you."

She lay back down with her hands over her head. Thinking about keeping them there was a lesson in control. She wanted to bury her hands in his hair as he coaxed her clit into submission until her body was vibrating with an ache she was dying to unleash. He curled his fingers inside of her, moving them at a slower tempo than his tongue. Suddenly, as both sensations hit her with the force of a moving vehicle, stars exploded in her vision. Her body convulsed, sending a shock wave from her middle all the way to her fingers and toes.

She heard a loud noise and realized as she came back to reality that it was coming from her. She had come so hard she didn't even know what sounds her own body was making.

Beckham released her. She felt like a puddle lying on the bed. Her limbs were jelly, and her brain wasn't functioning.

"You moved your hands," he observed with a sly smile on his face.

"I have hands?"

He laughed. She wanted to find a way to make all his sounds her everyday reality. That sigh, that grunt, that laugh. Oh, she would die happy for one more laugh.

"You have hands," he assured her. "And I would like you to get on them."

"On my hands?" she asked, her brain slow to process.

"Hands and knees."

He flipped her over, and then she adjusted her body to the position with her ass in the air, her hands on the comforter, her hair fanning out in front of her face. Beckham nudged her knees farther apart.

"That better?" she asked, swiveling her hips in place as she looked at him over her shoulder.

His eyes were on her exposed lower half. They drifted up to her face, and he smiled. A heart-wrenching smile that knocked the breath right out of her.

Her Beckham. Hers.

That smile. Hers.

She wasn't just his. Every inch of her heart, body, and soul didn't just belong to this man—every single part of him belonged to her, too.

She watched as he palmed his cock and settled it between her legs. The head pressed against her, and her body clenched. It didn't matter that she'd had one of the most mind-blowing orgasms of her life. Her body was greedy. It wanted more, more, more.

"Brace yourself," he said, placing his hand on the small of her back.

Then he thrust forward in one rough movement, seating himself inside of her.

"Oh fuck," she moaned.

So full. So fucking full.

She'd forgotten. Everything. Just everything. How amazing he felt. How big he was. How completely he filled her.

His hands gripped her hips, slicing past pleasure into pain and then mixing all together. If there weren't bruises in the morning, she would be shocked. She didn't care. Couldn't even find enough mental capacity to care. Because she wanted this—all that he had to give. The pain, the pleasure, the intensity. Nothing would ever feel as good as Beckham with his cock buried in her.

Then he moved and proved her wrong.

He pulled out of her and then sheathed himself once more. One more slow pull, like a drag on a cigarette before the blissful exhale, as he crashed back into her. He rocked her entire body forward, and the bed creaked with the force of it.

She'd be lucky if she could walk tomorrow. Or maybe she'd be lucky if she couldn't…

He didn't slow his pace. He drove into her over and over again. Not taking his time, just connecting with her until she was face-first in the comforter, her hands gripping it in tight fists, body shaking with the need for a second release.

"So…close," he got out through gritted teeth.

With another thrust, he buried himself in her and then reached down to pull her up. He pressed her back against his chest, holding her tight to him as a finger swirled around her clit. She lay her head on his shoulder, unable to move as he thrust into her.

His fangs dragged across her exposed neck. If he bit her now, she would completely lose it. She could sense the tension in him between wanting to take what was his and how close he already was to release. She still let him take complete control. Bite or no bite. This was the best fuck of her life. Beckham was the best anything in her life.

He leaned forward, and she expected the bite. Anticipated it. And then he kissed her as he stroked her clit more vigorously. She exploded a second time, and Beckham followed, holding her pressed against him as he came hard and fast deep within her. Only when they had both finished did he release her to fall forward onto her hands. Her breathing was ragged as he gently pulled out and she fell into a heap on the bed. Her eyes drifted to where he was standing, an arm braced against the wall, his chest rising and falling rapidly.

He was magnificent. The most beautiful thing she had ever seen. She could live a thousand lifetimes and never find anything better than post-orgasm Beckham.

"Becks," she whispered, holding a hand out to him. When he was fully back in control, he crossed the room and crawled into bed beside her.

"This is how I always wanted that night to go," he confided against the shell of her ear. "What I imagined would have happened if I hadn't lost control."

"This is perfect."

He kissed her ear and lapsed into silence. She lay there, her eyelids drooping. She didn't want this night to be over. She didn't want to wake up and find that it had just been another miraculous dream. Yet she couldn't seem to stop the exhaustion from hitting her.

Chapter Twenty-Two

Beckham was gone when she woke up. The indentation where he had slept was still visible. Evidence that their perfect night had really happened.

There was other evidence, too. Like the groan when she tried to stand. The pain as she hobbled across the room to the shower. Her lower half was tender. They'd definitely gone harder than she'd thought. The bruises on her skin were a road map of their pleasure. She traced them across her hips, thighs, and ass. She liked them. It was proof this life was real. Perhaps next time she wouldn't need such a powerful reminder, but it wasn't as if she hadn't wanted it. She'd begged for it—and she'd do it again.

Her only regret was that in the heat of their evening she'd never gotten around to asking Beckham about Laura's wedding dress. She'd had it on her to-do list, and then it had just slipped her mind, like most things did when they were together. She'd make it a priority for next time.

Reyna spent the rest of the day in bed, savoring the lingering smell of Beckham on her sheets. Her stomach was grumbling so ferociously by dinner, though, that she finally had to change and go downstairs. She was too hungry to care how she looked.

She was heading toward the door when a knock rang out through the room. "Come in," she called.

Jodie poked her head in. "Where have you been all day?"

"I haven't been feeling great." Not entirely a lie.

"I brought you some dinner," she said, holding up a bag.

"You're amazing."

Jodie shut the door and wandered into the room. Reyna took the bag from her and eased her way back to the bed.

"Why are you hobbling like an old lady?"

"I told you, I don't feel well."

"Uh-huh," Jodie said, unconvinced. "Explain these symptoms."

Reyna's cheeks heated. "Don't worry about it."

"Oh man, please tell me that you got fucked so good you're waddling. You look like you've been riding a horse."

"Jodie!"

"Come on. Tell me you got some."

"Fine," Reyna said. She pulled herself together and picked at the sandwich and water Jodie had brought her. "I had sex last night."

"So…vamp, huh? What's it like? Did you let him bite you?" When she just looked up at her in exasperation, Jodie continued. "Girl talk, Reyna. Give me the goods. I was locked up for ten years. I need this."

"Ten years is a long time," Reyna said slowly.

"Yeah. Yeah. And I have a lot of lost time to make up for. So spill."

"It's amazing. And he didn't bite me. He didn't want to lose control."

"I heard it makes it ten times as intense."

"Well, last time, it got out of hand. That's… Well, afterward, I ran out, and then I got kidnapped and taken to Visage."

"Damn. Was it better with the bite?"

Reyna considered. "Different. It was already the best sex of my life. Like he understood exactly what I needed and then took it. When I had the bite, it was a complete loss of control. It took over and heightened everything. I'd take either as long as I have him."

"Well, sign me up," Jodie said with a laugh. "Where do I find my own vampire boyfriend?"

Reyna shook her head. "You're outrageous."

"Sounds right."

"Did I miss anything today while I was gone?"

"Nah," Jodie said, slouching back into a chair. "Laura has been out of commission, too. Meghan disappeared early this morning. I'll tell you…I'd really like my own room sometime soon so I don't have to hear her come and go."

"Yeah. I think most people are bunking up. I'm surprised I don't have to share."

Jodie rolled her eyes. "With vampire boyfriend on your side? Puh-lease."

Reyna laughed. "Vampire boyfriend. I love that."

A knock came at the door. "Come in," Reyna called.

Meghan stuck her head in the doorway. "Hey. Just the people I was looking for." She stepped into the room and closed the door behind her. "I talked with Reyna the other day, and I've been thinking a lot about our conversation. And I want to help you. Both of you. I know what you went through was horrible, but we are not Visage. We want you to be happy. We would love to help you find anyone if you have people you want to bring in. Do you have someone we could look for?"

Jodie shot a look at Reyna, who held up her hands in surrender. She'd asked Meghan to look into it, but she hadn't given out Jodie's private details. Still, it was important for Jodie to open up just as much as it was for Reyna.

"You want to help me?" Jodie asked.

"Yes," Meghan said. "I do."

Jodie glanced down into her lap, where she threaded her fingers together. "Then why did you never come for me? Why did you leave me in there for ten years?"

Reyna could feel something slice open in Jodie. Could see her heart rip and spill all her inner turmoil onto the floor. The abandonment, the years of captivity, the hopelessness. It all came tumbling out.

Meghan's eyes welled with tears. "Ten years?"

"You saved Reyna after eight weeks but left me forever. Left all those other kids. How could you do that?"

"I didn't know," she whispered. "I didn't know, Jodie."

"No one knew?" Jodie asked.

"I don't know, but I personally didn't know. I didn't have access to that information. I had no idea that they had done this or that they had you or even that there were others like you. I found out when we got you out. I would get everyone out of there if I could. That is what we want long term. What we have always been fighting for."

Jodie looked skeptical. "You really didn't know?"

"No. And if I had, I would have done something about it. We're still building up to the resources we need to make a jailbreak of that caliber. But I don't want anyone in there any more than you do, Jodie."

Jodie deflated as all the righteous indignation she had been riding on dissolved. "I have a cousin, June Gardner. They took me from her." Jodie looked up into Meghan's face. "Can you help me find her?"

Meghan shot both of them a bright smile. "Of course. I would love to help you find your cousin. Why don't we start now?"

"What's the catch?" Jodie asked.

"There's no catch, Jodie. I don't know how many times I have to tell you we're not Visage for it to sink in."

"Probably a few more."

"Come on. With a name, maybe Tony in tech can point us in the right direction."

Jodie's gaze shot between Reyna and Meghan uncertainly. "Reyna, do you want to come?"

Reyna's smile was bright as she said, "If you don't mind me

hobbling around?"

Jodie snorted. "I don't mind."

"Why are you hobbling around? Are you injured?" Meghan asked.

"You could say that," Reyna muttered.

"Why didn't you come to medical?"

Jodie choked on her laugh. "She's been fucked properly."

Meghan held her hands up. "Oh dear God, I don't even want to know."

Reyna carefully got out of bed and limped behind Meghan and Jodie. The idea of finding June had clearly already brightened up Jodie. She seemed more relaxed and less wary. If they could help her, maybe they could help everyone who had been stuck in Visage.

And then, someday soon, she was going to make sure Harrington paid for what he had done.

Chapter Twenty-Three

Beckham was back in her room only a few days later, and the novelty never wore off. All that time imagining him. It didn't feel real that he was here.

"Reyna?" Beckham said.

He was dressed in a bespoke black suit. It was distracting. All she could think about was tearing it off and seeing the magnificent man underneath.

"Hmm?" she asked.

Her eyes snapped back up to his. She got lost in the obsidian staring back. The gleaming dark eyes that sucked her in like a black hole.

"Were you even listening?"

"Um…my mind's on all the ways I was quite adept at paying attention a few days ago." She slid her hand up the front of his suit, feeling the expensive fabric.

He smirked. "Don't change the subject."

"Why not?" she asked, reaching his jaw and running her knuckles against the slight stubble. "I think I'm pretty good at following your commands."

"Is that so?"

"Well, I think I got...*open your mouth* down pretty well. And *get on your hands and knees*." She threaded her hand around his tie and dragged him closer. "I'm not sure I'm the best at *keep your hands over your head*, but I'd give it another shot."

"Fuck," he growled as he grasped both of her wrists in one hand and pressed her back into the wall. His head dipped to the spot between her neck and shoulder. He placed a deliberately slow and enticing kiss there. "You are impossible."

She shivered at the touch. "Uh-huh."

She envisioned all the ways he would take her against this wall. The bed wasn't enough. She wanted to fuck him on every surface of this room.

He met her eyes again. "What are you thinking?"

She grinned as she told him.

"Every surface?" he all but purred.

"I'd like to not be able to walk for two days again."

"Two days?" he asked, his eyebrows climbing higher. It wasn't often that she shocked him.

"Jodie said I looked like I'd been riding a horse."

She thought maybe he would worry that he'd hurt her. That had always been his MO before. The monster was going to come out and break her. He couldn't be trusted. Something or other.

Instead, a self-satisfied smile crossed his features. "Good."

"And here I thought you'd be appalled that you rode me so hard I was incapable of basic human function."

His hand drifted down between her legs. "I like the idea that you can still feel me after I'm gone." His hand stroked circles lazily against her center. She closed her eyes and leaned into his touch. "Look at me."

Her eyes snapped open. He hooked his fingers into her underwear and slowly stroked one finger inside of her. Her body reacted to him like a finely tuned instrument.

He moved his thumb to her clit, circling it greedily in his hand and palming her pussy. She gasped as her body contracted around him. She thought she was going to come right then and there, her body aching all over. But he paused, drinking her in.

"Becks," she breathed. "Don't stop."

The self-satisfied smirk returned, and he continued stroking her deftly. His pace intensified, and soon she was crying out as she came. She slumped forward against him as he removed his hand and released both of hers.

"I thought you did pretty well with your hands over your head," he said.

"Did you just tease me? Are you *teasing*?"

His laugh was everything as he lunged for her, dragging her to bed. No more talk happened after that. Neither of them came up for air for a long time.

Beckham trailed his fingertips over Reyna's naked back. She was lying face down on the bed, somewhere between asleep and awake. Beckham hadn't been quite as rough this time. Despite his claims that he wanted her to feel him the next day, he didn't really want to hurt her. Their passion was palpable, and the joy of having these moments was enough.

"Can I ask you for a favor?" she murmured into the silence.

He pressed a kiss to her shoulder. "Anything."

"I need a wedding dress."

Beckham stiffened next to her. "Who are you marrying?"

She laughed and rolled over. "It's not for me."

He tilted his head in a way that she knew meant *go on*.

"My brothers, Brian and Drew, are here at Elle. Did you know?"

He nodded. "I arranged it."

Her heart swelled. How could he think himself a monster? When he did such things for her without even trying to take credit.

"Thank you," she said, her throat burning with emotion.

"I know what they mean to you."

"Brian got engaged to his girlfriend, Laura, while I was…gone," she said, stepping over the topic nimbly. "They're getting married on Christmas."

"That is less than a week away."

Reyna cringed apologetically. "I know. I meant to ask you last time you were here, but we kind of got distracted."

"Indeed."

"Well, Laura is pregnant, and they want to get married as soon as possible. She says she doesn't care about having a dress because she didn't even think a real ceremony could happen. But Meghan, Jodie, and I have been working with her to get everything together. So it's happening."

"But there's no dress."

"Right."

"And you think I could get her a dress?"

"You make things happen."

"Hmm, I could probably get her a dress. Just tell me what she wants, her measurements, and I'll have it delivered."

"That's sweet, but I was thinking more along the lines of…you would help get us out of here so she could try on dresses at a dress shop."

He raised his eyebrows. "Why? Leaving isn't a good idea."

"I know, but it's not for me. This is for Laura." Reyna sat up with her knees tucked under her, the sheet covering her body. "It's the magic, Becks. It's standing in a dress shop and trying on a million dresses and finding *the one*. So much has been robbed from us. I don't want this robbed from Laura, too. Even if we were in the warehouses, she would have gotten that moment, you know? I'm the reason she was uprooted from that life. I want to give her that one magical moment."

"Say I have a contact at a bridal shop who would work with us. I could probably get it to close for the day," he confessed. "But if *I* had it done, it would get out, and people would talk."

Reyna chewed on her lip as she considered it. There had to be a way to make it work. Her stomach flipped uncomfortably as she realized how it could happen. "I have an idea. It would involve a big favor from Penny."

"Reyna…"

"Hear me out. You two are still fake engaged. You can have the store close for her, and then we can bring Laura in."

His expression gave nothing away. "I have a feeling she will not like that plan."

"I would be on my very best behavior. I would put aside all differences and be extremely appreciative for her help." Reyna winced. "This isn't about me or you or Penny. This is about Laura."

He looked like he wanted to disagree, but then he sighed. "I will consult with her and see if she'll agree."

"Thank you. Thank you. Thank you!" Reyna beamed at him.

"I haven't said yes."

"But you're very persuasive."

He tugged her against him and pressed their lips together. "It is you who is persuasive."

She trailed her hand down his bare chest. "So what are you doing for Christmas?"

He frowned and glanced away. "Christmas isn't a holiday I celebrate. It's laced with bad memories."

There was a haunted look on his face. She wondered what had happened to him on Christmas, even as she knew that was a story he wasn't ready to tell.

"Well, would you like to make new memories?" she asked, drawing his face back toward her. "Would you like to be my date to my brother's wedding?"

When he didn't say anything, she kept talking. "It's a small thing. I don't think that many people will be there. I just thought it might be nice. It's a thing couples do. You know…boyfriends and girlfriends." She was rambling, but she couldn't stop. Then added hastily, "If you don't want to, you don't have to."

"I do."

"But?" she asked, instinctively knowing it was on the tip of his tongue.

"I don't know if I can get away."

"Oh." She looked down at the bed. Her cheeks warmed.

"I will try to. I want to come."

"I wish there wasn't this secrecy around our relationship."

"One day, things will be different." He swept a lock of her dark hair out of her face. "Then we won't have to hide anymore."

"I look forward to that day."

"More than my next breath."

He brought his lips down to hers, and she sighed into the embrace. She, too, wished for the day when there were no longer barriers between them. But she didn't know when or even *if* that day would ever come.

Reyna must have fallen asleep, but she didn't remember doing so. She woke up groggy from an afternoon nap to find Beckham on the phone in her room. A computer and a stack of paperwork were in front of him. He looked so serious, back in his suit, all professional. It was a strange juxtaposition to the image of him being naked in her bed what felt like moments ago.

His eyes drifted up from the computer as if he knew automatically that she was awake. She crooked a smile and tucked the covers around her still-naked body as she sat up.

Work? she mouthed to him.

He nodded and then spoke into the phone. "I understand. Yes, that sounds perfectly reasonable. I will be back in the office tomorrow."

After a short pause, Beckham frowned at whatever was being said on the other line. She could tell he didn't like it—what was being said or how it was being said. He looked as if he was about to rage on the other person. But when he spoke, none of that was in his voice. "Of course. Penelope is busy for the evening. She wouldn't mind giving me up for another ball." Slight pause. "That is a personal matter." Another pause. "Understood."

Beckham ended the call and tossed the phone next to the computer.

"Who was that?"

"Harrington."

Reyna recoiled at the name. It still stung like a viper's bite every time it was mentioned unexpectedly in her presence. Sometimes she forgot that Beckham worked for him. The reminder was a slap in the face.

"You're leaving to go see him?" Reyna asked.

"Yes. It's my job."

Reyna suddenly felt very naked. "Right," she said, scrambling out of bed and searching for her clothes.

"I still have some time before I have to return."

"What did he ask when you said it was a personal matter?" She threw a shirt over her head before glancing back at him.

"He asked what my fight with Penelope had been about."

"You didn't just lie?"

"Harrington can usually tell when I'm lying," he said simply.

That made Reyna shiver. "How do you avoid that?"

"Try not to get into situations where he is asking questions I do not wish for him to ask."

"How much longer are you going to work for him?" she asked, her voice unintentionally rising.

"As long as it takes."

Reyna waited for further explanation. Beckham stayed because it gave them insider information into what Harrington was doing and where Visage was going, but it didn't make it any easier.

"I need to talk to you." Beckham gestured to the place he had vacated. "Have a seat."

She plopped down, anxiety swirling through her. What the hell was Beckham going to talk to her about? From the look on his face, it couldn't be good.

He put his hands behind his back and stood tall over her. "I want you to work with Washington regarding your blood."

"What?" she asked, jumping back to her feet. "How can you ask me to do that? You do know what I went through at Visage, right?"

"Sit," he instructed, then waited for her to return to her seat. "Your safety is my number one priority. I won't let anything happen to you. You trust me. I trust Washington."

"Okay," she said uneasily.

"I can sense you. That day at the ball was not a coincidence. I knew you were standing outside the door that day you came back from Five Points. I knew when you were awake just now. It is all the same feeling." When Beckham glanced at her, all she could see was worry on his face. Or rather…him trying to conceal his worry. "If I can sense you and your blood, what is to stop anyone who has drunk your blood from sensing you?"

Reyna hated the implication, but she had to ask, "You think Harrington…"

"I don't know. And I do not like not knowing."

"You think Washington can figure that out."

"Wouldn't you rather know if he could?"

"Yes," she whispered.

"Then will you meet with him? I will go with you." He reached his hand out.

"Right now?"

"I don't have much time. I thought you'd prefer I go to make sure nothing happens to you."

She saw in his fierce expression that he was telling the truth. He would destroy anyone who tried to hurt her. Though the last thing she wanted to do was work with Washington or ever give her blood again, Beckham raised a valid point. If she wanted to leave HQ, she needed to know what kind of danger she was putting herself in.

She reached out and placed her hand in his. "Let's go."

CHAPTER TWENTY-FOUR

Beckham directed Reyna through the network of corridors to the back entrance of the medical wing. Reyna memorized the way in case she needed to do it again. Following Beckham inside put her even more on edge. Even though she trusted Becks, that didn't make it any easier.

Beckham put his hand on her lower back. "Your pulse is through the roof."

"Nerves."

He stopped her. "Will I let harm come to you?"

"No."

"Would I willingly put you in a position where you are unsafe?"

"No."

"I would kill before letting a single person lay a hand on you. You know this?"

She nodded. "Yes."

He threaded their fingers together, then brought her hand to his lips and placed a kiss there. "You are mine, Little One."

She breathed out a sigh of relief. She hadn't entirely calmed down, but there was something in his eyes that told her she had nothing to fear. It was incredible to think she had once feared him, or that he still believed he could ever be a threat to her.

Beckham directed her the rest of the way down the corridor until they reached an open office door. He knocked twice and then entered. Washington was seated behind a desk so cluttered Reyna could hardly see an inch of the surface—just paperwork, notepads, pens, a clipboard, and various medical supplies that disappeared beneath more papers.

"Beckham," Washington said with a genuine smile. "To what do I owe the pleasure?"

"I am here about Reyna."

Washington's eyes drifted to Reyna, who was still standing like a scared mouse outside of the office. "Hello there, Reyna. Good to see you back in the medical wing."

"Hi," she said softly.

Beckham looked at Reyna, checking that she still wanted to do this. He held his hand out, and she finally stepped inside. Her heart was thudding once more, but she knew Beckham was right. She needed to do this.

"I need to find out what's wrong with my blood."

"Wrong with it?" Washington asked.

"I can sense her," Beckham said, explaining all the strange incidents. "It has happened many times."

"Fascinating," Washington said as he came to his feet.

"How do we make it stop?" Reyna asked.

"Stop?" Washington asked, perplexed. "Hmm…I doubt you can make it stop. Why would you want it to stop?"

"I don't," Beckham said with finality. "But I don't want Harrington to have the same access I am privy to. I don't want anyone who has tasted her blood to have the same reaction."

"Well, we could have someone else drink her blood and see if it works," Washington said simply.

Beckham growled. Actually growled.

"Or…we could try something else," Washington said hastily, taking a step back.

Reyna could see the death in Beckham's eyes. She placed her hand on his sleeve. "It would be okay."

"It would not."

"I was merely suggesting the simplest test," Washington added.

"Reyna's blood is not for feeding," Beckham snarled. "No one else will taste her. Not ever."

"Becks," she whispered.

"If her blood does allow the ability to sense her, then another vampire will have claim on her. I won't allow it."

"I have heard of this sort of thing before," Washington said, obviously trying to redirect the subject. "But it's been many years. Long before we had the technology we do now. Might I be able to take a sample of your blood to run some tests?"

Reyna nodded. Washington glanced at Beckham, who nodded as well. All three of them moved out of his office and into a lab.

Reyna took a seat and tried not to think about the needle by focusing on her breathing. In through her nose, out through her mouth. Beckham came to stand next to her.

"Hey, look at me." She slowly did as he asked. "This will be over soon."

She didn't nod or do anything. She just stared at him and waited. Not watching usually helped some. She didn't anticipate it, but it didn't lessen the fear. It was like trying not to wait for someone to jump out at you in a haunted house.

The prick of the needle happened. Beckham inhaled deeply. His hand clenched on the chair, but he never broke eye contact. She could see him retreating deep into himself, fighting for control. Could see the hunger buried there. Then, as quickly as it happened, it was over.

"There we go," Washington said. He cleaned up her arm, put a

Band-Aid on it, and then swept the blood vials up and onto the counter. "That was interesting. Your blood smells very sweet."

"I've heard that before," Reyna said. "Do you know what that means?"

"Well, all blood smells different. Especially to vampires with our more enhanced sense of smell. But I personally only know of one other person who has ever smelled like that."

"I've never smelled anything like it," Beckham said, still in a bit of a trance.

"You were not even born yet when I discovered this woman." Washington finished with the rest of his work and then came to stand before them. "One of the lords had a favorite who smelled similarly."

Reyna's head swam. "Lords?"

Washington gave her an apologetic look. "I am afraid vampires were not as we described when Visage took power."

"Not *all* was as described," Beckham clarified.

"I don't understand."

"Not all vampires were crazed, animalistic monsters," Washington told her. "We spun that tale to make it more palatable for the humans when Visage rose up from the ashes of the collapse."

Reyna felt like her entire world had been flipped upside down. "But there were mass killings. People couldn't go out after dark except in well-lit places, and even then it wasn't advised."

"That's true. Vampires committed atrocities you could not even imagine," Beckham told her. "However, we were on an elevated plane."

Reyna blinked up at him. "But everyone said you were so fearsome. You yourself said you were the deadliest of them all," she breathed, lapping up this bit of his history.

Beckham frowned as if realizing how much he was giving away. "Yes, we were worse."

"Regardless," Washington said, "this woman's blood was incredibly enticing. It was clear that, had she not found someone to protect her, she would have been dead long ago."

Reyna let that settle between her and Beckham. The same could be said for her.

"What happened to her?" Reyna asked.

Washington frowned, clearly not liking where his own story had turned. "He sucked her dry and remade her. He wanted her to be at his side forever."

"So, he made her a vampire?"

"He tried," Washington said wistfully. "But she did not survive the change."

"She died?" Reyna gasped.

"Not all do," Beckham said.

"You mean some people try to become vampires and are killed?" How had no one ever told her that? She'd never heard of that happening.

"A shockingly large number, actually," Washington informed her. He seemed oblivious to her discomfort about the subject. "Vampirism itself is sort of like a virus. A human must drink a vampire's blood and be completely drained of their own blood. They effectively 'die' and are remade. The vampire virus latches onto the host and restarts the heart, producing vampire blood to refill the arteries. The new blood conveys the increased strength and speed. It makes our eyes naturally better adapted to the darkness and prolongs our life far beyond a normal human's. Thus, with all the changes that occur, it would make sense that not all humans are sufficient hosts for vampirism to latch onto."

"And the woman with the blood that smelled like mine—she wasn't a proper host?" Reyna asked softly.

"She wasn't," Washington said.

Reyna knew she shouldn't jump to conclusions. There were a million different things that could have prevented this woman from changing into a vampire. It felt too close for comfort, though.

If this woman with the exact-same-smelling blood couldn't turn, then could Reyna turn? Could she become a vampire? The smell of her blood must mean something. Surely it had something to do with her very rare blood type and the way Beckham could sense her. If all those traits were connected, that meant it was even likely the woman had been an Rh null human.

Of course, Harrington was Rh null, so obviously the blood type alone didn't determine a suitable host. So maybe her blood smelled different because of something else. Maybe she was similar to that woman in another way and *that* would prevent her from turning. She shuddered at the thought of dying. Of course she didn't want to die. And since when did she want to turn into a vampire?

She didn't. Did she? Her heart pattered away as anxiety took over. If she didn't turn into a vampire, she couldn't stay with Beckham. She would keep getting older, and he would stay the same age. Brian had flung that in her face when he found out about her and Beckham—as if Reyna turning into a vampire was the only option for them to continue to be together. She clearly must have taken that to heart.

"Reyna," Beckham said warningly, as if reading her weighted silence.

Reyna swallowed and pushed forward with her heart in her throat. "Can you…can you tell if someone isn't a proper host?"

Washington stared down at his equipment, still oblivious to the turn of this conversation. "Well, I haven't discovered a way without infecting a person. And then I'm afraid it's too late."

Reyna let the conversation lapse into silence. She could feel Beckham's eyes boring into her, but she didn't dare look at him. She needed a second to mourn the loss of that option. Because how could she risk something like that? There was no way Beckham would if there was even a possibility she could die—her safety was his number one priority—and she couldn't fathom the thought of having someone else turn her. There was always the possibility that it could work, but it still felt like driving away from the mountains and seeing them fade in the distance.

"This should suffice," Washington said with a bright smile. He looked between Reyna and Beckham and their stern expressions quizzically. "Well, thank you for allowing me to collect your blood,

Reyna. I know it is not something you had otherwise wanted to do."

She nodded, still not sure she had words.

"If you want to check in with me, I would love to have you in the lab. I could use an assistant," he offered.

Reyna's gaze shifted to Beckham's. He trusted Washington. That made a difference to her. It made her see Washington differently. He wasn't just the vampire who had created the blood type cure, who had gotten her mixed up in all of this to begin with. Though donating her blood and being in a hospital still made her queasy, she felt more at ease around him. She'd always known her helping would further the greater good, but her own fears had gotten in the way. She didn't want to be that person. Maybe she could be brave enough to help out. To overcome her fears for this.

"All right," she said softly. "Let's see how it goes. I can't promise much, but I'll try to help where I can."

"Will you wait outside a moment?" Beckham asked. "I want to have a word with Dr. Washington."

"Sure." She hopped off the chair and hurried out of the room.

She didn't want to know what they were talking about. She was sure Beckham was pissed Washington had revealed some of their history and scared her in the process. She knew she *should* be scared, based on the history, but all she felt was numb.

Beckham appeared a few minutes later like a thundercloud. "We should get you back. I need to return to work."

"Okay."

Beckham frowned at her compliance but didn't object. In silence, they walked together back to her room.

When they reached it, Beckham tilted her chin up, forcing her to look in his eyes. "You are shaken."

She tried to grasp at what she felt. "It's sort of how I imagine it would feel to find out you can't have children. You didn't really consider whether or not you wanted to have them, but now that you can't, all you can think about is the loss."

Beckham's eyes looked haunted by her words. He remained silent.

"I thought that maybe…one day…you and I…" She trailed off.

"I never wanted you to be this," he told her, gesturing to himself. "No one deserves this hell."

Reyna turned her face away. "I guess I see that turning me was never a possibility."

"You make it seem like a tragedy."

"The fact that our time is limited *is* a tragedy."

"Such is the way of the world."

"My world," she countered. "Not yours."

"We cannot undo the mistakes of our past. Just hope to make better choices in the future."

Except, it suddenly felt as if she had no choice in the matter, and she hadn't even known whether it was what she wanted before that moment. Now she might never know.

CHAPTER TWENTY-FIVE

With only four days until Christmas, Penelope had agreed to help Laura get a dress. She received a note from Beckham with the pickup time for her and Laura. Reyna raced out of her room and found Meghan, Jodie, and Laura seated around a table in the rec room, which was crowded for early afternoon.

"Hey!" she said, running up to them.

"Reyna." Meghan jumped to her feet. "I need to talk to you. Can we do it outside?"

"Can it wait? I want to talk to Laura. I have good news."

Meghan grabbed her arm and tried to all but drag her out of the rec room. "It'll just be a minute."

"What the hell," Reyna said. "Meghan, stop!"

"Go with her, Reyna," Laura said cajolingly, her face wan.

Only Jodie seemed too interested in the television to bother trying to corral Reyna out of the room.

Reyna yanked her arm out of Meghan's grasp. "What is going on?"

That was when Reyna noticed the television and, more specifically, who was on it. Beckham and Penelope's smiling faces and a bridal shop.

"Looks like he's taking her to pick out her wedding dress. I guess they're closing down the entire boutique just for her," Jodie said with a sigh. Her eyes finally turned back to Reyna. "Sorry. Seems he played you again."

Reyna laughed at Jodie. At all of them. "He didn't play me. This is for Laura!"

Laura looked confused. Jodie disbelieving. Meghan a little sad.

Reyna took a seat across from Laura and took her hand. "It's a setup, and it was my idea to begin with. We asked Penelope to pretend like she was going to get her dress there so we could get the shop to close. Then we can sneak you in the back to get a wedding dress."

"What?" Laura gasped. Tears came easily to her eyes. She swiped at them. "Pregnancy hormones."

Jodie laughed. "Holy shit, bet Little Miss Mayor is super thrilled about this."

"Wow, Reyna," Meghan said, sliding into a chair next to her.

"I cannot believe you did this!" Laura squealed. She threw her arms around Reyna. "You are the best soon-to-be sister-in-law."

Reyna hugged her back. "You're welcome. I'm glad it worked."

"This is great, but…" Meghan began.

"Oh God, here we go," Jodie grumbled.

"It's not safe for you or Laura to leave Elle."

"We'll be with Beckham. I'm pretty sure he knows how to secure a facility. He would never put me in any danger."

Meghan glanced at the floor. "Except that time he did."

"I put myself in danger. Not him." Meghan opened her mouth to respond, but Reyna beat her to it. "And if he thinks it's okay for us to go to the bridal shop, then it is."

"Okay. Okay," Meghan said, holding her hands up. "I'm just looking out for you. I really am excited about the dress."

Reyna hugged Meghan and promised to be careful, then dragged Laura away to her room to meet their pickup window. Laura was abuzz with excitement, chatting nonstop about how incredible it was that Beckham could pull this off. A knock came to her closet door at precisely the time Beckham had said, but when Reyna opened the door, she didn't find Beckham.

"Ladies," Gabe said with a wink. "Slight change of plans. Come along, you two."

Laura scurried forward as Reyna made the introductions and they headed out of the room. Laura blushed when Gabe worked his charm on her. Reyna had to refrain from rolling her eyes.

"So…a wedding dress, huh?" he asked Reyna.

"For Laura. She's marrying my brother."

"Lucky guy."

"Oh, shut it," Reyna said with a laugh.

They took the elevator up to the top floor, went out the steel door, and hurried out into the cold. Reyna was glad they'd once again bundled up downstairs as they hurried into a heavily tinted black van.

Reyna sat in the passenger seat next to Gabe while Laura peered eagerly out the window in the back. She had forgotten that it had probably been months since Laura had left the safety of the underground bunker. She was soaking everything in, because who knew when it would happen again?

"So, why you and not Beckham?" Reyna asked, turning her attention to Gabe.

"I was in the area. Thought it'd be easier."

Reyna doubted that was the entire story but decided to let it drop. "Can I ask you a question?"

"Do you normally ask for permission?"

"No," she said with an eye roll.

"Then shoot."

"The first time I was at Five Points, I ended up two floors up in a black-market blood bank."

Gabe swerved the van. Laura grunted from the back seat, her

hand on her belly, and Reyna clutched the side panel.

"Watch what you're doing," she groaned.

"How the hell did you come across that?"

"On accident?" she said with a shrug. "There was a riot. We escaped and fled up two floors and found it when we were hiding."

"We?"

"Everett and I," she clarified.

"Motherfucker."

"I just wanted to know if it belongs to Elle?"

"Well, it's a side business I was running out of Five Points, but we relocated it somewhere safer shortly after that riot. Elle has some of it. I have some of it." He shrugged.

"That's an interesting side business."

"Hey, it's hard to make money on the streets, and blood is no different than drugs or sex. It all sells."

Well, she couldn't argue with that—but it did leave her with a lot of questions. If Everett was working for Visage when they found the blood bank at Five Points, had he reported it? He had to have known it would have been of interest to them. She had so many questions about Everett's behavior—his friends' distrust and hatred of vampires, his knowledge of Elle, his interest in her rebellious photography. How could a man like that also work for Visage? How could he have betrayed her?

She sighed and decided it would continue to be a mystery. She needed to focus on the present anyway. Getting Laura a wedding dress and dealing with Penelope.

Gabe turned them down an alley and parked the truck in an underground garage. "The store has been cleared, and paparazzi have been removed from much of this area, but it's never a guarantee with those fuckers. Wear this hat," he said, tossing it to her and one to Laura as well. "Keep your heads down."

They all hopped out of the van. Gabe ushered them into an elevator that shot straight up to the ground floor and opened up on the opposite side into a deserted corridor. They walked partway down the hall to a back entrance, and he slid a key into the door. It popped open, and Reyna and Laura both hurried inside. Gabe glanced once more down the hall before ducking inside and locking everything back up.

Reyna yanked the hat off her head and breathed a sigh of relief. She hated this sneaking around. She could tell by Laura's expression that she didn't like it, either.

They were standing in the back room of the bridal shop where dozens of gowns in various states of unpacked took up much of the space. There was a corner for a seamstress to work, a small shipping and receiving area cluttered with boxes, tissue paper, and tape, a door to the owner's office, and a second one to the boutique itself.

The boutique door opened, and Gabe immediately thrust himself in front of them. In strode a shrewd-looking woman in her early thirties wearing a slim-cut black dress.

"Olivia," Gabe said with a grin. "Good to see you."

"Gabriel," she said with a tight-lipped smile. "I wasn't aware you would be joining us."

"Just here for the delivery." He gestured to the two women behind him. "Olivia, this is Reyna and Laura. Olivia is part of the cause."

"Indeed. Now come along, ladies," Olivia said, clapping her hands twice. "Let's get you inside. I hear we have a bride we're shopping for?"

Laura grinned like a fool and joined Olivia. They immediately began chatting up a storm about the impending wedding.

Reyna nudged Gabe. "Heartbreaker."

"As if I'm the only one." He disappeared back through the door.

Reyna hurried to catch up to Laura and Olivia, only to be stopped by none other than Penelope Sky herself. Reyna swallowed and tried to remember that she needed to be nice. Nice and happy and appreciative. Penelope had gone out of her way to help set this up. Without her, Laura never would have gotten to pick her own dress.

"Hey, Penny," Reyna said, forcing a smile on her face. "Thank you so, so much for doing this for Laura. It's super nice of you. I know both Laura and I really appreciate it."

"Oh, it's just you," Penelope said with a frown. "I thought Beckham had come back, finally."

"Gabe said there was a change of plans."

"Yes."

Reyna waited, expecting her to elaborate. "What happened?"

"Don't you already know?"

"I don't."

"Maybe he'll tell you when he comes back for me," she said, then turned and walked back into the boutique.

Reyna closed her eyes, took a few deep breaths, and counted to ten. She understood why Penelope was uncomfortable in this situation. They were using her fake engagement to help someone else. It couldn't be easy, being reminded that the engagement was fake. Still, Reyna was trying to be on her best behavior, and Penelope's attitude didn't make it any easier.

After she calmed down, Reyna walked through the doors and into the boutique. The place was breathtaking. The walls were lined with evenly spaced white gowns in every shape and cut imaginable. Some were the starkest white while others were a dark cream or off-white or even an array of colors—red, green, blue, and black. Glitter and lace and sequins and crystals abounded. Gossamer and tulle and silk and satin and all kinds of brilliant materials made these incredible creations. Reyna couldn't stop staring at them. The cost of one of these amazing gowns could likely feed the entire Warehouse District for a day.

Of course, Beckham could afford it, and he was footing the bill.

She ignored Penelope and went to help Laura pick out a dozen dresses. Luckily, her baby bump wasn't showing yet. The only real issue was that the dress had to fit her perfectly, because there was no time for alterations. At least she was tall. All the dresses would have been several inches too long on Reyna.

Olivia hustled Laura and her many gowns into the enormous dressing room and stayed inside to help her change. Reyna took a seat near Penelope, who was texting away on her phone, oblivious.

Reyna cleared her throat in the awkward silence. "I wanted to reiterate how thankful I am. Truly. It means a lot to Laura to have a dress."

Penelope slowly turned to look at her. Up close like this, the damage from the burns was more noticeable. Plastic surgery was a miracle, considering what she had gone through, and she didn't look any less beautiful. Her fine white scars were endearing. Enhanced an already perfect visage.

"I really appreciate you doing this for Laura," Reyna added when Penny said nothing. "It's very nice of you."

"Oh, please," Penny finally said with an eye roll. "Let's not pretend that I'm doing this for anyone but Beckham."

"Well, then, thanks for doing this for Becks."

Penelope shot her an amused face. "Becks?"

"Uh…yeah?"

"Have you seen that man? He's hardly one for nicknames."

Reyna couldn't stop her smile. It was all she could do to keep from laughing. Penelope was right. To the rest of the world, Beckham was not the kind of person to have a nickname. Her Beckham, though, the man he showed only her beneath the monster, was most definitely Becks.

"Okay," Reyna said.

"Does he let you call him Becks?" she asked, her voice low. Her doe eyes were round with concern she couldn't quite mask that she had missed something big about Beckham.

"Um…"

"Ugh!" Penelope said, turning away from her. "I don't even know why I bother with you. Or why he does, for that matter. You're like all the other girls who came before you. I was the one who changed him. I'm going to be the one at his side in the end."

Other girls? Reyna knew she shouldn't ask Penelope what she meant—she knew the other woman was baiting her—but she couldn't completely keep the confusion off her face.

"You do know about the other girls, right?" Penny asked in a sickly sweet tone. Reyna bit the inside of her cheek. "I mean…has he told you anything about his past?"

"I don't see how our relationship is any of your concern."

Penelope laughed a short little chirp. She seemed back in her element. "I see. So, he hasn't. Well, if you're not dead in a couple of months, I'll be shocked. I guess getting kidnapped appears to have prolonged your life. Go figure."

Reyna's temper flared. "It's one thing to insult me and to insinuate that you know Beckham better than I do. It's quite another to suggest that when I was kidnapped it was a good thing. Perhaps it was good for you, Penny, because you were able to continue living in your deluded world where you believe Beckham wants to be with you."

Penny pursed her lips. "Things were better before you showed up."

"I have no intention of apologizing for that. I didn't ask for this life. This life came to me. But now that it's mine, don't think I'll go down without a fight. You might think that you saved Beckham, that he changed because of you, but then you'd be just like every other woman in history who thinks that a man changed because of them."

"You weren't there when we first met," Penny said, jumping to her feet. "You don't know what it was like. Harrington sent him to me to test him. And considering he didn't kill me or turn me into a vampire"—Penelope made a face of disgust—"it's obvious that he passed. He's a different man now than he was then because of what we went through together. The fact that you now get to reap the benefits is so fucking ridiculous."

"I don't care what you two went through together. Or whatever *test* you were to him. None of that matters to me, because it clearly doesn't matter to him. Beckham chose me."

The words hung in the air between them. Penelope, red in the face and angry, stormed out of the changing area and into the back. Reyna didn't know where she was going or what she was doing, and frankly, she didn't care. She'd had every intention of being nice and conciliatory, but it was clear doing so would have meant crossing the line into doormat territory. She was not going to let Penny walk all over her because she felt she had some claim on Beckham.

"What do you think of this one?" Laura asked, finally appearing in a dress.

Reyna's mouth dropped open, her argument forgotten. "Holy shit!"

Laura bounced up and down with excitement. "It's so soft. I've never worn anything this dainty."

"Brian will fall over himself at the sight of you."

Laura tried on half a dozen more dresses while they were at the dress shop, but none compared to that first one. It was the dream dress. Magic was sewn into the fabric. It was the one, no matter how many other dresses she looked at.

"Just one more," she said, though she fingered the soft layers of the first dress again.

She was back in the changing room with Olivia when Beckham burst into the boutique. Reyna shot to her feet.

"What's wrong?" she asked upon seeing his face.

"We have to go."

"What happened?"

His eyes were dark and ominous, his voice deep and barely controlled. "Everett."

Chapter Twenty-Six

"He's back?" Reyna asked with wide eyes.

Beckham nodded once tersely. "Where's Penelope? We need to get her out of here, too."

"She's not in the back?"

"No."

"Then I don't know. She stormed out there like an hour ago and never returned."

His face darkened. Just then, Olivia and Laura came out of the dressing room, Laura in some poofy monstrosity. Olivia's eyes widened when she saw Beckham.

"Pack up whichever dress she wants," Beckham said to Olivia. "We have to leave."

"Of course, Mr. Anderson," Olivia said evenly. "Come on, Laura."

Beckham frowned and glanced down at his phone.

"Did Penny message you?"

"No." His eyes caught hers again. "Did something happen?"

"Well, it didn't go well."

He sighed, pocketed the phone, and nodded for her to follow him. They had barely entered the back room of the boutique when Beckham pushed her against the wall. He put his hands on either side of her head and leaned in. His lips caressed hers, and she breathed into him. It had only been a couple of days, but she had missed him.

He pulled back abruptly and stared deep into her eyes. There was something off about him, like he wasn't entirely sure how to act or he was afraid that she might disappear.

She placed her hand on his cheek. "Hey, whatever is going on, it'll be fine."

"I want to take you back to Elle."

"All right. Are you going to tell me what's up with Everett?"

Beckham turned his head away from her palm, and she let it drop. No, she had read him wrong. This wasn't fear or worry. This was anger. Bristling and spitting right under the surface. He was trying to control it and not let it erupt out of him. She was sure it had to do with Everett, but what could Everett have done that would make him this angry? After orchestrating her kidnapping, there couldn't be much worse than that.

"Will you go back to Elle?" he demanded instead of replying to her question.

"Becks, look at me." He finally did, his eyes black molten lava. "I will go back if I have to, but there's something you're not telling me."

"He wants to talk to you," Beckham ground out.

"What? Why?"

"He won't say. He won't say anything except that he has important information and the only person he'll tell is you."

Reyna's head swam with the possibilities. "Do you think he has info?"

Beckham considered for a moment. "I think he's a threat. He'll do anything to get close to you."

"So...you think it's a trap?"

"That is how it appears."

Reyna gnawed on her lip. It *could* be a trap. If Harrington was looking for her, it would make sense for him to use Everett to draw her out.

"What if he does have information?"

"I know a way to get it from him without letting him talk to you." The sinister glint in his eye said everything he hadn't—they would torture him until he revealed it.

Reyna hated Everett. She despised his part in all of this. That didn't mean she agreed with torture. She didn't want Elle to become the bad guys. She wanted them to be better than that. She wanted Beckham to be better than that.

"I'll do it."

"Reyna..."

"Find me a secure location. I can get the information from him. I know that I can."

He clenched his jaw. He'd anticipated she would want to do it. She liked to take chances. He liked that about her, even if it made his job to keep her safe more difficult.

"He's going to manipulate you."

"I won't forget what he did. Plus, you'll be there, right?"

His body went rigid, and he shook his head. That was the biggest obstacle—he couldn't be there. Everett wanted to talk to her, and Beckham couldn't be there to protect her.

"You won't be there."

"I will be there, but I can't risk him knowing that I'm Elle. He might not know you and Gabe are with Elle, but you two are connected now. We can't risk him figuring out more."

"But finding out about you would be worst-case scenario."

"Undeniably."

Olivia strode into the back room carrying an enormous white hanging bag before Reyna could respond.

"We chose a winner," Olivia said, handing it to Laura, who took it and thanked her profusely.

"The first dress?" Reyna asked.

Laura nodded. "It's perfect."

"Let's go," Beckham said, nodding toward the back door.

They exited into the corridor, then went down in the elevator again to where a nondescript black Mercedes idled.

Beckham turned to Laura. "My driver, Gerard, can be trusted. I've known him longer than you've been alive. He's going to take you back and will inform me if anything goes awry."

"Okay. Where are you going?" Laura asked.

"Business," he said, gesturing for her to enter the car.

She turned to Reyna. "Please be safe."

"I will," Reyna said and hoped it was true.

Laura stuffed the wedding dress into the back seat and crawled in after it.

Beckham knocked on the passenger window. It rolled down. "Gerard, please drive Laura back. Reyna and I will take my ride."

Gerard put down the historical romance novel he had been reading and nodded at Beckham. "Yes, sir."

Reyna watched the car speed off. Beckham tugged her close, directing her farther down the darkened garage. She shivered in the chilly temperatures and wished she'd thought to bring the hat and gloves Beckham had given her for the rooftop. Especially once she saw what Beckham's ride was.

"Is that *yours*?" she gasped.

He quirked an eyebrow as they approached the sleek black motorcycle. He responded by tossing her a helmet.

"It's December," she reminded him. "I'm going to freeze."

Next, he handed her fur-lined black leather gloves, a black beanie, and a black mask that covered the lower half of her face.

"You knew I would come with you."

"Do I ever expect you to willingly sit on the sidelines?"

She grinned fiercely as she pulled on everything he'd brought her. Beckham easily secured the helmet's clasp under her chin. He kicked one leg over the beast and waited patiently for her to work up the nerve to do the same. She'd never been on a motorcycle.

"I will not let you come to harm, Little One."

She swallowed and swung her leg over. She wrapped her arms around Beckham's middle, plastering her chest against his back and her thighs against his. She was surprised to find him warmer than she would have expected. She was about to freeze, but this was going to be worth it.

Beckham revved the engine, and the bike jumped forward. Reyna squeezed tightly as they zipped out of the alley and onto the city streets. The wind whipped at her masked face. Buildings rushed past her in a blur. Everything happened in a rush. Her heart leaped in her throat, but her fear quickly melted away. This was real freedom. No boundaries and endless possibilities. They could go anywhere. Do anything. Be anyone they wanted. She wanted to open her arms wide and let the bike carry her away.

When all of this was over and the weather became warm again, she was going to insist he take her out on this every day. Every single day. It was a travesty he hadn't told her about it before.

When Beckham pulled off of the road about fifteen minutes later, she was shaking and stiff, but she could have done that so much longer. Beckham parked the bike on the street in front of a boarded-up building and helped her off the back. When she tugged her mask down, her smile was huge and she was bouncing with energy.

"When do we do that again?" she asked.

"Danger doesn't just find you. You go looking for it."

"You put me on that motorcycle. You can't expect me not to love it."

He leaned forward, brushing a fang across the shell of her ear. "All I can think about is bending you over it."

"Well," she said breathily, "I hadn't thought of that, but now that I am…"

"Next time."

He slipped his hand into hers, and they headed off the street through an innocuous black door into the most glorious warmth. A small entry room with nothing on the walls and only one broken chair in the corner. She'd been cold on the bike, but adrenaline had taken over. Now she realized belatedly that she was shaking.

"You brought me an icicle," Gabe said from the doorway with a grin.

"I may actually be frozen," she grumbled.

"We should get you warmed up," Beckham said. His phone rang noisily, and he cursed, retreating to the end of the room to answer it.

"Come on, you," Gabe said.

He steered her down a hallway and into a cozy sitting room. It was nothing fancy, but it was more inviting than the boarded-up exterior indicated. He set her down in front of an electric fireplace, wrapped a couple of blankets around her shoulders, and brought her some hot chocolate.

"What is this place?" she asked between her chattering teeth.

"Safe house."

"Oh. I've been to one of those before. Are they all this shitty?"

"Helps with the cover." He winked at her. Typical Gabe. "You ready for this? I know with your history…"

"I'm ready."

"He didn't try to talk you into this, right? You came of your own free will?"

Reyna shot him an exasperated look. "If anything, Beckham tried to talk me out of it. Why would you think otherwise?"

Gabe glanced back down the hallway to where Beckham was still speaking animatedly on his phone. "Just wanted to make sure. You can never be too careful."

"He thinks this is a trap. *Am* I walking into a trap?"

"We did everything we possibly could to make sure that doesn't happen. There's no bug on him—we made him change clothes and burned his old ones. No tracker in his skin. We confiscated his phone, and it's not in the building. The guy seems legit scared," Gabe said thoughtfully. "I've seen enough shitbags like this to know when they're faking it. And maybe he is, but he doesn't look like it."

"So, you think he actually has information for us? He's not just trying to get to me?"

"He's a spy and a good actor. You're proof of that. I wouldn't trust a word he tells you, and I'd expect some serious mental manipulation in the process. But...yeah, I think he has something."

"If I can get it, I will," she said. She was warm again, so she gave him her empty hot cocoa mug and squeezed his hand.

Gabe motioned for her to follow him. He showed her to a bedroom at the back of the safe house.

"He's in there. We're going to mic you so we can hear everything that's being said. There's already a video camera in the room. And there's nothing he can use to hurt you. But if he tries, I'll be on the other side of this door."

"Okay." She swallowed.

"Beckham will be watching from another room, because I don't trust him not to barge in at the slightest provocation."

Reyna nodded. That sounded reasonable.

"How did Everett find me?" she asked. "How was he brought here and everything?"

"He didn't find you. He found me. I guess he did see me that night. He's been piecing together who I am and finally tracked me down. I nearly blew his brains out when he approached me alone in a dark alley. All I can say is that he seems desperate."

Reyna quelled her fear. She couldn't show any to Everett when she walked into that room. It also wasn't helping her now, thinking through how exactly Everett had been able to track her down.

"All right. Let's do this."

Tony, Elle's resident techie, hooked her up to a microphone. When he was done, Gabe nudged her with his elbow. "Knock 'em dead."

Beckham appeared in the doorway, and Gabe made himself scarce. "Are you ready?"

"As I'll ever be."

"If he harms you, I will kill him," Beckham said.

Reyna ran her hands up into his dark hair. "Nothing is going to happen to me."

His kiss was urgent and chaotic. It made her entire body tremble with need. Her bones ached with desperation. Her lungs burned to breathe him in. She could have gotten so lost in him.

She pulled back. "Wish me luck."

"Luck is rarely on your side, Little One." He brushed back her hair. "But *I* am on your side."

"Even better."

She managed to disentangle herself from him and stepped back into the hallway. Gabe gestured that they were ready. She grabbed the handle and pushed the door open.

There sat Everett, on a wooden chair in the center of the room. His hands were handcuffed in front of him, and it looked like someone had already tried the torture tactic on him. He glanced up, and his hazel eyes sparkled at the sight of her.

"You came," he said earnestly.

She took a deep breath and stepped into the room. *Here goes nothing.*

Chapter Twenty-Seven

"I didn't think that you'd come," Everett said.

She raised her chin an inch, taking him in. His boy-next-door good looks were bedraggled. His chestnut hair was mussed, one eye swollen, blood dribbling out of a cut on his lip. The clothes they'd given him didn't quite fit. His frame was swallowed by the oversize T-shirt and sweats he wore instead of his crisp valet uniform.

And yet…he wasn't downtrodden. His spirits were high. His smile was the same friendly grin she had known for so long. The one she had foolishly trusted. *That* had backfired in her face.

"Yes, you did," she finally said.

His lips quirked downward. "I wasn't sure."

"Don't try this act on me. I believe we're past that."

"It's not an act."

She laughed brusquely. "Everything about you is an act. So, let's skip the pleasantries. I'm here. That's what you wanted. Why don't you tell me the information you're withholding?"

Everett straightened in his seat. "Why don't you take these handcuffs off me?" He held his hands out in front of him. "Then we'll chat."

"Yeah. Not happening."

"You don't have to be afraid of me."

"I'm not afraid of you," she spat. Her anger was fuel to a fire.

"If you're not afraid of me, then I don't need these."

Reyna rolled her eyes. "Okay. So, you're not going to tell me. I guess I don't need to be here."

She turned around and started toward the door. Her palm was on the handle before he called out, "Wait."

She stilled. Forced herself to wait. To draw out his unease. Then she faced him once more. "I'm not here to play games with you. I've done that enough."

"Okay," he said evenly, leaning his elbows on his knees. "Can I start at the beginning?"

"Start wherever you like. Just get started."

"Will you sit?" He gestured to the seat before him.

She wondered if Gabe had done the initial interrogating. She knew he was good with his hands. A fighter at heart. It couldn't have been Beckham—he didn't want Everett to know he was part of Elle. Plus, Everett wouldn't just be bruised; he'd be bloody.

She swung the chair around on its rear legs and straddled it with the back as a barrier between them. Then she sat with her arms resting across the top. "I'm sitting. Get started."

Everett grinned. "You always were a surprise."

She sighed as if she were totally bored with him. "Let's start with—how long have you been a spy? Is that a good place to start?"

"A while," he said with a shrug. "Long enough."

"Do your friends know?"

"No. They are exactly as they seem."

"Why were you spying on me?"

"Well, I wasn't spying on *you*," he said nonchalantly.

"You didn't spy on me? Explain that."

"I didn't have to spy on you, Reyna. You were so desperate for someone to notice you that you would have made the easiest mark in the world."

She flushed. That was true. She had been that girl. Out of her depth and in need of a friend. No wonder he had been so kind to her. The only person who had been.

"But you weren't the mark," Everett added calmly.

"You turned me in to Harrington, and *I* wasn't the mark?" She had to fight to keep her anger in check.

"Why would Harrington give a shit about you?"

Reyna bit the inside of her cheek. "Then why did you turn me in?"

"Because Beckham was the mark." His handcuffs jingled as he pointed toward the door. "He's out there, isn't he?"

"Then why did you turn me in?" she repeated, ignoring his question.

"I did what I was told. I was supposed to report on anything interesting in Beckham's movements, changes in his demeanor, differences in his schedule. That sort of thing. He's a rather boring and predictable person, to be honest. Until you came along."

Reyna swallowed. "What changed when I showed up?"

Everett cocked his head to the side. His eyes were bright, as if he found the question interesting or maybe hilarious. "Everything."

She knew she shouldn't feel excitement at that thought, but still it curled inside of her.

"Didn't you ever wonder why I never turned you in for all your obvious rebellious behavior? That camera?" He laughed. "If I could figure out that you were behind the *Perspective* website in a half second, did you think no one else was going to find out? Do you know how many times I covered your tracks?"

Reyna sat motionless. He was manipulating her. He was trying to get to her, like Beckham and Gabe had said he would. There was no way to know whether he had covered for her. Beckham had set up the website, and he knew what he was doing. Everett didn't have enough power to do more than Beckham had. She wouldn't sympathize with him because of this.

"So?" She narrowed her eyes. "Do you think that absolves you of your part in my kidnapping?"

"Reyna, I didn't even know that was going to happen to you. I called in the bite because it was out of character for Beckham," he informed her. "I thought Beckham would finally be arrested. Even though I was spying on Beckham, Harrington somehow trusted him against all reason. Until you…"

"Yeah, well, he didn't come for Beckham. He came for me."

"And now you're out," he said breezily. As if this whole thing had been a walk in the park.

Reyna jumped up from her chair and kicked it to the side. She stormed toward him, grabbed him by the collar, and bent down low into his face. "Do not ever talk so flippantly about what happened to me. You have *no* idea what I went through. The fact that I'm out doesn't make it better. Nothing is better."

Everett's eyes widened in shock at her aggression. If he thought he was going to get the naive girl she once was, he was sorely mistaken. He'd played his cards wrong. She might have once been that girl, but now she'd grown teeth.

He held up his hands in supplication. "What did they do to you?"

She threw him away like a piece of trash. "Ripped away my innocence."

She prowled back to her overturned chair. She righted it, adjusted her dark hair, and took a seat. "Now…about that information?"

"They have someone I love, too."

Reyna wanted to not care, but between her and Jodie, she didn't have it in her. "Who?"

"My brother, Edmond. We were in the same program. He washed out, and they kept him as my collateral. I haven't heard from him in three years."

"I'm sorry."

"Me too, Reyna. When I called it in, I thought it was for Beckham. When they said they were coming to get you, I didn't know where they were taking you. I just knew I was protecting my brother."

"I really don't want to hear your tale. It seems everyone has someone. This world hasn't been kind. But it didn't turn us all into sniveling snitches."

"No, but it seems to have done its damnedest to harden even the best of us."

Reyna ignored his comment. Was she harder? Sure. She had to be. Part of that was his fucking fault. If she hadn't gone through what she had at Visage, she might still be that daydreamer. She might still be looking for the good in everyone. Hoping she could right the world through her photography and helpful programs for the poor. Visage was a last resort for a lot of people, including her. She knew there should be some other way. She just didn't know if she believed it was possible any longer.

"Why did you want to talk to me?" she asked.

"Because you know me, and I thought you would understand."

"No, when you saw me at Five Points, you saw the same frightened girl you thought you knew. I was so shocked to see you that I freaked out, but I'm not afraid anymore. So, if we're going to keep going around in circles, then I'll leave." She flung her hand toward the door. "There's someone else out there who will be happy to get the information in a different way. I'd think it'd be much less pleasant, but hey, that's your call."

Everett's eyes dropped to the floor. All the bluster and bravado slipped right off him. She saw him for exactly who he was and not the person he had always appeared to be. Broken. Kicked down by the system, just as she was.

Her heart went out to him. She had seen that same expression from Jodie time and time again. From everyone Visage had hurt. Even herself.

Yet, she guarded herself against it. Everett was a spy. It was his job to manipulate people like this. His first tactic hadn't worked; maybe this one would.

"You do realize I'm risking Edmond by telling you this." His eyes slid up to hers, piercing and terrified. The eyes of someone who was putting their life on the line…and the life of everyone they cared about.

"You haven't told us anything yet."

"I'm risking it all just by being here. By talking to you and admitting there's even something to talk about."

"Then why are you here?"

A chill ran through her at the haunted look in his eyes. "Because I couldn't ignore what I discovered."

"Then spit it out."

He shook his head. "I need some assurances."

"What kind of assurances?"

His eyes shifted to her chest, where the microphone lay against her bra strap, even though there was no way he could see it. "Did they get that? I want assurances for my safety. That I'm not going to be killed off as soon as they get what they want. That they'll find Edmond, too."

Reyna bared her teeth. "I don't even know what you have. It might not be worth my time."

"It is." His confidence was unwavering. "Go talk to them. Get my assurances, and…and I'll start from the beginning."

"Fine." She vaulted out of her chair and burst through the door. She slammed it shut behind her, frustrated by the entire ordeal. She'd naively thought she'd be able to walk in there and he'd tell her everything she wanted to know. Fuck, she should have known better. Nothing ever went her way that easily.

Gabe rounded the corner and dragged her away from the door. "Great job so far."

"What? He hasn't told me anything."

"He's told you a fuck ton. A spy for Harrington himself? Beckham as his mark? We're getting so much out of this."

She entered the second room and found Tony leaning over a series of monitors. Gabe moved to stand next to him and give her privacy as Beckham scooped her up. She threw her arms around his neck and buried herself into his chest.

"You're okay," he said soothingly. He traced lazy circles into her back. Then he kissed the top of her head and pulled away. "You're okay."

"Gabe said I did good."

"You're doing brilliant."

"He was spying on you."

"I heard."

"Motherfucker," she spat.

"You're almost done." He grinned and kissed her again.

"Well, what should I tell him? Do I meet his demands?"

"They only have to be met if he cooperates," Tony said, not even bothering to look up from the computer. "Then we toss him in a prison cell and let the bastard rot away forever."

"Then how are we any better than Visage?" she demanded.

Tony looked up at her and blinked. He was clearly used to living in a world of zeros and ones. What she was suggesting didn't compute.

"Reyna, we can't let him go," Gabe said.

"I didn't say we should. But if we imprison him, how is that any better than what happened to me?"

"He turned you in," Beckham growled.

"And he turned himself in for this. For the beating he got and the interrogation. He did it knowing someone he cared about could be killed. Could you imagine making that same sacrifice?"

"Are you suggesting we rehabilitate him? A man who admitted to being a trained spy?" Gabe asked.

"No. I don't know." She held up her hands. "I'd be happy if he was gone. I don't want to lose sight of the reason we're fighting against Visage, but we don't want to become as bad as they are."

"Give him the assurances," Beckham said.

"Beckham," Gabe grumbled.

"We're not going to kill him. And we might be able to use him."

"Thank you," Reyna said. "I'll get what we need. If he doesn't deliver and this is really a trap…I don't care what you do to him."

Beckham nodded. She knew the bargain she'd struck with him. Everett could be dead by the end of the night. The option was entirely up to him.

She left the guys in the room and strode back to Everett. She heard someone call out behind her, but she was already inside, and as soon as she closed the door, Everett grabbed her and wrapped his handcuffs around her neck, cutting off her air supply.

Without a second thought, her self-defense training with her brothers kicked in. She stomped her foot onto the top of his. Something crunched, and Everett howled, but he didn't release her. She tried to jab at his kidneys or do anything that could incapacitate him, but he dodged her arms, still cursing her for his foot. Then she grasped Everett's arm, bent forward, and jerked him over her shoulder. Unprepared, he rolled up onto her hip, and she slammed him down onto his back. Her foot landed on his throat.

"Don't fucking move," she growled.

Gabe dashed into the room, holding a pistol in his hands. His eyes widened in shock at Everett lying flat on his back and Reyna on top of him. She knew she wouldn't have been able to deliver that so effectively if Everett hadn't completely underestimated her, but it didn't matter, because it had fucking worked.

"Well, I guess you handled that," Gabe said, keeping his weapon trained on Everett as he sidled up to them. Gabe manhandled him into the chair again.

"Why the hell would you attack me?" she shouted at Everett.

"No one wants to be a prisoner," Everett said calmly as Gabe reattached the handcuffs. "You would have been good leverage."

Gabe handed Reyna the gun. "If he moves a muscle, shoot him. I'm going back for some rope."

Reyna had never handled a gun before in her life, but at point-blank range, she had a feeling that she could manage it.

Everett gulped. "Don't shoot."

A few minutes later, Everett's hands and feet were tied to the chair and Gabe took the gun back and finally left. Everett watched her. His eyes still hadn't quite lost their shock.

She touched her throat where the handcuffs had dug into the skin. "I had assurances for you. Unclear if I should hold to them now that you pulled that shit." He winced. "But if you don't tell me, they'll kill you. And I'll let them."

Everett couldn't deny it. She had shown him what she was capable of. "I was spying on a new mark. Roland Batiste."

Reyna wrinkled her nose at the name. Roland had stalked her and threatened her, physically and sexually, while she lived with Beckham. Death would be too kind for him.

"I was supposed to be doing the same thing I did with Beckham. But I found out sensitive information about the company that I shouldn't know. I don't think anyone else is aware yet that I do. But in all my snooping, I found it."

"Found what?" she snapped anxiously.

"They bought a huge tract of land and are building facilities on it."

"We already know that."

"Do you know what they're for?"

She didn't respond.

"Camps," he whispered in horror. "Human feeding camps."

CHAPTER TWENTY-EIGHT

"I would have heard about this," Beckham snarled later that night, back at headquarters.

Reyna paced agitatedly. Beckham, Gabe, and Tony had recounted what had happened to Sydney and Washington. She couldn't wrap her mind around it. Couldn't fathom how it was possible. How Harrington could get away with it. How he thought that everyone would just allow this to happen.

"You're on the outs," Gabe said. He almost sounded satisfied at the insinuation.

"Which means we're blind," Sydney snapped at Gabe. "Without Beckham in the know within Harrington's inner circle, we're blind."

"I don't think Everett's lying," Reyna spoke up. "He was shaken. I saw all his acts in that room. This wasn't one."

"And you're an expert on spy tactics, are you?" Sydney asked dryly.

"It sounds like William," Washington said. "It's in line with his basic philosophy in life."

"Philosophy again, Roger?" Sydney asked with a sigh. She massaged her temples and sank into a seat at the head of the conference room.

"We know William works within a certain set of core beliefs. Human subjugation is fundamental among those. The blood type cure only facilitated that goal—a means to an end. It would make sense, then, that he would want to push forward with his own agenda while he's in power. A conqueror claiming more territory."

"Will he overextend himself? Will Rome fall?" Reyna mused.

"Wishful thinking," Gabe said.

"Let's say this is Harrington's endgame," Sydney said. "How is he going to structure it? He's not going to come out to the public and say he's starting feeding farms. He's going to cache it in something the people find permissible."

Everyone was silent as they thought about the million scenarios Harrington could possibly use to make these camps work.

"It could be anything," Gabe said. "He's just as likely to commandeer the military and march people into the camps as he is to kidnap them or offer them a job in some new factory he owns. Who knows what's going on in his twisted mind?"

"That's precisely why we have people here who know him," Sydney snarled.

"He'll do it out in the open," Beckham finally said. "If he can make Visage seem like a savior, then he can make people want this, too."

"I agree," Washington said. "Easiest way to hide is out in the open."

Sydney sighed. "Perhaps Penelope has some inside information. She might know if something is coming up that we need to direct our attention to."

Reyna couldn't suppress her cringe. She'd forgotten about Penelope. The argument they'd had this afternoon felt like a lifetime ago rather than a matter of hours.

"I'll get in touch with her," Beckham said.

"Good. Let me know immediately if she has any idea what might be coming," Sydney said, standing. "Otherwise, I'm going to have to reach out to Tye to organize a group to scout the camps. I need someone on the inside to verify Everett's information. I won't act until I know for sure what we're up against."

Sydney strode out of the room, dismissing everyone. Reyna felt a wave of exhaustion hit her. She'd thought today would be a fun day of wedding dress shopping, but nothing could be that simple. It never was.

Beckham tilted his head toward the door, and she followed him out into the empty hallway. The idea of feeding farms was so outrageous that all she could feel was disbelief. She wanted Sydney's people to find out Everett had lied to them. That it wasn't possible for even Harrington to stoop that low. She had firsthand experience with how low Harrington would stoop, though.

She and Beckham returned wordlessly to her room. She flopped back on her bed and stared up at the ceiling. "Are you going to Penny's?"

"Yes. Our conversation needs to be had in person."

"She's going to love that."

Beckham crossed to the bed and hovered over her. She could feel his dark shadow looming over her, but she didn't look at him.

"Why didn't you pick me up?" Reyna asked quietly instead of talking about Penny.

Beckham tensed. "Why?"

"Because you were supposed to get me, and then you weren't there. Penny didn't know where you were, either."

Beckham glanced away from her when he said, "I must eat."

"Oh."

Beckham tugged her off the bed and deposited her on her feet. "I must eat and eat regularly. It is a necessity. Before, I could go a week, sometimes two, where I didn't need to eat anything unless I wanted to regain strength. Now I must eat anytime I am going to be with you."

"Why?" she asked.

He clenched his jaw and then released it. "If I did not, then I could not be around you as I am. The bloodlust would be overwhelming. Even eating as I do, I want you. To taste your blood and drain your life force and take from you all you will give me and more that you won't."

She trembled at the dark words and the force with which he delivered them. This was her predator. The one who could destroy her with a flick of his hand. And yet, he spent so much time actively trying to keep her fragile body alive.

"I don't believe you would do it," she told him with her chin tilted up.

"Believe me. I would." His fangs flashed. "I desire you even as we stand here. I can feel your blood pumping through your veins. I can scent you. I want nothing more than a taste. But I won't stop at a taste. Especially not after I saw you take down Everett."

Her eyebrows rose. "Oh yeah? You liked that I was able to hold my own?"

He brushed her hair off her face and knotted it in his hand. He tugged her head gently to the side and trailed his lips down her throat. "I enjoyed watching you stand your ground. You are not quite as fragile as when we first met." Then he moved. Infinitely faster than a human. Before she could even blink, he had her body laid out on the bed, her neck bared, while he straddled her hips. Then he came down on her as if he was about to devour her. "Do not think the same moves would work on a vampire. It is best to allow me to protect you instead of constantly putting yourself in danger."

Her core heated despite his harsh words. She knew getting turned on probably wasn't the right reaction, but her body didn't seem to care. Nor did she. He was on top of her. So close to biting her. She ground her hips in circles against him, begging for whatever he had to offer.

"Little One, look what you do to me," he groaned, releasing her gently.

"Don't stop."

"I threatened to kill you, and you beg for more. What manner of creature are you?"

"One who is not afraid of the monster lurking under the surface. One who desires the monster and the man equally. I'm not ashamed to admit it."

"This monster chose to work with Harrington. I *chose* to work with him. For nearly fifteen years."

Reyna swallowed. "So? You changed your mind."

"He kidnapped and tortured you. Do you think that's the worst I've done?"

"I don't care what you've done."

Though she was curious. How could she not be? Especially after the hints Penelope had thrown out.

"I can see it in your eyes." He rolled off her and stood by the edge of the bed as if he needed space to think.

"What you see in my eyes is the unknown," she told him, following him off the bed. She refused to give him that space. "It's you telling me you're this horrible monster, other people saying you're a scary motherfucker, and even Penelope saying I'm just like all the other girls and will be dead soon. It's hearing over and over again that I should fear you, but I don't."

They met each other, stubborn stare for an even more stubborn stare. Beckham would not win this. She wanted answers, and she'd wait however long it took. He must have seen it in her face. He released a breath and looked away.

"I was what we called a lord when I met Harrington," Beckham said.

"Washington used that term. Sounds antiquated."

"Yes. Well, the name has been passed down for many generations. Vampires are kind of stuck in our ways," he said wryly. "The term *lord* is reserved for the most powerful vampire rulers. They traditionally have a court, though by the time I was a lord, it had evolved into an army." He gauged her reaction to see if he should continue. "There are only two ways to become a lord: rise up in the ranks and eventually unseat the ruler, or raise an army big enough and lethal enough to take down the current lord and all their minions."

"Which did you do?" she breathed.

"Rising up from within is easier. Unseating a ruler can be done if you can assess their weaknesses and then gain the support of the other vampires already within the organization. Building a force big enough to contend with the lord's army and then slaughtering hundreds of well-trained vampires is nearly impossible." He paused and met her eyes. "I did the latter."

She shivered. "Wow."

"And I did it in five years. Here. In this city. In territory that had been ruled by a lord for three centuries longer than I'd been alive. I was the youngest lord to ever rule a territory of this magnitude. I was thirty when I was turned, and it had only been another twelve years when I became a lord. I ruled on high like that for a decade before it all fell apart fifteen years ago."

She did some quick math in her head. Thirty when he was turned. A dozen years as a vampire before becoming a lord. Ten years as a lord. Fifteen years since being a lord.

"You're sixty-seven?" she gasped out.

He nodded resolutely. "Thirty-seven years since I was turned. Relatively young for a successful vampire. I was extremely young for a lord."

"How did you do it, then?"

"I was a ruthless murderer, and I gained the loyalty and respect of every single person who worked under me from my second all the way down to the lowest dreg. No one was ever going to turn on me. Not in my organization. Not the way I worked."

Reyna saw suddenly how he had gotten where he was. How he was such an incredible businessman. He had been running a different sort of business for much longer.

"How did you end up going from being a lord to working with Harrington?"

His face was carved out of marble. His onyx eyes were dark gems cut into the hard surface. A deep sorrow suffused him all at once. It enveloped the room, sweeping everything into its orbit.

"My second was killed."

The way he said it made it perfectly clear that his second-in-command had been incredibly important to him and that loss still shaped him.

"When my second was gone, I wanted to walk away from everything I'd earned and burn the city to the ground. William showed up a couple of months later as I tracked down and killed every person who had been related to the death. He offered an alternative. He offered me the blood type cure."

"And you accepted it, just like that?"

Beckham laughed harshly. "No. I told him to go fuck himself. He said he knew who had killed my second and that he was able to think more clearly because of this cure. More clearly than I ever had before. If we brought the vampires out of the darkness together, he would help me hunt down the person who had done it and kill them."

"Did you find out who did it?" she whispered.

"Yes. And he paid dearly for what he had done." His eyes were unfocused, returning to what had happened that day.

"So, Harrington offered you a new life, and you accepted it."

"Yes. We orchestrated the financial collapse. Between the four of us, we had enough resources tied up to cripple most countries relatively easily."

"Four?"

"Harrington recruited two other lords—Roland and Cassandra."

"Ah," she said. Roland's name made her stomach turn. "Cassandra wasn't a lady?"

"Ask her that and she'll tear your throat out."

Reyna tried not to think about the fact that he'd been a part of the financial collapse. Of all the things, that was the one that hit her strongest. If the economy hadn't collapsed, her uncle wouldn't have turned her and her brothers out on the streets. They might never have ended up in the warehouses. She never would have joined Visage.

"What about the girls?" she asked, forcing the words out.

"Penelope said something about...about her being a test?"

"Harrington thought I'd kill her. He thought if I did it would keep her father in line. Her father was trying to revitalize the slums and doing too good of a job."

"You were preventing him from helping people?"

"The crash keeps people desperate enough to work for us," he said without emotion. "It did for you."

Fuck. She felt sick. It was worse, knowing all her fears were real. If the world knew this, they'd hate the vampires so much more than they already did.

"Yes. I helped ruin your life. Only to have you show up at my door and let me ruin it a second time."

"You might have been a part of it the first time, but you saved me the second time."

He shook his head. "You still don't understand."

"No, I think *you* don't understand. You can throw anything at me, Becks. You could kill mothers and children and puppies." She paused and grinned slightly. "Okay, maybe not puppies. But whatever it is you did that you thought was so terrible isn't going to be enough to turn me away. I see you. I know you."

"I hunted people," he spat. "For fun. For sport. I'd find prey that were weak. I looked for them. I tortured them. And I killed them. Like you and Penelope and many, many others."

She swallowed at this revelation. She had known, but hearing it in his words was still hard. "You're not going to kill me now."

He stared at her, blank-faced.

"Beckham, all of this happened before the blood type cure. There's a reason you and hundreds of vampires just like you changed after the cure. You were an animal, and you couldn't control yourself."

His voice was hollow when he said, "I still hate myself."

"Further proof that you are no longer the animal that you once were." And she had to believe that. No matter what had happened in his past, that wasn't him *now*. What he'd done had been a terrible act by an animal. Not her Beckham. Not Becks.

Still he looked unconvinced.

"You didn't kill me. You didn't kill Penelope. Why?"

"The cure," he said on a sigh. "But also because I picked up photography again. I'd done it as a child long before I was turned. And everything changed when I looked through the lens."

"That's why you gave me a camera."

"Yes. I saw a different perspective, and I wanted you to as well." He sighed. "And as for Penelope, she wasn't any different than the other girls. She was never different. I simply opened my eyes. And when I did, she happened to be there." He slowly reached out and touched her face. "It was another year before I found what I was looking for."

"What's that?" she whispered.

"You."

Reyna reached up onto her tiptoes and pressed their lips together. He hesitated, as if he couldn't believe she would still want to kiss him after those revelations.

"Becks," she said softly against his lips. Coaxing him to relax. She didn't like his past, the things he'd done, or the things he'd had to endure, but he had been a different person when he went through those things. He was a different man when he was with her. He'd told her his deep dark secrets, and she still wanted him. She still wanted this.

"Little One," he said. "I did want to tell you—I can get away for your brother's wedding."

She reared back, and a broad smile lit up her face. "Really?"

"If you'll have me."

She fell into him, wanting nothing more than this moment. She pushed all her emotions into one blissful kiss. Finally, slowly, he relaxed and kissed her back.

CHAPTER TWENTY-NINE

Four days later, all she could think about was the wedding and her impending date with Beckham. She knew the mission to scout the camps was happening before the new year. She knew her brothers were going on that mission. She knew there were a million other things that should fill her head, but today, she would be happy.

She stretched and opened her eyes to Christmas morning.

She had forgotten about it in the midst of the wedding planning, but now here it was. Her family had never had much, but they usually managed something. Meghan had helped her pick out things for them this year. But she was blown away when she saw a pile of presents on her desk, including an unusually large black box.

She grabbed her sweats from the floor and dragged them on as she dashed across the room. She surveyed the pile of presents, but her hands trailed to the black box first. On top of it was a single white rose.

Her heart stuttered. Beckham.

She smelled the rose with a sigh and lifted the lid on the box. Her gasp was audible. Her hand went to her throat, and she bit her lip as she lifted her camera out of the box. The note inside read simply *Perspective*. The familiar weight of the camera made her feel as if she were holding an old friend. Someone she had desperately missed.

A knock on her door broke her from her reverie. "Come in!"

Jodie stood in the doorway. Reyna brought the camera to eye level and pressed the button. A picture of Jodie, with her perfect dark skin, coily hair, and dismayed expression appeared on the screen.

"Whoa. Fancy camera. Where did that come from?" Jodie asked. "Wait, let me guess—vampire boyfriend?"

"Vampire boyfriend," she confirmed with a laugh. "Becks got it for me when I was living with him. I used to wander around the city and take pictures of all the things I wanted to change in the world."

"You're so dramatic."

"Pretty much. I figured Visage must have confiscated it because he never brought it back. I guess he was just waiting for the right moment."

"Makes a perfect Christmas present. This is the first Christmas I've celebrated in a long time," Jodie said with a frown. "I just wish that June was here."

"Me too." They hadn't had any luck locating Jodie's cousin. Reyna hoped for Jodie's sake that June was still out there. Jodie had made so much progress; it was amazing to compare who she was now to the fierce, combative person she had been when they had taken her out of Visage. They both had changed a lot. For the better.

"I feel like we're close," Jodie said, "but Meghan is distracted with other stuff. That mission thing the guys are going on."

"Yeah. I wish I could help more." Reyna reached out and took Jodie's hand. "I'm sure you'll have a breakthrough once you have more time."

"I hope so." Jodie squeezed Reyna's fingers and handed her a wrapped gift. "I wanted to give this to you myself."

"Jodie, you didn't have to get me anything," Reyna said. She took it from her and peeled the red paper back. Inside were two books—a slim copy of the *Complete Works of John Keats* and Aldous Huxley's *Brave New World.*

"They, uh, got me through some dark times. I thought, if anyone would understand, you would."

"I do. I can't wait to start them." Reyna pressed them to her chest.

"Books keep me sane. They transport me to a thousand new worlds. They let me escape into a different reality. A better one than my own."

"Sometimes we all need to escape."

Jodie nodded, and an understanding passed between them.

Reyna placed the books next to the camera. Then she linked her arm with Jodie's and drew her out of the room. She couldn't imagine Christmas had been a pleasant time for Jodie inside Visage. She hoped today, with presents and a big meal and the wedding, Elle would maybe start to feel like home for the both of them.

When Reyna returned to her room to get ready for the wedding, she was surprised to find a long black bag hanging in her closet. For a second, her mind returned to that time Harrington had sent her a dress to wear to Penelope's mayoral ball. The shadows lengthened in the room. Her mind felt fuzzy. The walls closed around her, slowly constricting her breathing and narrowing her focus. She felt queasy, unsure if she was going to vomit or not.

She closed her eyes against the pain of the memory. This wasn't real. She took deep breaths in through her nose and slowly released them from her mouth. There were no shadows or monsters lurking in the darkness. There was no Harrington, no B, no captivity waiting. She was fine. She was safe. He couldn't get her here.

When she opened her eyes again, the shadows had disappeared. The room was the same as it had ever been. She let out a shallow breath and crossed to the closet. There was a note pinned to the bag.

You are my greatest temptation.

She grinned despite herself and slid the zipper to the floor. She opened the bag to reveal a bloodred floor-length gown. She salivated at the sight of the gorgeous dress. It was silky and stunning. As much as she liked it, though, she worried she would look way overdressed. Everyone else she knew was going to the wedding in clothes they already had, except Jodie—Meghan had gotten her a dress for Christmas. Reyna had been planning to wear the single dress in her closet. The boys were wearing jeans and button-ups. This was too much.

She ran her hands over the fabric once more and then zipped the bag back up. She wouldn't wear it. She couldn't.

Retreating to the bathroom, she took her time getting ready. She had just finished her hair and makeup and slipped into some unmentionables when she heard the door click in her room. "Hello?"

Beckham appeared in the doorway. His eyes crawled the length of her nearly naked body. "Hello, Little One."

She choked on her reply. He was in a tuxedo, crisp and black and fitted to perfection. He looked like a god walking among mere mortals.

"You're early," she finally stammered.

"I believe I am right on time."

They stood there staring at each other, completely enraptured. She felt like at any second they might tear each other's clothes off.

"I should probably get dressed."

"Probably." Except he continued to block the doorway. She stepped into his space, and he reached out, running his hands down her sides. "Or you could stay like this."

She laughed breathily. "You can have your dessert after dinner."

"Rules were meant to be broken."

"Is that so?"

"You're wearing lingerie."

"You bought it for me," she said with a grin.

"Remind me to buy you more, because I'm tearing this off of you tonight."

She shivered with excitement at his words. A promise for later.

He moved to the closet and reappeared a minute later with the black bag. "Your dress," he said, opening the bag for her. "Put it on before I change my mind."

"I can't wear that."

"You don't like it?"

"It's just extravagant for the occasion."

He slipped the straps of the beautiful dress off the hanger and passed it to her. "Wear it."

"Becks."

"I took care of it, Reyna."

"What do you mean?"

"Why don't you put it on and find out?"

She narrowed her eyes at him. What had he *done*? He was so sneaky. Was this attention to detail one of the reasons he'd been so successful in life? Part of his charm.

She vacillated only a second longer before taking the dress out of his hand. After all, she *wanted* to wear it. She slid it over her head and sighed with satisfaction. It felt like water on her skin, and it hugged her figure like a dream. The neckline was V-cut, and the thin straps crossed at the nape of her neck. It had a fully open back, which meant she'd had to remove her bra, but the rippling of the material made that less noticeable. The only issue was that it was about four or five inches too long and she only owned Converse.

Beckham held out a pair of shiny gold high heels that crisscrossed up the front, with red-lacquered bottoms.

"Holy shoe porn," she whispered in awe.

Beckham laughed, that rare unguarded one that made her toes curl. "I never thought you would actually like heels after your fit about them in the penthouse."

She snatched them out of his hand. "They're perfect for the right occasion. Not for everyday wear, when I have to…you know, walk and run and kick some ass."

"Duly noted."

She slid the shoes on. Beckham's feral grin was a seal of approval.

"You're missing something," he said.

"Am I?"

He withdrew a red velvet box from the inside pocket of his tuxedo jacket. "This."

Her eyes widened. When she didn't move to take it, he popped the top open and revealed a stunning teardrop-cut diamond pendant on a long chain. He twirled his finger, motioning for her to turn around. She did as instructed as if lost in a dream. She pulled her hair off her back and felt the cool metal touch her skin as it dropped down right between her breasts. He clasped it into place.

"Wow," she whispered. She was mesmerized by the huge rock. She knew it was a drop in the bucket for someone who could engineer an entire economic collapse, but it was still magical. "This is…beautiful."

"I'm glad you like it."

"I love it. But you didn't have to get me anything else. My camera was enough."

"Your camera was returning property that already belonged to you. I should have brought it long ago."

"Thank you."

"Merry Christmas, Little One," he said, dropping a kiss to her crimson lips. Then he held out his arm for her. "Shall we?"

She placed her hand on his elbow and followed him through the secret door. Her mind was racing with the extravagance of this gift. What she had gotten him was nothing compared to this. What could you get the man who had everything? She pushed it out of her mind. It didn't matter. Beckham didn't care.

They took the elevator down a few floors and entered the main corridor. Reyna was surprised to find it cleared. Had he done that, too?

At the end of the hall, a set of double doors stood open to reveal the wedding space. Reyna's jaw dropped. She had sat in meetings with Meghan, Jodie, and Laura for hours the last two weeks discussing the small wedding they were planning and fantasizing about the elaborate affair Laura wanted to have but knew was impossible. That fantasy was now a reality.

The room was no more than a large conference space, but it had been transformed into a stunning rose garden. White, red, and pink roses bloomed on a large archway at the end of a path of red rose petals. White wooden chairs were artfully arranged in a semicircle with flowers on either side of the chairs. Twinkling white lights lit the ceiling, mirroring the stars of the night sky.

And everyone…everyone was dressed to the nines.

Brian and Drew stood by the flower arch in lush black tuxedos. Meghan had on a forest-green floor-length gown, and Jodie wore a dusty pink dress that shimmered in the lights. There were about a half dozen other people in attendance who Laura had gotten to know in her time at Elle, and all of them were dressed in similar attire. It was as extravagant and gorgeous as any ball Reyna had ever been to…maybe more so. Because this was for her…for Brian and Laura.

This was a gift. The real Christmas gift. A real wedding for them amidst these hard times when they had never expected to get anything. Let alone…*this.*

"You did this?" she whispered.

Beckham plucked a white rose from a high-top table at the entrance. "White roses are for new beginnings," he said, passing the bloom to her. "This is our new beginning."

"You're incredible."

"I do it all for you." He swept a lock of her hair behind her ear. "You make it all worthwhile."

CHAPTER THIRTY

Beckham took her hand and kissed it once before guiding her down the aisle to their seats in the front row on the groom's side. Just as they sat down, instrumental music filled the room. The guests rose, turning to see Laura appear. She looked like Cinderella in her wedding dress. Reyna peeked back at Brian to find his mouth open and his eyes wide with shock and admiration. Laura swept down the rose-petal aisle to her beloved. As they stared at each other, Reyna realized she had never seen either of them look so unbelievably happy.

Elle had given them this. Elle and Beckham and security they hadn't known back in the warehouses. It was a magical thing to witness. She squeezed Beckham's hand as tears came to her eyes at the sight. He squeezed back, and when she turned to look at him, she saw that his gaze was on Reyna and the joy this moment brought her.

"Thank you," she whispered, leaning her head onto his arm as

Brian and Laura said "I do."

"Anything for you."

The ceremony ended, and everyone helped to clear the chairs to the side of the room for the reception. Meghan and Tye wheeled in refreshments, and music played from the speakers.

Reyna approached her brother and tugged him into a hug. "Congratulations, big brother."

"Thanks, little sister."

Beckham held his hand out to Brian. "Congratulations."

Brian shook his hand. "I appreciate what you did for us. Maybe I had it wrong about you the first time."

"It's an easy mistake to make."

Reyna liked that he didn't try to correct Brian, didn't disagree and say he wasn't one of the good ones. It had to be a sign of progress.

"Well, thank you again. We owe you. Big time."

"Absolutely not. It's a gift. A wedding gift."

"It was very generous."

"We're going to let other people say hi. I'm so happy for you," Reyna said, pulling Beckham away. "You made their life. You know that, right?"

"I hardly did anything."

"When you have nothing, anything is a miracle."

After all the congratulations, Brian led Laura into the first dance. The rest of the party joined in on the next song. Reyna saw, with some amusement, Gabe slip in and pull Meghan into a dance. Tye looked disgruntled. When he tried to dance with Jodie instead, she flipped him off and grabbed Xavier. What a lovers' quadrangle.

Reyna's eyes widened even farther when she saw Drew work up the nerve to ask his roommate, Gregory, to dance. She was even more surprised when the man's smile lit up his whole face and he all but dragged her brother out onto the dance floor. They'd joked that Gregory was his boyfriend, but this was the first time she'd gotten real confirmation of that without Drew blowing them off.

"Would you care to dance?" Beckham asked, holding his hand out.

"I'd love to."

They moved forward into the crowd of people as a slow song came on. Reyna slipped both of her hands around his neck, and he placed his hands on her hips. The moment felt surreal. Here she was in Beckham's arms, surrounded by the people she loved. It was impossible to believe that after what she had suffered…all was right with their world, at least for this one night.

They danced through the night, laughing and cheering and celebrating this blissful union. Taking all the happiness they could where they could. In the midst of a rebellion organization, these moments were rare. No one wanted the night to end.

Even Reyna.

Though she was having a hard time keeping her hands to herself after the bottle of champagne she split with Jodie. Her head buzzed. She felt amazing. All she could think about was Beckham's promise to shred her lingerie. She was ready to take him up on that.

Meghan and Gabe slipping out of the room was the first sign the festivities were winding down. Reyna kissed Brian and Laura as they decided to return to their own room. He squeezed her hand, and then they were off.

"Oh, Reyna," Beckham said as she twirled back toward him. "You are intoxicated."

She trailed a hand down the front of his tux. "I'm fine."

He hefted her into his capable arms against her protests and carried her all the way back to her room.

"Okay. Okay. Put me down. I can walk," she insisted.

"Perhaps I enjoy carrying you."

She leaned her head onto his shoulder. "I like when you're a gentleman."

"I am no gentleman."

"Beg to differ."

He gently set her on her feet, holding on to her waist to steady her. "Do you always see the good in people?"

"You paid for an elaborate wedding for my brother, who up until today wasn't even sure he liked you."

"But you love him," he said as he opened the door and they stepped through it.

"That's what I mean. You do it with no expectation of return. 'A wedding gift.'" She reached up and cupped his jaw. "You are a good person."

"My present does not erase my past."

"No, it doesn't. But your past doesn't define your future, either."

Beckham stared down at her as if he were seeing his future written in her eyes. He branded a kiss against her forehead. She closed her eyes and breathed him in. He slowly walked around her, found the zipper at the base of her spine, and tugged it down. He slid the straps off her shoulders and let them fall. The fabric caught on her hips before pooling in a puddle at her feet.

She could feel him assessing her from behind. Her breathing hitched when he grabbed her ass fully in both hands, then traced her skin up to the thong she was wearing. She heard a tear before the slinky material shredded and fell on top of the dress.

Beckham nudged her feet apart, urging her into a wider stance. She moved to kick her heels off, but Beckham gripped her hips.

"Leave the shoes."

She raised an eyebrow as she turned to look at him over her shoulder.

"I like them," he confessed.

He leisurely trailed his hand back down to her ass. Around her cheeks and down the backs of her thighs, mapping all the things he liked that the heels accentuated.

"Bend over."

With exaggerated slowness, she leaned forward until she had enough balance to bend over and grasp the footboard of the bed. Her ass was in the air and completely on display for him. His hand slipped back up her thighs, and then he was spreading her cheeks wide for him. She groaned as he pressed two fingers in her already soaked pussy. He used his slicked finger and circled the wet digit around her clit. She bucked against his hand, but he held her steady. He drew out her pleasure until her legs trembled and she thought they might buckle.

"Becks," she pleaded. "Please."

"What would you like, Little One?"

"Fuck me."

"Don't move," he said.

He withdrew, and she nearly fell over at the absence. She heard each piece of his tux fall to the floor. It was agonizing, not being able to see him slowly undressing. But she could picture it with vivid clarity. The muscled torso. The long, strong legs. The length of his hanging cock as he approached her.

She trembled in anticipation as he returned to her in distressing slowness. His hands traced her body—up her back, over her hips, grasping her ass, down her inner thighs, and then back to her clit. She clenched to keep from bucking back against him at the stroke of her most sensitive bud. The soft husky chuckle as he removed his hand only made her want him more desperately.

The head of his cock angled toward her, sliding through her wetness. She wanted to push backward and beg for him to take her, but she just dug her fingers into the footboard and tried to hold still.

"Is this what you'd like?" he teased.

"Please."

"You did so good following instructions. Will you come when I tell you?"

"Yes," she promised.

"Hold on tight. I won't be gentle."

She nearly melted at those words. Her desire was on such an edge that she could barely brace herself for what was to come. He slammed forward into her, seating himself in one power thrust. She cried out in pain and pleasure and the mix of both that had delighted her so much in the past.

"Beckham," she moaned, seeing stars as he pulled back and then thrust deep inside of her again.

"Look at how well you take my cock," he said, his hand on the small of her back for leverage as he hit deeper each time. "Look at what a good girl you are."

"Oh fuck," she said. The dirty talk was going to send her over the edge even faster than the rest. Her body was primed and ready, and she could barely contain herself.

This was primal. A claiming. She was Beckham's. Beckham was hers. They belonged together.

"Almost there," he promised, rutting faster until every movement felt layered upon the next one. Like it was all one deep thrust and there was nothing else in the world.

Sweat beaded on her body, and her legs trembled to hold her up in her high heels. But Beckham guided her forward another step and pushed her body down into the mattress. Her entire awareness returned to where he was pumping into her. Claiming, owning, taking. And she wanted nothing more than to give.

"My name when you come," he commanded.

"Now, please," she gasped. "Now."

"Now," he agreed, fucking her thoroughly.

Her body exploded at his command. She cried out his name over and over again until it was almost unintelligible. Her pussy tightened around his cock nearly to the point of pain as he unloaded inside of her. A feral roar came from him as he finished, holding her down and commanding her body.

She could be claimed by Beckham Anderson any day of the week. All days that ended in "y"—and all days that didn't, for that matter.

He released her gently and then pulled out. She would have hit the floor if he hadn't been there. He picked her up in his arms and lay her across the bed.

"Let me clean you up."

She reached for him again before he could go. Still wanting.

"More," she breathed.

He grinned that insufferably attractive smirk that got her hot all over again. "Are you sure?"

"I need you."

His cock was already lengthening again. She wrapped her fingers around him and stroked up and down until he was hard and unyielding beneath her grip. He didn't argue further, just pushed into her. She wrapped her arms around him, pulling him down onto the bed as their lips touched. Their breath mingled. Their eyes met. The world stopped.

"Bite me," she whispered as their bodies moved in tandem.

"Reyna," he groaned. He slowed his movements. "I don't want to get carried away like last time."

"Then don't."

"I can't promise…"

"I want all of you, Beckham," she said sincerely, wrapping her legs around his powerful body. "And I want you to have all of me, too."

She knew the moment he decided to give in. His breathing slowed. His pupils dilated. His fangs flashed.

"Just a small amount."

"Yes," she gasped, turning her head to expose her neck for better access.

His fangs pricked into her neck.

The second the venom hit her, she sighed with sweet relief. Endorphins flooded her system. She felt incredible. Beyond incredible.

This was nothing, nothing at all, like getting venom through an IV. She'd gotten too much in her system every time. She floated away and couldn't have cared about anything.

This was pure bliss. It was heaven. It was *Beckham.*

Nothing else could ever compare.

Her body ignited, and as he drank, he continued moving inside of her. Everything hit her at once, and almost without warning, she came apart a second time. When she hit the peak, his control slipped and he released into her. Blood dripped down her neck and chest. It should have terrified her, but all it did was heighten her orgasm. She could have gone a third time, with the rush of his venom and orgasm still pulsing through her.

She could have died. She would have gladly turned.

But Beckham returned to himself. His fangs retracted, and he pulled back, his breathing still rough. His eyes swept her naked chest, dotted with her own blood. He eased out of her tenderly.

"Are you all right?"

"I've never been better."

He assessed her neck. "Those should heal quickly."

"Mmm-hmm," she mumbled.

"I stopped." He seemed shocked he'd done it.

"I knew you would."

Beckham still stared at her as if she were a miracle and a vision and also somehow impossible. Like he'd believed all along that what had happened the first time they were together would always be the case. He'd just proven that wrong.

"We should get you cleaned up."

Beckham carried her to the bathroom and started the shower. He stepped under the hot spray and gently wiped the remaining blood from her skin and took care with her body. She'd be sore tomorrow, but right now, she felt nothing but restored. After he toweled her back off, they returned to the bedroom.

"I have something for you," she told him.

"I think you already gave me everything."

She extracted a carefully wrapped present from under her bed. "Here."

Beckham stared at the package as if he wasn't sure what he was seeing, but he took it out of her hands and opened it. Inside was a stretched canvas print of the city skyline photo she had taken when she was with him on that rooftop all those months ago. It was the night they had first really known they had feelings for each other. It was also the first night Beckham had told her about the rebellion, about looking from a different perspective, about seeing Visage as it was and not just how it appeared.

His eyes were wide with consideration. “From the rooftop?”

She nodded. “I thought it would look nice in your apartment or at work. To have a piece of me in the heart of the beast.”

“You already have my whole heart.”

CHAPTER THIRTY-ONE

Reyna entered the cafeteria bleary-eyed the next morning. Beckham had slipped out at an early hour. She'd been mostly dead to the world, and all she remembered was a kiss on the forehead. She grabbed a tray and piled it high with eggs, bacon, and orange juice. Drew and Gregory were sitting together in a corner, and she headed in that direction.

She plopped her tray next to Drew.

"So," she said in greeting.

Drew smiled. "Hey, Rey."

"So, is this official, then?" she asked, pointing her fork between Drew and Gregory.

Drew looked at Gregory. "I guess it is?"

Gregory smiled brightly back at him. "About time. We've only been hooking up since before you moved in."

"You said you weren't together! Why didn't you say anything?"

"I've never had a boyfriend before," Drew said.

"You've never really had a girlfriend before, either. Doesn't mean your sister has to be left in the dark."

"All right. All right. My bad," Drew said.

Gregory smirked at him. "I told you so."

"Yeah. Yeah," Drew said, nudging him with a blush.

"Brian and Laura still locked in their room?" she asked.

"As far as I know. Brian has to come out sometime. We have to leave once the sun goes down."

Reyna frowned. She'd tried not to think about the mission her brothers were going on. She knew they were going to check out the site and try to discover if it was really being set up as a human feeding camp. They'd been on plenty of missions like this before, but it didn't make it any easier to see them leave.

"Make sure you and Brian say bye before you go."

"Will do."

Reyna finished up her breakfast, listening to the adorable banter between Drew and Gregory. Jodie showed up just as Reyna was returning her tray to the front.

"Reyna," Jodie cried. She jogged over to Reyna, holding a piece of paper.

"What happened?"

"We found something."

"About June?" she gasped.

Jodie nodded. "An address."

"Oh my God, where?"

"Here in the city. It's not verified, but it looks like she lived here at some point. All we have to do is get Elle to approve us to go into the city." Jodie's eyes were lit up. Reyna had never seen her look this excited or happy. Not in the entire time she had known her.

"Then we should go!"

"Meghan is on it."

Reyna pulled Jodie into a hug. "I hope you find exactly what you're looking for."

"Me too." Jodie followed Reyna out into the hallway. "What are your plans for today? I'm so anxious. I don't think I can go back to my room alone."

"I actually think I'm going to the medical wing."

Jodie stopped in her tracks. "Why?"

Reyna faced her. "I promised I'd help out."

"Why?" she repeated.

Reyna linked arms with Jodie and forced her to start walking again. "Because there's something wrong with my blood."

"Duh. You and I are peas in a pod, sister."

"But I mean…more wrong. Beckham can sense me."

"Kinky."

Reyna snorted. "Not like that. I mean he knows where I am, even from long distances away, and when I wake up. He's worried that if he has the ability, Harrington might also have it. He thinks it's something in my blood, and we're checking it out."

"Whoa. That's freaky."

"Yeah. It's fine if Becks has that capability, but I don't want anyone else to have it. It'd be like having a beacon over my head."

"True. So, you think you can figure out what's happening?"

"There's a doctor here who's looking into it. I thought I'd check on his progress. He said I could come anytime and be his assistant."

"And you trust him?" Jodie asked skeptically. "I wouldn't want to set one foot in that medical wing. No matter what Meghan says or does for me."

"Beckham trusts him. And I trust Beckham."

"Let's hope vamp boyfriend knows what he's doing."

She understood Jodie's fears; they mirrored her own. She was still having panic attacks and flare-ups of her PTSD from what she'd endured. The thought of donating blood, of working with her blood, of any of that nonsense, made her sick. She knew she couldn't keep running from her fears, though. She needed to face them if she wanted to get answers.

Despite Jodie's feelings about the medical wing, she followed Reyna into the empty med bay. It was so sterile and silent. Only the slow whir of machines and the air-conditioning kicking on broke up the stillness. Reyna headed to Washington's office. The door was propped open and the room was empty, so she moved from there to the lab where she had last seen him. Success.

He was wearing his usual white lab coat, staring into a microscope. Petri dishes and graduated cylinders and pipettes and tongs and a bunch of other equipment were scattered all around him. She was sure there was some order to it, but she couldn't begin to navigate it.

"Dr. Washington?" she said, rapping on the door to announce their entrance.

His head popped up, and he smiled brightly. "Ah, Reyna, have you finally come to help me with all this work?"

"Yeah. And I brought Jodie with me."

Reyna gestured to her friend, but when she looked up into Jodie's face, she was pale with terror.

"Jodie?"

Jodie shook her head. For once, words failed her.

"What's wrong? What's going on?" Reyna asked, reaching for her. Jodie shuddered away.

"Miss Gardner," Washington said. He took a step forward.

Jodie took a step back. "Don't." Her voice rasped, and she withdrew even farther.

Reyna's gaze moved from one to the other. "Do you know each other?"

"You're a fucking monster," Jodie said savagely. "How dare you stand there as if you're part of this rebellion. And if you really fucking are, then this entire thing is a sham. I knew it was all too good to be true. How could I have ever believed this wasn't going to end exactly where it started?"

"Jodie," Washington said. A look of absolute despair crossed his face.

"Fuck you! Just fuck you!" she spat and fled the room.

Reyna's eyes widened, and she dashed after Jodie. She was already out of the medical wing and down the hallway before Reyna caught up with her.

"Jodie." Reyna grabbed her shoulder and hauled her to a stop.

Jodie slapped Reyna's hand away. "Don't touch me."

"What happened? Tell me what happened. You know Washington?"

"Know him?" Jodie hissed. "He was the monster who started the experiments on me!"

Of course. Washington had developed the blood type cure, and he was working on the blood disease. He'd been one of Harrington's best doctors. It made perfect, horrible sense that Jodie had been one of his test subjects at some point if she had been at Visage for ten years. Still, it hurt.

"How long has he been here?" Jodie asked. "No. Fuck it. It doesn't matter."

She kept walking down the hallway. She took the stairs instead of the elevator down to the floor where she still shared a room with Meghan.

"Jodie, what are you doing?"

"Getting the hell out of here."

"You're leaving?" Reyna asked.

"Well, I can't fucking stay. If that man is a part of Elle, then this place is no better than that hellhole."

"Jodie, I know Washington worked with Visage in the past."

"If you knew, then how could you allow this?" she asked. "You were there in Visage, too, Reyna. He was part of that."

"I know. He's the one who invented the blood type cure in the first place. He worked with Harrington, but he's not working with him anymore. He's not still the person he was before. I have to believe that."

"Well, you do you, then."

"If Beckham can change, then Washington can, too."

"This isn't about your vampire boyfriend. This is about my life. Ten years of my life. I thought you understood."

"I do," Reyna said quietly. "I don't want to work with Washington. I don't want any of this. But I want him on our side, not Harrington's."

Jodie faced her, stuffing a pair of tennis shoes into a backpack. "That's the difference between me and you, Reyna. I don't believe that anyone can change. They're not on our side. They're on *their* side. Vampires are our *enemies.*"

"They're not our enemies."

Jodie snorted. "They *feed* off us. They drink our blood. They want to kill us. Nothing changes that. Nothing."

"Okay," Reyna said, holding her hands up. "I hear you. We both were put through shit. I'm not telling you to trust Washington. Or to even trust Beckham. It's understandable that you'd hate them."

Jodie's shoulders shook as she clutched her backpack. "I can't stay, Rey."

"Seeing Washington fucked you up. It triggered you, and it's totally understandable. If I saw Harrington right now, I'd want to bolt, too," Reyna admitted, reaching her hand out for Jodie. "But I don't want to lose you. You're my friend. My sister."

Jodie dropped her head. "You're all I have, sister. The rest of this…" She glanced up at her. "It's yours, not mine."

"What's mine is yours," she told her. "Always."

Jodie threw her backpack down. "He's a monster, Reyna."

"I believe you. And I'm sorry for what he's done. I'm sorry for everything that happened to you. That happened to both of us. But it isn't any safer out there right now. And I don't want you to get hurt. Running isn't the answer."

"Then what *is* the answer?"

"Take it one day at a time. We're not going to get through this in a few weeks. It's going to take a lot longer to recover. Even longer to change the world. You don't have to forgive him or forget what he did to you. Just don't leave."

Jodie chewed on her lip and glanced away. "You and I see the world very differently."

"That's okay. As long as you're still in my world."

Jodie nodded. "I'll stay…for now."

"Thank you," Reyna said, wrapping her into a hug.

"Just be careful when you're working with him," Jodie said. "I don't want anything to happen to you."

"I will," she promised and prayed that Washington never proved Jodie right.

Chapter Thirty-Two

After the sun set, Reyna stood with Laura as Brian and Drew prepared to leave. Laura had silent tears running down her cheeks. She buried her head in Brian's shoulder and clung to him. There was nothing to say, though. The mission was imperative—Elle had to know what was inside those camps, if they were really what Everett said they were. That didn't make it any easier to see them go.

Reyna wished she was going with them. She hated sitting on the sidelines. It wasn't in her nature. There were too many reasons she couldn't be out there, though. Besides the fact that nobody wanted her in the security crew, she still didn't know if Harrington could sense her blood, and if she got injured, there was no other blood to save her. She was still the only person alive they knew of who had Rh null negative blood. So she stayed behind and prayed nothing happened.

Drew pulled her into a hug. "We'll be back soon. It will only be a couple of hours."

"Be safe, okay?"

"No problem." He nudged her and grinned that playful smile.

Laura finally released Brian, wiping away her tears. She tugged Drew in for a hug next, and Brian moved to Reyna.

"You're all making such a big fuss," he said with a laugh.

"I don't like where you're going or what you're doing," she said softly.

His eyes moved to Laura's. She didn't know exactly what they were doing tonight; the information was sensitive. "It'll be fine. Come here, kid."

"I'm not a kid anymore," she said, falling into his arms.

"I guess not."

"Just be careful, okay?" She repeated what she'd said to Drew.

"All right, Rey."

He hugged Laura once more, and then they were gone.

"I hate this," Laura mumbled.

"I know."

Reyna urged Laura away from the door the boys had walked through. If she hadn't moved her, Reyna was sure Laura would have sat there until they came back. Reyna made sure to spend time with her for the next couple of hours until Laura's exhaustion won out and she reluctantly headed to bed.

Reyna couldn't go back to her room. She needed to get out and do something. But what? She had nothing to photograph. Beckham wasn't around. She couldn't stomach seeing Washington yet and hearing the paltry explanation he would be sure to offer.

She sighed as her feet carried her through Elle's strangely silent corridors. It was better to be walking. She could get lost in the labyrinth. Anything was better than wondering what was going on.

It wasn't until she stopped in front of the guarded room that she realized where her feet had taken her. She frowned. Had her words to Jodie earlier sparked this impulse? This world wasn't black and white. People could change. Not everyone would, but wasn't it a disservice not to see if they'd try?

"Is he taking visitors?" she asked the guards.

"Uh," the guy said, turning to look at the woman on his right.

She shrugged. "No one told us one way or another."

"Okay. I'll only be a few minutes."

"Just knock when you want to come out." The woman nodded at the guy, and he produced the key, opening the door for her.

"All right," Reyna said, walking through the door. Her heart was racing. This was probably a bad idea. And yet…she didn't turn back.

Everett sat on the floor of the sparse room in the lotus position. His hazel eyes opened slowly and weighed her standing there. He didn't move. She didn't move. They just stared at each other across the small divide.

"Well, it's not a prison cell," he finally said.

"More than you deserve."

"Did you come here to tell me that?"

"I don't know why I'm here."

She didn't know why she admitted it. She hated that she was here at all. That thinking about people changing had brought her here. He was a spy. He'd turned her in. And yet…he'd come to find her when he'd realized the damage Visage was really doing. Not to mention, someone he loved was on the inside, and she knew what the inside was like.

"Probably because you know I did the right thing and yet I'm still in this room with armed guards."

"You did one good thing. And you've spied on how many people?"

"Countless." He tilted his head. "But not you."

"You were spying all along. You fed me information about Elle before I even knew what it was. You followed me to find out about my photographs. You took me to that fight and walked me right into that blood bank. You already knew about all of it, didn't you?"

He shrugged. "Yes."

"Why? Why did you do it?"

"I long suspected Beckham was involved in the rebel group. I thought helping you along would tip his hand. That he'd reveal himself."

"Why did you think he was a part of something like that?"

"He disagreed with the permanent positions and developed a lasting relationship with a human." He smiled. "Penelope, that is." Reyna kept her face neutral. "That prompted my interest, but it wasn't until you arrived that he started acting different. So I thought you could help move things along."

"But I wasn't a rebel."

"No. I never thought you were. You were too naive for that."

Reyna glared. "So, you just used me?"

"I did actually like you. Spending time with you was refreshing."

"Why? Because I was so naive?"

"Because you were so *genuine*."

Reyna rolled her eyes. "Amazing that a spy can't seem to find anyone to be genuine with him."

Everett didn't take the bait. "What did they do to you?"

"They?" she asked. "*You* did this to me."

"You've changed."

"Yeah, I have. Being tortured for eight weeks does that to a person. I'm never going to be the victim like that again."

"Tortured," he breathed.

"Kidnapping victims tend to have psychological issues."

"I bet it doesn't help anything that you're trapped here."

Trapped. That word. She couldn't fully suppress her shudder. "I can leave whenever I want."

"Just as much as I can." He tilted his head. "Just a captive playing a different game."

"God, what am I even doing here?" she said, throwing her arms wide and stepping away from him. "This is a waste of time."

"Why *are* you here?" he asked quietly. "For real."

She had her hand on the door, poised to leave. She didn't have to talk to him. She didn't have to tell him anything. She might have considered him her friend once, but that had been based on a lie. She didn't want to fall into his trap again, but she still hoped. Hoped he could be rehabilitated. That they could get his brother out, like they were working to find June. That all would be right with the world.

"My brothers have gone to check out the camps," she said to the door. "I guess I wanted to think about anything but my fear for them."

"Wait...what?"

She glanced over her shoulder to find that he had surged to his feet. This entire time, he'd remained seated, but now he looked frantic.

"They went to the feeding camp?" Everett demanded.

"Yeah. We had to corroborate your story."

"When did they go?"

"I don't know. A couple of hours ago. Why?"

The look on his face—like there was a Rubik's Cube before him and he only had a matter of minutes to get all the colors on the right sides—made her body turn to stone. When he looked at her again, her blood ran cold.

"What?" she demanded.

"It's a trap."

"What's a trap?" she whispered, though she already knew.

"They set me up. They know you're coming." He held his hands out. "Tell them all to come back. Get them home."

"They have precautions against it being a trap," she told him.

"Not enough. They must have let me find the information on purpose. Shit, shit, shit!" His fear permeated the room. "Reyna, go. Go now!"

She saw the truth in his eyes and slammed her hand on the door. It opened slowly. She slipped out and was running down the hallway before either of the guards could ask what was wrong. Her heart was slamming in her chest.

She needed to get to Sydney. She needed to hear from her that all was going to according to plan. That she was freaking out over nothing. Everett had planted the idea in her head, but his fear was what had triggered this reaction. She was sprinting, running at top speed, grateful for all those hours on the treadmill pushing herself to her limits. She skipped the elevator entirely and took the stairs three steps at a time.

She was panting by the time she burst into the conference room.

"It's a trap," she gasped. Her hands were on her knees. "Everett thinks…it's a trap."

Sydney had her hands braced on the table at the head of the conference table. Only Gabe and Washington stood at her sides. She knew Beckham had to be visible anytime a mission was going on, so he always had an alibi.

"We know," was all Sydney got out.

"You…you know?" she said in shock. Her voice rose as her anger did.

"We mapped all the contingencies. We didn't know ahead of time," Sydney told her. "But they were ambushed once they got to the facilities."

"What happened? Is anyone hurt?" Reyna demanded.

"We don't know."

"How could you not know?" she asked, panic rising.

Gabe crossed to her. "We should talk about this somewhere else."

"Don't you dare fucking placate me."

"Communications went down. We're blind. We have no idea what's happening in the field."

"Then send people to find out!" she nearly shrieked.

"We don't have the resources, and we can't send more soldiers out into an uncertain situation," Sydney said.

"Soldiers. Soldiers!" Reyna laughed manically. "My brothers aren't soldiers. They're people. Brian just got married. He has a baby on the way. Drew is coming out of his shell here. They're so young. Too young."

"We know," Gabe said.

Reyna only had eyes for Sydney. "You send these men into war and call them soldiers. To you, they're another piece on your chessboard. To us, they mean everything."

"Do I relish sending boys like your brothers out there?" Sydney bit out. "No. But sacrifices are the only way to accomplish anything."

"My brothers are not a sacrifice!" she screamed at her. "How can you speak so frivolously of a potential casualty?"

"Don't speak to me about casualties. I lost my *life* to this war. I sacrificed everything for it."

"I don't even know what that means. You seem to be doing all right," Reyna spat.

Gabe winced, and even Washington seemed to recoil at the comment. Sydney, however, straightened to her considerable height.

"You know so little to make such accusations. This rebellion was founded by Elle. She guided her 'toy soldiers' into battle and lost her life to the cause. And Elle did die that day," Sydney told her. "Because the person they turned her into after they captured her was no longer that idealistic woman. She was tortured into a hardened soldier herself, until she fought her way free of the chains that enslaved her. Until she came back as someone stronger, more realistic about the cause. Elle's death sparked a fire in this revolution, and I was born from the ashes."

Reyna's world turned upside down. Elle was Sydney. Sydney was Elle. She couldn't believe it. Couldn't believe Elle hadn't died, had instead been made into the one thing she had fought against. No wonder she hated Visage so fiercely. She had died for the cause, after all.

A crackle came from the radio sitting in front of Sydney. "Carpenter reporting in," a voice echoed through the scratchy radio.

"Drew," Reyna whispered.

Sydney snatched up the receiver. "What's happening out there, Carpenter?"

"I got away. I'm out, but the range on this is shot. Can you hear me?"

"We can hear you. Who else is with you?"

The radio crackled and then went out.

Chapter Thirty-Three

Drew was out there somewhere, alone. She didn't know where Brian was or what had happened to any of the other soldiers who were out on the mission. All she knew was that it had gone horribly, horribly wrong.

"Gabe, get Tony in here. Now," Sydney snapped, immediately launching into action.

Gabe flew out of his seat, rushing for their tech guy. He gave her a passing look of sympathy before leaving the room, but she hardly noticed.

"I'm going to find Meghan. If we have injured…" Washington said, trailing off.

"Go," Sydney barked.

He hurried toward the door but stopped to put his hand on Reyna's arm. "You should take a seat. I will have Meghan bring you water. You're in shock."

She shook him off and turned away. Shock. Yes. That was the

correct word. She knew it was true and yet couldn't seem to process anything past that.

To Sydney's credit, she didn't try to console Reyna. Perhaps she knew Reyna was past that. Or that she had caused this. Or maybe… she just didn't care.

People flitted in and out of the room, coming and going. Tony tried to fix the radio, listen in to microphones he'd attached to people, adjust earpieces. Nothing worked. All the cameras were down. All the radios were out. It was like an electromagnetic pulse had gone off inside the camp they were infiltrating. It was a technological black hole.

Tony's head jerked up finally. "Someone just pulled into the parking lot."

Gabe was out of the room in a second. Reyna felt her heart race, wondering who was there. What could possibly have happened.

"It's Tye," Tony confirmed. "He just scanned in."

Reyna deflated. Tye. Thank God. She was so relieved for her friend. He had helped her escape. She couldn't imagine what would happen if the others were…

She didn't even know. Caught? Captured? Killed? She shuddered at that thought.

Gabe burst back into the room, holding Tye up. He looked like utter shit. He was favoring his right ankle. His clothes were covered in black soot. He coughed and collapsed into a chair. Meghan was at his side in an instant.

"Oh my God, Tye," she gasped. Her hands fluttered over him. All of her calm demeanor had dissolved.

"I'm okay, Meghan. It's just my ankle, and I inhaled something." He coughed again violently. "Knocked most of us out, but I covered my face with my jacket and got far enough away."

"Tell us what happened," Sydney said, only slightly gentler than her normal command.

Reyna took a wary step forward. Her eyes were wide with terror and barely concealed hope.

"It was a decoy," he gasped. He clutched his lungs. Meghan brought him a glass of water. He took a long drink, draining the entire glass before continuing. "They knew we were coming the entire time. I don't know how they did, but they did. I should have known it was too easy to get past the guards on duty. Too easy to get over their fence and inside the perimeter. All my training for shit." He ran a hand through his black hair. "We split up. Carpenter took one team. I took another. Xavier took the third."

"Carpenter," she whispered.

"Brian," Tye said with a grimace.

Reyna hadn't known he was leading a team. It made her even sicker.

"My team had only just made it inside when we noticed none of our comms were working. That was my first sign. But when we got inside, it was empty."

"Empty?" Sydney asked.

"Just a warehouse. I mean, it had shit in it. But like, building supplies. Guarded and all that shit for some building supplies. They'd set us up. And then the smoke rained down." He coughed again, trying to expel whatever toxins they'd hit him with. "I called a retreat. Tried to warn the other teams, but there was no way."

"What happened to your team?" Meghan whispered.

"We scattered."

"You had a rendezvous point, right?" Gabe asked.

Tye nodded. "No one showed."

"Fuck," Gabe spat.

Meghan covered her mouth. Reyna's eyes welled with tears. Washington sat back hard in his chair.

"I don't know if anyone else got out."

"Drew did," Reyna said softly. Tye's eyes snapped to her. "He was able to radio us right before everything went out."

"Anyone else?"

"We don't know," Sydney answered for her.

There was a long silence in the room as the possibilities swept over them. An ambush. All communication down. Tye and Drew the only people they'd heard from. It would be an incredible loss to their cause.

"We should get that leg looked at," Meghan said.

"I'm fine," Tye said.

Meghan glared at him. "You need medical attention. We have a long night ahead of us. I don't want you to do more damage to yourself than necessary."

He relented. "Fine."

"Gabe, help me get him upstairs."

The trio retreated, leaving the bomb Tye had just dropped behind. Reyna's heart was in her throat as she realized she'd have to wait longer to get more information about her brothers.

"We're going to need to interrogate Everett," Sydney said. "He set us up for this. We need to know all the information he has. I'm going to give Gabe the go for whatever methods prove fruitful."

Reyna's gaze snapped to her. "Everett didn't know."

"He clearly did. He told you it was a trap."

"He pieced it together when I told him we sent a team there. He didn't know before then. Why would he tell me it was an ambush? He wouldn't want me to know he was involved."

"He wants you to trust him. Providing you with key information once it was already past the point when it could be of value is an easy way to do so."

"I really don't think he had anything to do with it."

"Either he was manipulated or he manipulated us," Sydney said evenly. "Either way, we will find out tonight."

It was nearly dawn when Gabe returned to the conference room. Reyna had finally sat down, head resting on her hands, eyes drooping from lack of sleep—and yet she wasn't tired. Just exhausted.

"Either he's trained to endure this," Gabe said, flexing his fist and revealing split knuckles, "or he really didn't know what he was leading us into."

Reyna smiled faintly. She'd been right. But the smile didn't stay long. Everett's involvement didn't change anything. Her brothers were still unaccounted for, along with everyone else. Meghan had Tye ordered into a chair at the table when he wouldn't cease pacing.

"Lower-level entry access requested," Tony said in the same tone he'd been using all day.

"What?" Reyna gasped. Her head popped up.

"Hold. Let me get that camera up."

He typed furiously on his computer. Everyone crowded in around him, hoping to get the first glimpse. The screen flickered and revealed a person.

Reyna's breath released in a whoosh. Her legs gave out, and she clutched at the table. "Drew."

"Should I grant him access?" Tony asked Sydney.

"Gabe, go and meet him, then yes," Sydney said.

Reyna darted to her feet. "I'm going with him."

"We need to assess him and make sure there are no more threats," Sydney said.

"You want a threat?" Reyna snarled. "Just try to keep me from my brother."

Without a backward glance, she stormed from the room. Gabe dashed after her. He put a hand on her shoulder to move into place beside her, but neither of them let up. They raced down the stairs, their breath in tandem with their movements. He was faster, but he didn't let her fall behind as they finally hit the level where Drew had come in.

Gabe spoke into a radio. "We're here."

"Access: three, two, one," Tony counted down.

The door slid open.

Drew collapsed forward onto the floor. Reyna ran to him, cradling his head in her arms. She pushed his fine hair out of his eyes.

"Drew," she whispered. Tears streamed down her cheeks. "You're alive. You're okay now. You're here."

She barely noticed Gabe as he checked the underground garage entrance before manually shutting and relocking the door.

"He's alone," he said.

"Drew, it's Rey. I'm here."

"Rey," he muttered, coughing up the same stuff Tye had inhaled.

"Yeah, it's me. I'm here. You're safe."

"Hey man," Gabe said, leaning forward. "How did you get here? Did you see anyone else?"

Drew pushed himself up on his elbows. His eyes were red and hazy. "I…I walked and…I'm alone." He coughed again, so hard she thought he might cough up his lung. "Where is everyone else?"

"We're trying to figure that out," Gabe said.

Drew groaned and rolled in on himself.

"Hey, hey, are you hurt?" Reyna asked.

"Shoulder."

Reyna looked down at his shoulder and cursed. "He's been shot. We need to get him upstairs. He needs medical attention."

"No," Drew managed. "No, I need…Laura."

"Laura?" Reyna asked, horror sinking into her stomach. "Why?"

"Rey, I'm sorry."

"No, no, no," she whispered. "Don't be sorry."

"Brian."

Gabe radioed back to the conference room. "We need medical here. Carpenter has been shot in the shoulder. Plus smoke inhalation."

"Laura," Drew repeated. "I have to tell Laura."

He tried to struggle to his feet, but Gabe put a hand on his good shoulder, pushing him back down to the ground. "Hold it there, buddy. You can tell her when you're patched up."

"I have to tell her," he repeated, slipping in and out of consciousness as he collapsed back onto the floor.

"Tell her what?" Reyna asked.

"They got Brian," he whispered. "They captured Brian."

Then Drew passed out.

Drew was rushed to the medical wing, where Meghan and Washington both suited up to remove the bullet from his shoulder. Reyna sat in the waiting room with Gabe. She knew that she should tell Laura. That she should get Jodie. That anything else should probably matter at that moment. But…it didn't.

All that mattered was that Drew was in surgery. And that Brian was gone.

Gone.

Her heart broke. Shattered into a million pieces and scattered all over the floor. *Gone* was such a simple word. A word that didn't mean half of what she was feeling.

When she joined Visage, she did it for her brothers. All of this had been for them, and in the end, she was safe and they were fucked. What the hell had she done? What the hell had she brought them into?

She didn't know how long she sat there before Beckham suddenly appeared. Tears fell from her eyes as he picked her up and crushed her to him. She put her arms around his neck, and he wrapped his around her waist. She stayed like that, letting him hold her, giving him all her grief.

His lips landed on her hair. "Oh, Little One."

"Brian," she choked out.

"I heard."

"It's my fault. If I hadn't joined Visage, they wouldn't be here."

"No," Beckham repeated more firmly. He pulled back to look down into her red-rimmed eyes. "Do not place the blame on anyone but the person who deserves it—William Harrington."

"Can we kill him now?"

"Yes." The murderous vampire who had single-handedly taken

over a kingdom stood before her. She was glad for it. She would need him to win this war.

"Good."

His thumbs stroked across her cheeks, wiping away her tears. "Don't let them break you."

"Only you." She whispered the words he had said to her once before.

His lips were tender against hers. A direct contrast to his normal behavior. It settled her in a way nothing else had been able to.

"Will you wait with me?"

"To the end of time."

Meghan came out of surgery. Dark circles ringed her eyes, and her hands shook as she adjusted the braided bun on top of her head.

"He's fine," she told Reyna. "He told us the same information Tye did. I think he inhaled more smoke than Tye, though. We gave him a sedative so he'd sleep. He'll have to wait a few hours to tell Laura."

"Thank you," Reyna said, hugging Meghan. "For everything."

"Of course." She ran a hand over her face. "What a night."

"Beckham said there's a meeting. They're waiting for us."

Meghan nodded. "I should check in with Jodie first. She's been cagey lately."

"Yeah. I know. Let me know how she is." Meghan stumbled forward a step, and Reyna caught her. "Hey, maybe you should get some sleep. You're no use to anyone if you're dead on your feet."

"Everyone else is still awake. I can make it."

"When did you last sleep?"

"I don't know."

"You're not a vampire. Leave patients to Washington, okay?"

"Maybe just a few hours," she said reluctantly.

Reyna went to see Drew. She played with his hair where he slept on a cot in the corner of the recovery room. She kissed his forehead. "We're going to get Brian back, Drew. We're going to kill the monster who did this. We're going to fix everything. I promise."

Vengeance filled her cold heart, savage and wild. Eager to devour anything that got in her way.

Beckham saw the look on her face and offered her his hand. She took it, drinking in his strength as a beacon to ground her. The anger and Beckham were the only things keeping her afloat right now. If she gave up either, she didn't know where she'd be.

They returned to the conference room once more. Sydney remained at the head of the table. Tony had his computer up in front of him, still typing away frantically. Gabe had returned, and Tye sat next to him, ankle bandaged.

To Reyna's surprise and distaste, Penelope was also in attendance. Her eyes drifted down to where Beckham still held Reyna's hand. She pursed her lips, then looked away.

Washington followed Beckham and Reyna into the room.

"As many of you know," Sydney began, "early this evening, we sent a scouting team to look into the reported farming camp. That mission failed. It was an ambush. They knew we were coming. They planted the information for us to find. Which means we are no closer to locating the actual farming camp, we don't know how the camp will be utilized, and we have no idea when it will be functional."

"What *do* we know?" Penelope asked curtly.

Sydney shot her a furious look. "That nearly a dozen of our top soldiers were either taken or killed at this decoy camp. They are MIA. And Visage clearly wanted us to know about these plans. They sent Everett to us knowing he would reveal the information."

"Then how do we know there actually is a feeding camp?" Penelope asked. "Perhaps it was all just a lie to make us look a fool."

"It's not," Beckham said. "I found correspondence at Visage with coded information about it. Once I knew what I was looking for, I found it. They're doing this. I just don't know when or where."

"Which means Harrington no longer trusts you," Sydney said.

"Which officially confirms what we already suspected—you're out."

Everyone was silent at the realization that their top double agent was out of the game.

It didn't faze Reyna. She stood and slapped her hands on the table. "Then there's only one thing we can do. Only one thing we must do. We must stop the camp any way that we can. We cannot let it happen."

"And what do you propose?" Penelope asked with a sneer.

"We create chaos. We kill Harrington."

Chapter Thirty-Four

Sydney nodded. "I agree."

"What?" Penelope asked in shock. "How would we even do that?"

"I'll draw him out," Reyna said.

"No," Beckham said at once.

Reyna continued as if she hadn't heard him. It was so simple. So very simple. "I think it's time we test that blood theory you have, Becks."

His eyes narrowed. "Absolutely not."

"If Harrington can sense me, he'll come to me. I'll lure him out into the open. You finish the job."

"There are a million things wrong with that scenario."

"Where would we do it?" Sydney asked.

Beckham snarled at her. "You can't be considering this."

"I consider every option. Reyna is willing. She made the suggestion. I'd be a fool not to consider it."

"She'd be *bait*."

"Yes," Reyna said. "I'll be bait. We just need to find a time when Harrington will be out in public. Somewhere not as guarded as Visage or wherever the hell that monster lives."

"No," Beckham repeated.

"You will not change my mind," she told him with all the fires of a thousand suns.

"I'm throwing a New Year's Eve masquerade party," Penelope said. "Harrington was invited."

"That's only five days away," Gabe interjected. "Not much time."

"Then he'll never see it coming," Reyna said.

"We could have access to the event?" Sydney asked Penelope, who nodded.

Beckham flew out of his chair. "Have you all lost your minds? We are not sending Reyna out against Harrington."

"I'm going, Becks," she told him. "And I need you there to finish it off."

"If Harrington is out of the way, then you have a play for president of Visage," Sydney said. "Imagine what we could do, the changes we could implement, with you at the helm."

"You're sure?" he asked Reyna.

"Yes. Do this with me."

"I don't want to risk you."

"Some risks are worth everything." She tried to say with her eyes what she didn't have to: *You were. You were worth everything.*

"No," Beckham said again.

"I believe I am in charge of this operation, Mr. Anderson," Sydney said formally. "I think it's the start of a plan. We need to flesh it out, but if Reyna is willing, it's the best chance we have."

"Sleep on it," Beckham said.

"I won't change my mind," Reyna said defiantly.

"It's been a long night for everyone. Get some rest and meet back here at fifteen hundred hours," Sydney said as a dismissal.

With the decision all but made, Reyna felt a sharp sense of relief flood her system. She was doing something. Sacrificing anything to stop this camp from being implemented—to find a way to get Brian back.

Beckham herded her toward the exit. Her exhaustion was winning out; she stumbled through her steps, and her eyelids drooped. The adrenaline was wearing off, and she had nothing left to give.

They were in the hallway when Beckham growled, "You can hardly walk."

"It's been a long night."

She was far from okay. Even further from fine. *Catatonic* was the correct word.

"Beckham!" Penelope called behind them.

They both stopped and faced her. Reyna braced her hand against the wall to stay steady. She really didn't want to deal with Penelope right now.

"Where are you going?" Penelope asked.

"Reyna needs to rest."

"Okay…so she'll rest. But where are *you* going?"

His patience was clearly on a razor-thin edge when he responded, "I am going with her."

It felt like he was drawing a line in the sand. A line that he'd drawn over and over again, but never in this way. Never this forcefully. Never in front of Reyna.

Penelope crossed her arms. "I can't keep doing this."

"Then don't."

"I'm the one who's always been there for you. I'm the one who changed your life. I'm the one who brought you to Elle," Penelope said. She tilted her chin up. "It's me. It's always been me."

"You're really doing this *now*?" he asked.

"When else am I supposed to do it? I'm Penelope Sky. I'm the mayor. I'm exactly who you're supposed to end up with, Beckham. When are you going to get a clue that there is nothing better than what is right in front of your face? This charade has to end. You and I, we're perfect together. We *should* be together," she said, her voice rising an octave. "The mayor and a senior vice president of Visage, working together to make a better future. That's us. Everyone can see it but you."

Reyna's eyebrows rose at her entitled tone. "I…uh…maybe I should…" She hitched her thumb over her shoulder and started to back away. Beckham could handle the situation.

"Oh no," Penelope snapped. "By all means, stick around. It's not like what I'm saying should come as any shock to you. I thought it was already obvious that I was better than you in every way."

"Penelope," Beckham said, his voice low and disapproving.

"What? We all know it's true. I don't accept that this ends any other way for me. There is no way that you fuck me, drink from me for over a year, and then leave me for some warehouse rat. I always get what I want, and what I want is you."

"No, you want what you cannot have. I have already told you time and time again that this is *not* what I want. We are *not* together," Beckham said, putting himself between Penelope and Reyna. "I didn't want to have this conversation in front of Reyna, but you're leaving me no choice here."

"No choice?" Penelope laughed in a short burst. "You had every choice. You could have picked me. Look at me, Beckham. I am the most sought-after woman in this city. I could have anyone I want, but I want you. You and me against the world."

"Penelope, you and I were over long before Reyna entered my life. So, don't try to pin it on her," he said, holding up his hand to forestall her protest. "We were a dalliance. We had fun. But I never gave you the impression that this was going to be long term."

"You never gave me the impression?" she nearly shouted. Her eyes widened, round as saucers. Her eyebrows lifted incredulously. Her mouth dropped open. "Are you fucking kidding me? I just… I can't believe you're even saying this. We were supposed to be together, and now you're gaslighting me about our relationship. A fucking dalliance, Beckham?" She shook her head. "I have nothing to say to that absurd notion."

"I've been saying all this from the start. We're not together."

"Sure. Whatever. Go fuck yourself," she spat. Then she turned on her heel and strode away from them, down the hallway.

"Fuck," Reyna whispered. "Maybe we should go after her."

Beckham flexed his hands. "Just let her go. She needs to blow off steam. I think reality finally sank in, and she has to come to terms with it. I'll talk to her after she's cooled down again."

As soon as Reyna entered her room, she collapsed into bed. Beckham followed behind her, carefully stripping her out of her clothes and tucking her in. Her eyes fluttered shut as soon as she hit the pillow.

"I'm sorry," she whispered deliriously.

"Why are you apologizing?"

"For Penelope."

"You aren't responsible for her actions."

"Still sorry."

Beckham kissed her temple. "Don't worry about her."

"Okay." Reyna sighed. "Will you do me a favor?"

"Perhaps."

"Hold me?"

He crawled into bed, his movements as lithe as a panther. His hands moved around her body with her back pressed into his chest. They fit together perfectly. As one.

"Another favor?" she mumbled.

"Hmm?" he breathed into her ear.

"Stay through the morning?"

"It is morning."

"Stay all day."

"For you."

She sighed deep in her throat and then let the tension finally leave her body.

• • •

Reyna awoke with an arm around her waist. She rolled over to find Beckham perfectly asleep behind her. A statue carved of stone. Adonis in the flesh.

She had always wondered if vampires slept. She had never seen Beckham do it. Of course, he had a bed in his room back at the penthouse, but beds could be used for multiple purposes. She was well aware. She traced the contours of his face, allowing herself to forget for this one moment the horrors of yesterday and the new nightmares she would face when she left this room.

"Keep doing that and we're never leaving this bed."

Reyna smiled. "Is that supposed to get me to stop?"

His eyes slowly opened, revealing their dark depths. He captured her hand in his, brought it to his lips, and kissed her.

"How are you?"

She shrugged. "You're here."

"Yes."

"I didn't know you slept."

"Sometimes," he admitted. "We don't need to as much. Just like eating. It rejuvenates us, though we can go much longer without."

"It's not fair that you look exactly the same when you wake up, and I look like a bomb went off."

He tugged her closer. "Does it matter what you look like when you still have a sharp mind, quick wit, and fragile human heart when you wake up?"

"And here I thought my heart was hardening."

"I dread that day. Your struggle, emotion, and humanity are your best qualities. It makes you who you are."

"It also makes all of this so hard," she whispered. She hated admitting how she felt. That she knew she would have to face the day once they left this bed.

"Be glad you feel at all. For so long, I did not." He frowned. "You asked me once what changed me. Why I decided not to continue on as I had as a lord. I didn't give you the whole truth."

Reyna frowned. "What do you mean?"

"The camera came second. The truth is that I know what you're going through, because I lost a sister."

"You had a sister?"

He nodded once. His eyes were very far away. "Bronwyn and I were very close. When I was changed, I changed her as well. Brought her into this world." He paused with a sigh. "Made her my second."

Reyna covered her mouth. Oh God.

"She was murdered in a turf war. I mourn her death every year. She was my only real family. On the fifteenth anniversary of her death, I went to the home we grew up in. I sat there and watched a new family on the property—a young brother and sister, playing together—and I remembered that innocence. I wanted to find that again." His eyes bored into hers. She hardly breathed. "I started taking pictures soon after that, searching for it. I joined Elle hoping this rebellion would reveal it. But it wasn't until you arrived that I knew you were everything I'd been seeking. You were then and you are now.

"I love you," Beckham told her. "I have loved you since the first time I saw you, since you defiantly bared your neck to me while you trembled, and as you fought for the oppressed every way you could, and every moment you see me for who I am. I love you. I will always love you."

"I love you, too," she released on a breath, and then she kissed him. Because no other words could do justice to the way her heart expanded.

CHAPTER THIRTY-FIVE

Telling Laura about Brian destroyed any lingering happy feelings. Drew had been the one to utter the words, but Reyna had held Laura's hand. She'd been there when Laura fainted and collapsed backward. When Laura came to, Reyna sat with her while she sobbed and held her arms around her stomach, their child growing inside of her, oblivious to what might happen to their father.

She would have sat there all day if she wasn't required to report to Sydney's meeting.

"I'll stay with her," Drew promised, taking Reyna's seat.

Not that Laura was responding to anyone. Still, he took her hand in his.

Reyna dragged her defeated body upstairs and found Meghan pacing back and forth in front of the closed door. "What's going on?"

"There you are!" she cried.

"I'm not late."

"It's not that. Have you seen Jodie?"

"No? I thought she was with you."

"I've searched high and low. She wasn't in our room when I went to sleep. She didn't sleep in her bed. All of her clothes are gone. I don't know what to do." Meghan bit her lip. "Reyna, I think she left."

Her heart sank at the words. She thought that she had gotten through to Jodie. She knew their time in Visage was remarkably different, but they were each other's rock. The only ones who really knew what the other had endured. And she had just left?

"How is that possible?" Reyna asked.

"I think she snuck out behind the security team last night. I don't know any other way she could have gotten out."

"She told me she wanted to leave," Reyna said with despair. "I thought I'd convinced her to stay."

"This isn't your fault, but—I don't know how to find her."

Reyna considered where her brave friend would disappear to. "She went to find June," Reyna answered.

"Oh," Meghan said, releasing her breath in a huff as if it made sense. "Of course she did. We found an old address for her cousin right before the raid. We were going to check it out to make sure it was safe and to see if she still lived there, but we couldn't spare the resources yet. And now…" Meghan shook her head.

"I know. Now we're screwed." Reyna frowned. "We have to go after her."

"We're needed here, and she doesn't trust anyone else." Meghan ran a hand through her braids. "Hell, she doesn't trust me. I did everything I could." A tear came into Meghan's eye. "I don't want her to get hurt out there."

"We'll have to find a way to get her back."

"I know," Meghan said, defeated. "I'll talk to Sydney after the meeting, but with the huge defeat…I don't know who we can spare."

Reyna took her hand and squeezed. "We'll find our girl, okay?"

Meghan nodded, straightening back to the operative Reyna had first met. Neither of them wanted to abandon their friend, but Jodie had chosen to leave at the worst possible moment. Who did they have that they could spare in the midst of this utter chaos and the moment when they were finally taking the fight to Visage and Harrington?

...

The plan came together over the next several days as they prepared for Penelope's party. In endless meetings, they hammered out all the details. Every contingency. Every exit. Every single way things could go horribly wrong and blow up in her face. When she wasn't in meetings, she was on the treadmill or in the firing range with Gabe. He'd given her a crash course in how to use a firearm. She was far from a pro in less than a week, but at least she could handle the weapon. She would never be faster or stronger than a vampire, but a gun could level the playing field a bit.

"It's not going to kill them," Gabe reminded her, adjusting her stance again. "But you'll slow the fucker down."

She fired again and again. She missed as often as she hit the target, but her accuracy was slowly improving.

"Aim for the biggest sections. Torso is going to be your best bet. Don't try to get fancy. You want to keep them from reaching you or disable them enough to get away." He corrected her arm. "Try again."

So she did until everything ached.

"Good," he said with a genuine smile. "Much better."

Meghan popped her head into the firing range. "Gabe..."

Gabe grinned at Meghan. "Hey babe."

Meghan rolled her eyes. "I need Reyna."

"Guess that's all the time we have," he said, patting her back.

Reyna swallowed. "I'm not good enough."

"Worst-case scenario only. If all goes as planned, you won't even need this." Gabe released the clip and broke the gun down. "I'll be there. Try not to think about anything else."

She nodded. "Okay. Okay."

"Now go get pretty."

"I'm already pretty," she teased as she hurried toward Meghan.

They took the elevator to a room outfitted to look like a dressing room. There was a dresser full of makeup and hair products and brushes and every color of lipstick imaginable. Two garment bags hung against the far wall.

"Whoa," Reyna whispered.

"Yeah. I have a slight hair and makeup obsession." Meghan pointed at the chair. "Now, sit. I have to make you presentable for tonight." Meghan tossed her a button-up shirt. "Put that on so you don't mess up your hair when you change after."

Several hours later, both Meghan and Reyna were presentable for Penelope's New Year's Eve ball. Reyna wore a black sequined halter dress with a full tulle skirt from the waist down that had pockets allowing her access to the thigh holsters that held a handgun on each leg. Her dark hair was down around her shoulders in supermodel waves, and Meghan had mastered a cat eye and smoky makeup that transformed her face. Meghan looked like a movie star in a slinky gold glitter dress that sparkled with every movement. Her long red box braids were in an elaborate updo, and her light-brown skin glittered with a matching gold shimmer.

Tony came in for the final touches. They each had an earpiece, a microphone, a hidden camera in their bodice, and a diamond-encrusted ID bracelet that doubled as a tracking device. Spy 101.

"One last thing," Meghan said. She handed Reyna a box. Inside was a delicate black lace mask with sewn-in beads and glittery sequins.

"Wow," she whispered.

Reyna let Meghan secure it to her face. When she looked in the full-length mirror, she hardly recognized herself. She looked like some dark ethereal creature.

Death. She was death, come to claim her next victim.

Meghan nodded her approval. "Killer. Ready?"

Reyna turned away from the mirror and smiled grimly. She was ready.

A knock on the door surprised them both. Washington stood on the other side.

He seemed out of breath. "I had to come tell you that I have results for you."

Meghan glanced between them. "We only have a few minutes, Reyna. I'm going to make sure everything else is set up. Find me after this."

"I will." She turned back to Washington. "What results?"

"It's a scientific breakthrough! I realized I've seen blood like yours once before. Very early on when I was first studying blood type matches. Actually, the very idea for the cure came to me because I found a perfect blood match."

Reyna tilted her head to the side. "A blood type match? Aren't there millions of them?"

"Yes. But this was a blood match."

"What's the difference?"

"A blood type is exactly what everyone already knows, but a blood match is a snowflake. It's a fingerprint. It doesn't have to match the blood *type*—it matches the blood composition itself. It is an extremely rare, one-to-one match between two people's blood."

Her heart stopped beating. "What exactly are you saying?"

"I'm saying that the reason Beckham can sense your blood has nothing to do with him drinking it. William shouldn't be able to sense you, because there is only one perfect blood match for you."

Reyna held up her hand. "Hold on. Harrington can't sense me?"

"As far as I know, no. Though you should still be on your guard tonight. There might be more to your blood than I know," Washington warned with a stern look. "But the fact that you and Beckham found each other is truly incredible."

"Wait, so…Beckham is my…blood match?"

"A once-in-a-lifetime match. I never even considered looking for it again, because it's so uncommon."

"What does that even mean? I thought he was O negative. I thought I was Rh null. And when he bit me the first time…he reacted strongly," she said to put it mildly.

"Well, he *would* react strongly. It had to be the best blood he'd ever tasted in his life."

"So…because we're matched, he couldn't resist. It didn't make him go feral?"

"Assuredly not. He should be able to drink your blood with no negative side effects. And I suspect with many positive ones." Washington's smile widened. "I believe the concept is very similar to a soulmate."

"A soulmate," she said, the breath rushing out of her. The word sounded impossible. A fairy tale. And yet, Washington wasn't one for fancy. He was a scientific man, and if he was using the term, then he meant it.

"Yes. Your one true match. Beckham claims to be able to sense you at a great distance. Have you ever been able to sense him?"

"I don't think so." Though…had she ever tried? She'd always had an awareness of Beckham. The knowledge of him. The feeling of him. They had clicked. Even from day one, through her terror. "Though…I don't know. Maybe."

"We'll do more testing later. I simply wanted to bring you the good news."

"Thank you, Washington," she said and meant it.

"And I apologize about what happened with Jodie. I heard about her leaving and fear that might have been partially my doing. I can't change my past with her or William, but I do wish that it hadn't scared her away."

"Me too," Reyna said with a hitch in her throat.

"Let me wish you luck. Be careful out there."

"I will."

She turned back to the door with her head in a daze as the realization of what Washington had said washed over her again. Soulmate.

"And Reyna?"

"Yes?"

"Don't underestimate William."

Reyna's heart hardened around the words. Harrington. She needed to keep her head in the game. She was out to destroy the destroyer.

"I won't."

She met Meghan at the top of the complex, where the steel door was open and a stretch limo was waiting for them in the parking lot.

"Everything all right with Washington?" Meghan asked.

"I'll tell you about it later."

Gabe held the back door to the limo open and leaned against it in a slick black tuxedo. His red hair was gelled to perfection, his green eyes as charming and devious as ever. A plain black mask dangled from his hand.

"Ladies."

Meghan stepped forward and straightened his bow tie. "This is a good look for you, O'Connor."

His hand slipped to a lock of her red hair. "Everything is a good look on you, love."

Meghan laughed softly and then slid into the limo.

"After you," he said gallantly, gesturing dramatically into the vehicle.

She knew it was to lighten the mood, and she appreciated it. She gave him a small smile before pulling the folds of her dress in and entering the limo. Gabe slid inside last. The door slammed shut, and then they were off. No one spoke on the drive. Even Gabe's normal chatter was absent as anticipation clogged the car.

Reyna was glad for the anonymity the masks provided. She worried for Meghan. Her face had certainly been caught on cameras the day she had broken Reyna out of Visage. And Gabe—if Everett had guessed he knew Reyna, would Harrington know the Irish mobster Gabriel O'Connor and the rebel Gabe were one and the same? Would Harrington be able to sense her? Washington said no, but this would be the test of that.

She tried not to think about it. What would be would be.

Traffic obstructed their limo at every turn. New Year's Eve in the city was a nightmare. People had started to line up in Times Square at the earliest hours of the morning. But the elite who had received invitations to Penelope's party were whisked past all the banal theatrics and through to her event. Gabe insisted the crowd would give them cover if they had to escape, but to Reyna, the mass of people was just a barrier. She remembered what it had been like to get caught in a riot outside of City Hall. She shuddered.

The limo dropped them off on a red carpet, and, as planned, Reyna and Meghan were Gabe's arm candy for the night. They passed a row of flashing photographers, and when they reached the entrance, Gabe produced an invite from his jacket pocket.

"Welcome to Mayor Sky's New Year's Eve masked extravaganza. Proceed through the ID scanner and enjoy your evening."

"Thank you," he said.

This was the part Reyna was most afraid of. None of them had real ID bracelets. They had to trust that Tony had programmed their fakes well enough that no one knew the difference. Because if they failed here, everything would be for naught.

A woman used a small electronic device to scan Gabe's bracelet, looking as bored as ever. He chatted the woman up, keeping her attention on him. Gabe was a charmer, that was for sure.

"Mr. O'Connor, A positive. Cleared."

Gabe kept talking to the woman as she scanned Meghan's wrist, revealing her fake identity, Annabelle Donoghue, B negative. Cleared.

And then it was Reyna's turn. She tried to look as blasé as Meghan had when she held out her wrist, like it was a supreme inconvenience that anyone was even doing this. She wasn't sure she quite managed it.

The woman scanned her wrist. The device pinged. It hadn't pinged for anyone else. Shit.

Reyna started to sweat. This was the end. They were caught. She'd be dragged to Harrington or kicked out of the party. They'd know it was a fake. They'd know.

"Oh, this damn machine," the woman said. She hit it twice with her hand. "I'm so sorry, miss. Sometimes new technology is such a pain."

"Isn't it?" Reyna managed to get out through her fear.

"Let me try one more time."

Reyna held her wrist out to the woman. She had no decorum left. Her fear pricked too high.

"Rachel Murphy, O negative." The woman smiled brightly at her. "Sorry for the delay. You're cleared."

Reyna contained a sigh of relief. Gabe took both of their arms once more, walking them inside.

"That was close," Reyna ground out.

"We're fine," Meghan whispered.

They stepped over the threshold and into the ballroom.

"Showtime," Gabe muttered.

The ballroom glittered from floor to ceiling. Balloons rested in netting overhead, ready to be dropped at midnight. Waiters meandered through the crowd in slim-cut tuxedos with tails. The waitresses wore faux tuxedos with tiny skirts and high heels. They all carried champagne and little hors d'oeuvres. Some even had trays of blood in tiny shot glasses, organized by blood type.

Reyna covered her mouth to keep from gagging at the sight. Meghan's sharp look made her remember her role. She dropped her arm and fawned over Gabe, letting her eyes roam the crowd. They made a slow circuit around the room. It seemed so much larger in person than when she had been staring down at the blueprints. Plus, the room was packed. She hoped she'd be visible in the masses.

Gabe had just reached for champagne for both Meghan and Reyna when a voice broke through the speakers.

"Your mayor, Penelope Sky," the person said.

Applause boomed all around them. Their attention shifted to the stage as Penelope Sky stepped out. She looked…radiant. For a woman who had just had her heart broken, she looked even more stunning than normal. Her typical blue dress was so pale it was almost white. Her matching mask covered her entire face. She looked utterly unique and otherworldly beautiful.

Gabe directed them into position. It was a step above the rest of the room with a light overhead. There were several around the room, but they'd picked this one because it was closest to an exit.

Reyna stepped into the spotlight. She cleared her mind, ignoring Penelope's final steps to the microphone. She wanted to test if she could sense Beckham in the same way he could sense her. She had never even considered it before Washington had suggested it, but if she was his blood match, then he was hers.

She tuned in to that sense she had always had of him. That moment where everything had always felt right. Where she inherently knew him. It bubbled up inside of her. An awareness. A sense of rightness.

She turned her head. And there he was.

He was standing between Cassandra and Roland to the right of the stage. As if in response, he faced her, cocked his head to the side, and a small smile graced those perfect lips.

Her heart thudded in response. It had worked. She couldn't wait to tell him. Her soulmate.

"Ladies and gentlemen," Penelope said, drawing Reyna's attention back to the matter at hand, "thank you so much for being here tonight. This was one of my father's favorite occasions. While I miss him dearly, I am so happy to continue his legacy. As with every New Year's Eve, the mayor brings an honored guest up onto the stage. I'm pleased tonight to have the CEO and president of Visage, William Harrington."

Penny greeted Harrington as he strode onto the stage. This was the moment. She waited to see if he would find her in the crowd. If he could sense her, he would do it now. But his eyes never flickered toward her. He just continued until he reached the microphone.

Reyna gritted her teeth and forced herself to applaud along with the rest of them. This was the first time she had seen him since she had escaped. He looked…healthy.

It made no sense. He shouldn't look this hale when he didn't have access to her blood. He still leaned on his cane, but she'd seen him fake that before. His face wasn't pasty. His hair was full. All he needed to do was straighten his back and she knew that the monster would reappear.

The crowd cheered enthusiastically for him. He'd fooled them all—the entire world. He'd made them think the blood type cure was the only way for vampires to use their intelligence—but Beckham had explained that not all vampires functioned on the same animalistic level without the cure. Harrington had pulled humanity back from the brink of collapse by employing humans at Visage, but no one knew he had caused that depression. He'd offered this Blood Census as an olive branch to help with all registered vampires, but it was just a scheme to find more Rh null negative humans.

William Harrington was not an altruistic savior. He was a lethal, manipulative, conniving bastard. And he'd had centuries to perfect his act so everyone in this room salivated at his very presence. But she knew better.

"Thank you so much, Mayor Sky," Harrington said with the soft voice he used with a crowd. "I'm so pleased to be here as an honored guest tonight. Visage is a beacon in this city. It employs many of the people here in this room, including my senior vice presidents who are in attendance." He gestured to the side of the room where Beckham stood flanked by Roland and Cassandra. "At Visage, we always strive to be cutting-edge. To bring bigger and better to the world, to our employees, to our shareholders. This year alone, we've rolled out a new permanent enrollment, first with senior staff and then all of corporate. This is set to go fully public in the new year."

The crowd cheered. They *cheered*.

Reyna was sick. How many people at this party had any idea what it was like to be a blood escort? She doubted there were many other than the hired help.

"With the completion of the Blood Census, we'll be able to work toward even bigger gains going forward. A full registry only makes sense when you consider that vampires have been registered for more than a decade. But more importantly, we have a *huge* announcement coming early next year. It'll be groundbreaking." He grinned wickedly. "I wish I could say more, but be on the lookout for news."

Reyna's face paled further. The feeding camp. It had to be.

"And with that, I want to say thank you to our illustrious host, Mayor Sky. She's a wonder to work with, and I'm amazed by the transformation she's made in the short time she has been running this city."

"Thank you, William," Penelope said. "I feel like a new person."

Then her hand went to the back of her mask and the entire thing fluttered away, revealing her full beauty. Her completely seamless, perfect face. There was no sign of the multiple surgeries she had undergone to recover from the fires. She was the same, and yet…

Penelope smiled. Bright and bold and deadly.

Reyna choked.

"No," she whispered.

Penelope had been turned. Penelope was a vampire.

Chapter Thirty-Six

"Fuck," Gabe spat. Meghan covered her mouth with her hand. Reyna just stared. And stared. And stared some more.

Harrington waved his hand and said something into the microphone, but she heard none of it. All she saw was Penelope standing there healed and yet…rotten. Not that being a vampire automatically made you a bad person. She knew too many who weren't. But Penelope had done this post-Beckham. This was not a clearheaded choice. This was desperation.

"Abort," Gabe said into their earpieces. "It's a trap."

He tried to grab for her, to pull her out of the room, but Reyna yanked away from him. They had not come this far to turn around and do nothing. If Harrington obviously could not sense her, then she would make him *see* her. They still had this one shot to get at Harrington. She wasn't going to squander it just because of Penelope Sky.

With her plan clicking into place, she took a deep breath and pulled off her own mask, revealing her face to the entire crowd.

Harrington's head turned toward the back of the room. His eyes widened as he took in Reyna standing under a spotlight for all to see. A slow smile crossed his face as their eyes locked. His seemed to say, *Well met, little queen.*

Instead of walking off the stage as he'd come in, Harrington took the stairs down to the front. He ignored the excitement and congratulations of his fawning admirers. His vice presidents pulled in behind him automatically, but Reyna didn't dare glance at Beckham. She still didn't know how much Harrington knew and wouldn't tip her hand if she didn't have to.

"What are you doing?" Gabe hissed.

"Getting his attention."

"Fuck," he ground out. Then he and Meghan slid out of view to move into their designated positions.

Harrington was walking directly toward her, and as he got closer, she backed slowly out of the ballroom and through the exit. An empty patio opened onto the entrance to the secluded park that Penelope had cleared for her guests. She could see her breath in the frigid air as fear of the man striding purposely for her threatened to overwhelm her.

She had learned at a young age how to compartmentalize the horrors of her youth. Visage had only intensified that skill. Survival. She knew how to function when survival was her only option, and she put those skills to good use for what was to come.

Harrington cleared the doorway and followed her into the cold.

"My little queen," Harrington said in his lilting voice that made her teeth grind, "you have come home."

That fucking nickname. If she never heard it again, it would be too soon.

She saw the chessboard before her and made her move, praying no one would beat her.

"I'm here."

"Very elaborate attire for such a thing," he said casually

as if they were back underground and she had to listen to his insufferable chatter. "I do prefer you in white, though. Much more angelic."

"Black suits me," she said.

"Not in the slightest," Harrington said, taking another step forward. He swung his cane in circles. She had been right. He still didn't need the damn thing. "You are innocent and soft and so very human."

Reyna clenched her jaw and released it. She hated the way Harrington's words mirrored what Beckham had said to her earlier this week. How could both men enjoy these qualities in her and be so utterly different? Want such different things from her?

"However, you could have simply walked back into my life. You didn't need such a dramatic entrance."

"You like dramatic entrances."

He smiled. "You know me so well."

If she didn't know better, she would think William Harrington was infatuated with her. She knew he was not. He wanted something from her, and he was a master manipulator. He would play whatever game was necessary to get her to come to him of her own free will. That would be easiest for him. Kidnapping was an extra step. He preferred to cut out the middleman.

A shuffle from behind Harrington drew both of their attention. Reyna stiffened when she saw Roland exit onto the patio. Then Cassandra. Then Beckham.

"You know my colleagues," Harrington said, gesturing to Roland, Cassandra, and Beckham as they followed him outside.

"Yes," she squeaked out like a mouse.

She was prepared for the possibility of facing all of them, had even hoped that Beckham would be in attendance to protect her. But her preparation didn't meet with the reality of their horror. Harrington with his lethal calm. Roland, the devious sexual predator. Cassandra, the deranged sadist.

"Mr. Anderson is in a mood," Harrington said with a wide smile for Beckham. "He's not pleased that we turned his girl."

She finally steeled herself to glance at Beckham. He was not her Beckham. He was the senior vice president of this deplorable organization. He was a vampire lord. A murderer, a killer, a monster.

"Ruined her," Beckham spat instead. His arms were crossed, his eyes flat and lifeless.

"You'll find another O negative beauty. You always do, my boy," Harrington said dismissively.

Reyna couldn't believe Harrington still addressed Beckham as if he were a treasured son. A prodigy. They'd suspected Beckham was on the outs. Had they been wrong? What was an act…and what wasn't?

"We wouldn't risk you that way, though, dear Reyna," Harrington said. "You are much too valuable. But I see that I did it wrong the first time. You can come back and live a normal life. Come and go as you please. We'd be more careful with the blood donations. I'd negotiate to once a week, even."

He was…negotiating with her. She hadn't expected that. Truthfully, she hadn't expected any of it. Harrington was acting as if her presence was totally normal. What he had always expected.

"A normal life?" she asked, hoping she sounded earnest.

"Of course."

She was pretty sure her definition of *normal* was about as far from William Harrington's as imaginable. Any life in which she had to "donate" her blood to keep the biggest murderer in history alive was not a life she wanted to live.

"You've already seen what the alternative is like," Harrington said.

"Yes, I remember clearly what my alternative is."

He made it seem as if those were her only options. A life as a prisoner or a life as a willing prisoner.

"Certainly, you'd rather have what I'm offering."

Reyna frowned. The fact that he honestly believed he was

tempting her was ludicrous. She suddenly saw again exactly what her life had been like: a white bedroom, IVs ripped out, needles, insanity…B. Always B. The woman she could have been. The vampire Harrington had made into an unstable monster.

"I will not be like B," she spat, unable to keep up the facade. The idea still haunted her dreams. She suppressed them when she was surrounded by people who cared for her, but staring into Harrington's face, they all returned.

She saw Beckham's face crease. She was going off script. She couldn't mask the anger in her voice.

Harrington laughed. "Ah, B. Perhaps my demonstration was too severe."

His eyes darted to Beckham. There was careful calculation in that look. A person contemplating poking a bear to see if it would bite.

"But surely you know her name is not truly B," Harrington said, a slow, creepy smile crawling onto his face.

Reyna stared at him in confusion. She had never thought about B's name. She had assumed B was just a label. A designator.

After a heartbeat, Harrington said, "Her name is Bronwyn."

Everything slowed to a stop.

That *name*. Bronwyn. B was Bronwyn.

Bronwyn was Beckham's sister. B was Beckham's sister.

Reyna couldn't process that. How could that creature possibly be Beckham's sister? How could she have been his second?

"What?" Beckham snapped. He lost all sense of decorum and stalked forward. Cassandra and Roland blocked his path, standing between him and Harrington.

"Come now, Beckham. Don't hate me. I've had your sister exactly where she belonged all these years—locked up."

"You fucking bastard," Beckham snarled.

Harrington found that amusing. "You are the one who created her. It was only safe for the maintenance of a well-run society to remove the loose ends."

"My sister is not a loose end."

"She most certainly was when I encountered her. You tortured her into insanity over the course of several years, Beckham. What did you think would happen to her?" He smiled that wicked, pleased smile he wore when he was needling someone. When he was about to go on one of his soliloquies about how brilliant he was. "She certainly wasn't going to regain her sanity working as second-in-command of your army. If anything, she was only getting worse. I saw her for the menace to society that she was. So, I took her out of the equation. Killed two birds with one stone with that one. Her disappearance was the only reason you ended up working for me. All worked out in the end, don't you think?"

"You bastard," Beckham said. "I know what I did to Bronwyn, and there is no atoning for that. But she is my sister, and you lied to me and killed someone else to stage her murder. Yet you've held her all this time?"

"Well, it was an easy way to get someone else out of the way," Harrington said as if he were so clever.

Reyna's heart pounded in her chest. Her eyes darted to Beckham, though he had completely forgotten her, standing there in the cold. Beckham had done that to Bronwyn. Beckham was the one who had destroyed her mind. *She* was one of the people he tortured before the blood type cure. It pained her beyond belief to think Beckham had created her nightmare, even as her heart was breaking for him.

And suddenly a conversation with Beckham all those months ago in his penthouse came back to her. His words rang in her mind…

"I've sought people out, tortured them, drove them mad just to kill them slowly through their insanity. I've done horrible things and enjoyed it, Reyna."

She realized she had never truly examined that statement. He'd done this to Bronwyn, to his own sister. She'd seen firsthand exactly how thorough he'd been. How ruthless he must have been at the time to ruin her in such a way.

Her heart broke for him. For the weight he must carry around. How destroyed he must have been by it that he couldn't even tell Reyna the full truth to this day. And how difficult it must have been to hold that guilt and try to become a better person post–blood type cure.

"My sister is not a pawn for you to use," Beckham said.

Harrington shrugged. "I use all my pawns as I see fit, and she is not a menace I want walking the streets of my city."

"*My* city," Beckham growled. "I own this city. I bought it in blood. Bronwyn at my side."

"That was long ago. Cities no longer belong to anyone. The world belongs to me," Harrington said. "I did you a favor by getting her out of the way. Haven't you thrived without her?"

Reyna saw the instant something inside Beckham snapped. Harrington had kept Bronwyn from him all these years, and now he was trying to justify it by calling it a *favor*.

Beckham unleashed. He lunged for Harrington, who took a step backward in displeasure. Cassandra and Roland still stood in his path. Beckham would have to go through them to get to Harrington. Always another barrier. But there was nothing left in Beckham except revenge, death, and destruction.

He was savage and uncontrollable. She'd seen him fight Roland before, but this was beyond anything she could imagine. His movements were lightning fast. So fast she could hardly register them. He took on Cassandra and Roland as one, hands flying, arms moving, legs kicking. It was a blur.

Beckham was larger than both of them. Roland had a slimmer frame with equally quick movements, and Cassandra was tall and lithe. She had none of his supreme strength, but she was slippery like an eel, evading capture and delivering blows that would have incapacitated an ordinary man. Roland was the opposite of Cassandra's stealthy movements, diving right into Beckham's calculated advances.

And then the fight shifted.

Beckham had Cassandra in a neck hold, her back to his chest, his arm across her shoulders. His hand cupped her chin. A sickening snap rang out, and Cassandra's body went limp. The light left Cassandra's eyes. When Reyna's gaze snapped back up to Beckham's there was nothing in his eyes, either.

He didn't stop there. He used the rest of his strength and physically ripped Cassandra's head from her shoulders. He let the body drop, the severed spinal cord showing through. Blood coated the patio floor. Vampire blood. Beckham still held Cassandra's head. Her mouth was still open in shock and fear, her red hair blowing in the winter breeze.

He tossed the head at Harrington's feet, wiped his bloody hands on his tuxedo pants, and turned to face Roland. He lifted one hand and beckoned Roland forward.

"If you dare," he snarled.

Harrington toed the decapitated head of his ex–senior vice president with disdain. "Now you've made a mess."

Beckham and Roland weren't listening. They were circling each other like champion fighters.

"It will be with great pleasure when I finally end you," Roland said. "After what you did with that little bitch."

"You always were all bark and no bite," Beckham said and then lunged.

"Enough," Harrington said.

But neither of them were listening to him any longer.

Reyna's eyes were wide with fear. This wasn't how any of this was supposed to happen. Beckham had snapped. Finding out Bronwyn had been alive all this time had wrecked him. Would he be able to come back from the brink after this ended?

Then she felt Harrington's hand on her elbow. She shrieked and tried to wrench herself out of his grasp, but he was too fast. He put her body in front of his and held her in place in the same manner that Beckham had just held Cassandra.

He was going to snap her neck.

Fear rolled off her. As if sensing the danger, Beckham tore himself away from Roland and rounded on Harrington. His eyes cleared, and he saw the position she was in. That he should never have allowed her to be in.

One move, and she'd be dead.

Chapter Thirty-Seven

"Cease or I'll kill her," Harrington said.

"You won't kill her," Beckham said. He was breathless. The fighting was intense. He and Roland were nearly evenly matched. "You need her."

"As a matter of fact, I don't need her. I found one other. A little old lady who has gone her entire life without ever having to get her blood drawn. No children. No surgeries. Truly miraculous. Thank Visage for the Blood Census."

Beckham paled.

"But I don't *want* to kill her, Beckham. Don't make me the bad guy here."

Reyna laughed a short, hysterical breath.

Harrington ignored her, gesturing to the dead body lying between them. "Why don't we act civilized, hmm? Let's forgo our baser qualities for the moment. Look what we're going to have to clean up."

Harrington might actually kill her. Her hands trembled from the cold and terror as they moved into the folds of her gown. She could take a gun out now. She could turn around and shoot Harrington. She wasn't faster than him, but she might be able to catch him by surprise.

Beckham's eyes moved to hers, and he shook his head marginally. Just enough for her to see that he was telling her no. *Don't do it.*

She knew she could get herself killed trying it, but she had to try.

"Fine," Beckham said.

He prowled away from Roland. Roland straightened his suit and narrowed his eyes at Beckham's back.

"There we are. Back to manners," Harrington said. He released Reyna with ease and assessed her with cold calculation. "You are freezing."

Yes. She was actually trembling now. Cold was creeping into her bones. Beckham slipped his coat off his shoulders. He stepped forward, eyeing both Harrington and Roland carefully before slipping it onto her small frame. It enveloped her, dropping down nearly to her knees. Blood soaked the expensive material, and a trail from the collar smudged onto her collarbone. She could smell the tangy rust.

Harrington patted Beckham affectionately on the shoulder. It was as if all was well in the world. As if Beckham hadn't just killed someone.

"That's better."

Beckham brushed Harrington's hand off of his shoulder. "Hardly. You kidnapped my sister and kept her hidden from me for years. You kidnapped Reyna and tortured her. You treated me like a son, and yet you never trusted me."

"Trust," Harrington scoffed. "You had it. You're my prodigy, Beckham. You are a son to me."

"If you believed that, then you would not need Bronwyn as a

bargaining chip. Or Reyna, for that matter. I should have followed my instincts all those years ago and killed you the second you stepped foot in my city."

Harrington waved his hand dismissively. "More of this 'my city' business. If it was truly yours, then you wouldn't have handed it over to me so readily. I didn't even have to kill you like you killed your predecessor."

"You were offering us a utopia. I was a fool to have ever believed in it. Now I won't stop until I see it ended."

Harrington sighed. "Oh, Beckham, I do wish you hadn't said that."

"I was wrong about you. About all of you and all of this." His eyes moved from Harrington to Roland and back. "I will burn you to the ground."

"That's where you are wrong," Harrington said. "I am already burning *you* down. Your little bunker. Your little rebellion. All of Elle."

Reyna's hand flew to her mouth. She took a step forward without knowing she'd done it, as if she could somehow get him to take it back. What about everyone inside? What about her brother and Laura? What about Sydney and Washington and Tye? Even Everett. All those people working toward this moment of triumph. And now they were burning. Her throat closed up. She could almost smell the smoke from where she stood in horror.

"You burned down Elle?" Beckham asked, his voice as sharp as a razor blade.

"I'd thought you'd at least deny your involvement. Show me you are still the person I recruited so many years ago. It's a shame. I wanted it to be you." Harrington did look moved. But not repentant.

"I won't deny anything." Beckham seized Roland by the neck and then threw him backward. Roland collided with the building and crumpled, cracking the facade and taking a few bricks with him. He coughed and tried to rise, then collapsed again. "And now all of your guard dogs are down for the count."

Harrington laughed. Actually laughed. "I always loved your enthusiasm, Beckham."

Beckham reached out to grasp Harrington, to end this whole thing, but Harrington was fast. Much faster than Beckham had been anticipating. He moved out of the way and gracefully stood back with his hands in his pockets.

"You're missing something, Beckham," Harrington said. "You haven't quite realized that you've lost. If you fight against me, I'll kill Reyna. If you fight against me, I'll kill Bronwyn. If you fight against me, I'll crush your little rebellion. Oh, wait, I already did that, for your insolence."

"You can't kill them if you're dead," Beckham said.

"I have a kill order on Bronwyn if anything happens to me. Both will be dead before you can do to me what you just did to Cassandra."

Beckham snarled, but Reyna could see the moment Harrington's words sank in. He had the upper hand. Somehow, Harrington had managed to outmaneuver them.

"I have all the players on the board. I even have your little Penelope. What a treat that girl is. You know what they say about crossing a scorned woman."

Reyna's stomach sank even further. Penelope. Hell hath no fury. Of course, she hadn't just turned…she'd turned coat, too.

Harrington smiled at their shocked silence. "Checkmate."

Beckham's fury simmered, but this was a no-win scenario, which meant that they had no options left.

Harrington won. He fucking won.

All of this for nothing. Losing Brian for nothing. Putting her life on the line for nothing. Elle burning for nothing.

Her eyes snagged on Beckham. There was love. Endless, eternal love in those eyes. And an apology. For fucking up. For walking her into this. For not being able to fix all of it.

She'd made this plan. *She'd* walked them all into it. It was her fault, not Beckham's. He hadn't wanted to risk it, and she'd been so headstrong she hadn't stopped to consider the real possibility that Harrington could win.

Their rebellion was just and righteous. They *had* to win.

And yet…there was no hope that they could escape this. If Beckham moved against Harrington, he'd destroy everything he loved. And Harrington had another match. She was no longer one of a kind to him.

But her mind snagged on that.

A little old lady. He'd said that. No…sneered that. He must be drinking from her to be so healthy, but she couldn't be providing everything he needed. He wouldn't have tried to negotiate with Reyna if he truly didn't need her. In fact, he wouldn't have bothered with any of these charades if he hadn't needed Reyna.

She thought around that fact, looking it over from every angle, assessing its worth, and then made her decision. Her hand slipped into the pocket of her dress, and she removed the gun hidden against her thigh. Harrington's eyes snapped to the cool metal clutched in her hand.

"What are you doing?" he demanded furiously.

Then she chambered a bullet and put the gun to her temple. "You're bluffing."

His eyes widened. His hands fluttered at his side as if he wanted to snatch the gun from her hand.

"Just try," she dared him. "See if you can get to me before I pull the trigger."

"I already said that I don't need you," he said angrily.

"You *do* need me. You would *never* be so incredibly wasteful when a perfectly good blood type match is available."

"You know nothing."

"You exposed your queen." She spat back at him the words he'd said to her in Visage all those weeks ago. "You should never leave your queen unguarded. The game isn't finished."

Harrington's smug expression evaporated. She didn't dare look at Beckham. She couldn't look him in the eye for her next gamble.

"You let Beckham walk out of here alive and promise never to search for him, and I'll come with you now," Reyna finally said.

"No," Beckham cried.

"You think you can bargain with me?"

"It's the only deal I have to offer. My life for his."

"Reyna, don't do this," Beckham begged. "Your life is worth more than mine."

"We can agree on that at least," Harrington said.

"I'm sorry," she whispered to Beckham. She kept her eyes on Harrington. "I'm waiting for an answer."

"I watched you for weeks, my little queen," Harrington said. "I know you are a survivor. You value self-preservation above all else. You won't pull that trigger, and you will come with me regardless."

"I'll do it," she said, her hand shaking where it held the gun in place. "I care more for him than I ever will for my own life."

"Reyna," Beckham pleaded.

Harrington raised an eyebrow. "Oh, is this love? How quaint."

"You could never understand love," Reyna spat.

"Love is a weakness. I have no need for weaknesses, as I have no need for a traitor."

A blue dress appeared at the door, snagging everyone's attention. Penelope's shocked face took in the scene around her—Cassandra's dead body, Roland slowly getting to his feet, and Reyna with a gun to her head, standing between the two most powerful men in the world.

"What is going on?" Penelope gasped.

The distraction was all Harrington needed.

He moved so fast no one could even see what he was doing. No one could move to stop him. It wasn't until the dust settled that Reyna saw he had Beckham's head between his hands, that Beckham's head was wrenched to the side with his eyes turned away from her, and then finally…Harrington's triumphant smile.

She saw Harrington release him.

She watched Beckham's body slump to the ground.

Then she screamed.

And screamed.

Chapter Thirty-Eight

Reyna's blood ran cold.

Her world tilted. She swung off axis. Everything unraveled.

She was still screaming. She couldn't stop screaming. She would have no voice and she'd still be screaming. In her blood, in her mind, in her soul. She would go on like this for the rest of her life. Never ceasing.

Beckham was…gone.

Not gone. Dead.

She choked on the word in her mind. Flinched from the harsh, impossible reality.

She couldn't breathe. She couldn't think. She couldn't possibly process any of this. Beckham was infallible. He was a giant among men—enormous in size and personality. He took over every room he entered. He was larger than life in every sense of the words. There was never a day that she feared for his life in the way he had always feared so strongly for hers. Nothing could stop him. Nothing and no one could take him down.

Until now.

How had she lived all this time and never considered his possible end? She'd considered hers enough times. She had thought of any number of ways in which she would die. She had even been okay with it tonight. She'd held the gun to her head, determined to do what must be done. But not Beckham. Never Beckham.

The gun now hung limp at her side. A useless piece of equipment. It hadn't saved her. It hadn't saved Beckham. The gamble had failed. She might as well use it Romeo-and-Juliet-style, because she couldn't imagine how she could go on without Beckham in her life. Without him, it was no life at all. Yet her hands trembled. She didn't have the strength to lift the gun, let alone to pull the trigger. Everything had just fallen to shit. It was over. It was all over.

She barely registered the fact that Penelope had fallen to her knees at Beckham's side. That she was screaming at Harrington. Something about a deal. About this not being part of the deal.

Reyna watched as she cradled Beckham's head in her lap. Tears ran down her beautiful face. She held him like a lover. Like someone who could possibly understand the anguish coursing through Reyna.

But Beckham had never loved Penelope. How could he love a cold, heartless bitch like Penelope? If she hadn't sold them out, then *none* of this would have happened. Beckham wouldn't be dead.

This was *her* fault.

Reyna remembered how to move her feet. She ignored Harrington completely. He was nothing to her anymore. Consequences no longer mattered. Harrington would get his due next.

She walked right up to Penelope where she kneeled in the cold. How could someone so beautiful do such horrible things? How could she so freely give up her soul to the devil?

Reyna had fought and fought and fought. Even at the risk of losing everything, she had still told Harrington no. She had still done the right thing. When all odds were turned against her, she had stuck it out. She had endured. She had fucking persisted.

Penelope lost one thing, *one* thing in her entitled life, and she'd crumbled. Worse, that thing had never even belonged to her.

Reyna's fist tangled in Penelope's dark hair.

Dark hair. Reyna hated it, that they had the same color hair.

"What are you doing?" Penelope shrieked as Reyna wrenched her head backward.

Reyna raised the gun and pressed it against Penelope's head. Penny was shaking like a leaf. Terrified despite her now superior strength and speed. She hadn't quite gotten used to her new reflexes, and she was in shock in her own way.

"This is your fault," Reyna snarled.

"Reyna, stop," Penelope cried. Tears ran in rivulets down her face. "I didn't know! I would never have done anything to harm Beckham."

"Reyna, allow Penelope her time to grieve," Harrington said as if he were consoling a child having a tantrum instead of a woman who had lost the love of her life.

"You are a coward," Reyna spat in Penelope's face.

Then she moved the gun and shot Penelope in the heart. The jealous empty vessel that had ruined everything.

Penelope dropped backward, blood seeping from the wound. She screamed in pain and shock and revulsion. It wouldn't kill her; Reyna knew that. But it would keep her ass on the ground and get her the fuck away from Beckham.

Harrington was laughing in the distance, but Reyna had already fallen to her knees. She had to hold Beckham. She had to fix this. He couldn't be dead. Beckham would never leave her. Never. She could save him. She could bring him back. She was his soulmate. She hadn't even gotten to *tell* him she was his blood match, his once-in-a-lifetime, his soulmate. If their blood was perfectly matched, then maybe it could work a miracle.

Reyna did the only thing that she could think of. She opened his mouth and used one of his sharp fangs to slice her wrist. She vaguely heard a hiss and a sharp inhale. She was sure the sweet smell of her blood was permeating the air, but she didn't care. She couldn't care.

"You're only harming yourself and wasting precious blood. Beckham isn't coming back. No matter what you do."

She ignored his words and forced the blood out of her veins and into his mouth. The pain was nothing compared to what the pain of losing Beckham would become if this didn't work.

"Enough," Harrington barked.

This was her only hope. She had nothing left to give. She sank forward, resting her forehead on his chest. Tears wouldn't come. Just exhaustion and numbness. She wanted to lie down beside him in the cold and never wake up again. There would never be another Beckham Anderson.

"Come on, Becks," she cried, shaking his body. "Please. You can't do this to me. You can't leave me!"

Nothing happened.

Her blood, while unique and very, very rare, wasn't anything special. It didn't have magical healing properties. Their blood match wasn't saving him. Her chest was a black hole where her heart had been.

"Fix him," she screamed at Harrington.

"He can't be fixed, Reyna."

"How could you do this?" she demanded. But her eyes were on Beckham as she tried to rouse him. As she tried to do anything to save him.

Harrington was wrong. What did he know? He was a monster. A villain. A sadistic vampire who had taken away the best thing in her life. He'd played the game like a chessboard, and she'd walked right into his trap.

But he couldn't take Beckham.

Her once-in-a-lifetime. Blood match. Soulmate.

If her soul mate was dead, there would be hell to pay.

TO BE CONTINUED

Acknowledgments

Deep breath. This is my favorite ending I've ever written. When I wrote the book, I didn't know it was going to end like this. I sent the finished book to my agent and editor without telling them...and I waited. It was about two days later when my phone and email blew up with messages. Luckily, everyone was on board for the emotional bomb I'd dropped at the end of this book. So if you, too, are suffering at the end of this one, know that I'm waiting for my inbox to blow up again and looking forward to it. But know there's one more book!

So many incredible people went into the making of this book. First and foremost, I have to thank my crew who has been with me from the beginning of this series: Anjee Sapp, Sharon Goodman, Katie Miller, Rebecca Kimmerling, Amy McAvoy, and Christy Peckham. You all rock! To my early readers and helpful plotters—Diana Peterfreund, Lori Francis, and Staci Hart. I could not have gotten through this book without you!

To the author friends who gave me blurbs for this, you're the best.

This job is hard and isolated but better with you in it—Rebecca Yarros, Rachel Van Dyken, Geneva Lee, AL Jackson, Corinne Michaels, K. Bromberg, Kendall Ryan, S.C. Stephens, Susan Stoker, Carrie Ann Ryan, Mari Mancusi, Jessica Prince, and Erin Noelle.

To my wonderful agent, Kimberly Brower. Thank you for championing this series, fighting for Beckham, cheering for Reyna, and being generally all around awesome. To the team at Red Tower who created the gorgeous sprayed-edge edition of this book—LJ and Bree, thank you thank you thank you! Sylvan for your help with edits and seeing the vision for this one. And the rest of the team who put their hands on this book and helped bring it to readers worldwide—Liz, Hannah, Nicole, Rachel, Lauren, Riki. To the people who have fought fearlessly for this book all along and were on my team bringing it to life—Dani, Devin, Lisa, Bri, and Brooklyn. To all the new bloggers, TikTokers, and bookstagrammers who have found me through this series and all the recurring ones who tried out my vampires, thank you for your support!

As always, my husband Joel and son, who are here for me always. I love you both so much.

This book was written to the soundtrack of "Castle" by Halsey, "Breath of Life" by Florence + The Machine, "Dark Paradise" by Lana Del Rey, "Liability" by Lorde, "Blood Bank" by Bon Iver, and forever and ever "Bones" by MS MR. Thanks for creating the perfect soundtrack to my dark vampire romance.

Last but certainly not least, to all my incredible readers for falling in love with Reyna and Beckham. Two down and one to go. Can't wait to bring this to a close with you. Forgive me.

***SHIELD OF SPARROWS* IS A SLOW-BURN, HIGH-STAKES ROMANTASY PERFECT FOR FANS OF SARAH J MAAS AND EMILY THIEDE—WHERE ENEMIES BECOME LOVERS, MONSTERS WEAR CROWNS, AND A FORGOTTEN PRINCESS FINDS THE POWER TO BURN A KINGDOM DOWN.**

The gods sent monsters to remind mortals to kneel.

I've been kneeling my whole life—and I'm done.

As the overlooked second daughter of the kingdom's royal line, I was never meant to rule. Never meant to fight. And definitely never meant to marry the kingdom's deadliest monster hunter to seal a treaty soaked in blood.

But the day he walked into my father's court, everything changed.

Now I'm crossing cursed lands beside a stranger who sees me as a burden, bound to a future I never asked for, and watched by gods who delight in human ruin.

Everyone wants me to be something I'm not—a warrior, a symbol, a sacrifice.

But being invisible my whole life has taught me one thing: *there is power in the shadows.*

I just need to find the strength to take it.

AN ASSASSIN, A BAKER, AND AN EVIL SORCERER WALK INTO A TAVERN...

EXPECT SOME CHAOS.

CAN YOU LOVE THE DARK WHEN YOU KNOW WHAT IT HIDES?

Some things aren't supposed to exist outside of our imagination.

Thirteen years ago, monsters emerged from the shadows and plunged Kierse's world into a cataclysmic war of near-total destruction. The New York City she knew so well collapsed practically overnight.

In the wake of that carnage, the Monster Treaty was created. A truce...of sorts.

But tonight, Kierse—a gifted and fearless thief—will break that treaty. She'll enter the Holly Library...not knowing it's the home of a monster.

He's charming. Quietly alluring. *Terrifying*. But he knows talent when he sees it; it's just a matter of finding her price.

Now she's locked into a dangerous bargain with a creature unlike any other. She'll sacrifice her freedom. She'll offer her skills. Together, they'll put their own futures at risk.

But he's been playing a game across centuries—and once she joins in, there will be no escape...

THE EXPLOSIVE SECOND BOOK IN THE VALLENDOR SERIES — A SWEEPING ROMANTASY WHERE GODS BLEED, REALMS FALL, AND ONE WOMAN STANDS BETWEEN SALVATION AND RUIN.

A god's wrath is unforgettable. Her love, even more dangerous.

Kaivara Megidrail was once worshipped as the Grand Defender of Vallendor—until betrayal, punishment, and exile left her Diminished. Now, the realm she abandoned teeters on the edge of collapse. Monsters roam free. Gods whisper in shadows. And one man—Jadon Wake, prince, blacksmith, liar—may be the key to her salvation... or her final ruin.

Haunted by the past, hunted by divine enemies, and armed with only fractured memories and an unrelenting will, Kaivara must choose: reclaim her power and face the truth about Jadon, or watch Vallendor fall to a traitorous god's rising.

The realm called her a destroyer. This time, they'll learn what she was truly made for.

Doubling the Trees Behind Every Book You Buy.

Because books should leave the world better than they found it—not just in hearts and minds, but in forests and futures.

Through our Read More, Breathe Easier initiative, we're helping reforest the planet, restore ecosystems, and rethink what sustainable publishing can be.

Track the impact of your read at:

Connect with us online!

@RedTowerBooks

@redtowerbooks

@redtowerbooks

Join the Entangled Insiders for early access to ARCs, exclusive content, and insider news!

Scan the QR code to become part of the ultimate reader community.